AD LUMEN PRESS

American River College

PRELUDE

a novel by
SCOTT BUTTERFIELD

 Ad Lumen Press | Sacramento | 2021

Cover art Ángeles Santos Torroella, *Un Mundo* (detail)
Reina Sofia: Museo Nacional Centro De Arte
© 2020 Artists Rights Society (ARS), New York / VEGAP, Madrid

Ad Lumen Press
American River College | 4700 College Oak Drive | Sacramento, CA 95841
Part of the Los Rios Community College District

Library of Congress Cataloging-in-Publication Data
Names: Butterfield, Scott, 1982- author.
Title: Prelude / a novel by Scott Butterfield.
Description: 1st edition. | Sacramento : Ad Lumen Press, 2021.
Identifiers: LCCN 2020056507 | ISBN 9780997446913 (paperback)
Classification: LCC PS3602.U89254 P74 2021 | DDC 813/.6--dc23
LC record available at https://lccn.loc.gov/2020056507

1st Edition | 1st Printing

for my family, immediate and extended

No hay banda. And yet, we hear a band.

—David Lynch, *Mulholland Drive*

FIRST MOVEMENT

𝄞 I open my front door and walk down the porch steps to the flowerbed and my wife, sitting on her heels like a meditating monk. She is pruning. I slip on her a necklace of my teeth, my tongue for a pendant, because we have discussed the future names of our children, our funerals, dinner tonight, and this is all that's left to say. She rises, thrilled, and points to my parents who stand in the driveway. I unbolt my abs and haul out my guts, placing the pile at my father's feet, and he's so proud that he divides like a cell and is beside himself—one absolutely still, stoically nodding, the other drowning in the lake that pours out of his face. For my mother, I break open my ribcage and hand her my lungs. She fits them in her shoes for support and when she walks away I can already see the balance and bounce my breath gives to her step. The sidewalk is smooth. The street is clean. The usual screams of misery and pain float up from the grate cut into the curb, so I rip off my ears and toss them sewer-wise. My friends are everywhere, on bicycles, on porches, on the roofs of houses. We wave and come together for a bonfire in the backyard that eats up the air. I scissor off stripes of my skin and write down my forwarding address and fuck the barriers of Geometry and Time, we'll always keep in touch. The neighborhood shrinks and the city swells. A woman in a pinstripe suit is trying to hail a cab. I detach my dick and slap it in her hands. Perhaps she can get some use from it, hasn't done me much good. Two bored kids loiter outside a Laundromat. I give one a loose muscle fiber, one a stray vein, suddenly both run around, overcome by enthusiasmos, unwinding me like a spool of thread until they have woven a double-slide, monkey bars, a bridge, trapeze rings, and a swing-set with every last micro-filament. The sun is white and high and commuters shield their eyes from the gleam of my skeleton. At the doors of City Hall, I unscrew my skull and scoop out my brains, dip in my pinky like a pen in an inkwell and scrawl across the threshold *you want my brains you can have my brains—not my compliance.* A couple blocks down, there's a group of 3rd shifters standing in a stupor while waiting for the bus. I shake off my bones and rearrange them as a bench. They sit and sleep against each other like siblings. My sister plays in a dark hollow at the central city park, beside a silted stream, and under the umbrella of a willow tree. She's carving her initials in the trunk with a buck knife. She is so small. I pluck out my peachpits and drop them in her palm. She puts them in her pocket and says with a diamond smile, "They'll be fine." The wind rushes through the trees and the buildings and the corridors of the isthmus towards the on-ramp of the Highway. It's raining. The cars decelerate and congeal at the intersection, wipers going mad, and in the meridian, on an isolated patch of concrete, bathed in copper-penny colored streetlight, is a man with a sign that reads ANYTHING HELPS. ANYTHING HELPS slouches and hooks a thumb in his belt loop. He's still as a mountain, but his eyes are skittish, and his face reminds me of students before the beginning bell of class, drunks at the tail end of drinks, a crowd after a violent crime, families at cold meals, and every dismal lost driver at a stop sign. The rain quits, the gray wall drifts past, and the old universe unzippers itself into a new universe where there's not a pitiful person soaked to the bone but a fragrant and molting creature of light with a million shimmering marionette strings securing his body up to the sun in the sky. Nice trick. I'll give you the fist of my heart and its everyday rhythm, but don't spend this how I think you will in the concrete beyond.

SECOND MOVEMENT

A voice called her name from the other side of the door, and it lifted Vera Lyons out of her brown study. She shoved her brother's journal between the cat-shredded cushions of the couch and smoothed her hair with her hand, twice. She moved to the wooden trestle desk at the opposite end of the Mystery Machine. She sat in her tall metal chair and folded her hands in her lap and faced the attic window, as big and round as a bass drum, and pretended to escape. Vera, diffuse as she was, passed through the glass without much friction and floated down three stories, landing softly on the fine powder in the front yard. It had stopped snowing, finally, but the world wasn't white. The streetlights gave the trees and lawn and sidewalks and cars a sick yellow tint.

And she could hear it, the yellow tint, an annoying low buzz that never rose or fell in pitch, reminding her of gloomy parking ramps, supermarkets at night, and the basement of Horizon Elementary, a name which made Vera shudder even though she wasn't cold. She remembered Ms. Dewer's 5th grade classroom vividly. It smelled like a heap of dirty clothes in the closet. The desks in tight rows. The gray walls covered with faded watercolors on pastel construction paper. The geometry workbook didn't even have any proofs, just long word problems and every answer listed in the back pages. A stupid waste of time. Five minutes ago the class was discussing Geography, a subject Vera adored, but it was cut short by Ms. Dewer, who forced everyone to put away their maps and take out their math. The relative ease at which the class went along with this jarring tonal shift from the Deserts of Africa to the Area of Planes made Vera think of assembly-line robots, but not all the kids were fully programmed. Ms. Dewer, with a constant light touch of menace, directed their attention away from cell phones, tablets, and real live friends and back to the exact page they should be working on in the workbook, and yet, despite her lidless eye, this whole time, a lanky boy one row to the left and two desks ahead of Vera was being terrorized.

This boy combed his thin black hair to the side and had the nose of a smashed button. He picked this button as if searching for a frayed end to snip. He wore a striped orange and blue polo shirt that was much too small and the boys in adjacent seats were poking pens and markers and paperclips into the sides of his exposed belly. They poked and poked and poked and the lanky boy took it, as if the pokes were static shocks or mosquito bites to be swatted off. The boys didn't laugh. Only the slyest of smiles passed between them, some secret and satisfying language. Vera, watching it escalate, watching the boy flinch with each poke, sensed a deep and complex history behind the action, the weight of daily cruelty with each jab. She had a moment of bitter anger, at Bremen for being dead, at the school for its pride, at her mother and father who didn't trust her one bit. She looked down at the workbook and read *If a piece of square paper has a perimeter of 32 centimeters and Mark's dog, Yankee, tore off ¼ of the page, then what is the area of the remaining paper?*

Vera slammed her pencil down pretty hard on the desk with the intention of breaking it in half, but no one noticed, because at the same time the lanky boy spun around and attacked the kid jabbing him from behind. The fight went from zero-to-sixty in three seconds flat. Ms. Dewer rushed out of the room. The class was shouting, squealing, and enclosed the boys in a circle and tracked with them as they careened throughout the room. An adult male voice, a piercing and stable voice, belonging, she would soon learn, to the Vice Principal, cut through the commotion: *Stop this now!* The class went silent like a group of soldiers after an execution. The lanky boy, amped up to dangerous levels, took that moment to scream at the top of his lungs and pick up a chair and charge the VP, who was not intimidated. *Go ahead, Derrick. Go on. Are you going to throw that chair at me, Derrick? Only idiots solve their problems with violence. Are you an idiot, Derrick? If you throw that chair at me, you'll be an idiot and you'll be expelled. I guarantee it. I will make it happen.*

A striking image flashed in Vera's mind: a black rat with a gash across its stomach, bleeding, weak, and afraid, cornered in a garage by a crazed and frothing Doberman waiting for the best moment to go in for the kill. Derrick froze. He put down the chair, totally ashamed. Without another word the VP escorted the fighting boys out of the room. Ms. Dewer, who had been hanging back by the door, issued a bland apology to the class and instructed everyone to return to their Geometry workbooks. Just like that. Vera gazed around at the class, heads down, hushed, toiling away. She did not want to believe what was happening, how easily everyone forgot that a second ago, a boy was reduced to an animal and then hauled away. It made her want to throw up. She stood up from the desk and took three steps to the door.

Ms. Dewer, eyebrows arched, asked where exactly did Vera think she was going, in the tone of a cop to some suspected criminal, and Vera mumbled *the bathroom* with every single student gawking at her as if she was a criminal. Ms. Dewer understood it was Vera's first day and that not everything made sense, but she couldn't use the bathroom now because it was on restricted use, *the bathroom was a privilege.* Vera retched, she was not playing, she was going to be sick, and Ms. Dewer, perhaps foreseeing the mess she'd have to clean up, let Vera go to the bathroom without giving her a hallway pass, and Vera kept her head down and took the first non-classroom door she found, which led not outside, to freedom, as she hoped, but down to a basement of over-head pipes and damp concrete and that annoying yellow buzz. She explored the inner recesses until the Janitor who twisted her wrists too tight found her playing with the water valves, and the Vice Principal who never let her finish a sentence found her *the most emotionally disturbed student of the day*, and that was the night she had a nightmare about comets ripping apart her body in the field behind her house. In a cold sweat she stumbled to the third floor turret, the Mystery Machine, and slept on the couch and continued to every night after that and had no more dreams of fire and blood. She loved her little attic and the room loved her back. That's why it made her uneasy to feel—more than anything at this moment, sitting at the desk, staring out the window—that she needed to escape even from here.

Nothing could help her. Not her mother or father. Not her best friends, Ayla and Helene. Neither of them had a brother. Not her favorite book or painting, not a movie or a song, not a priest or rabbi or imam or philosopher or something called a Unitarian minister, which came up when she typed how to write a eulogy into Google.

Certainly not her brother, who helped her with everything, and who the eulogy was for.

She had no idea what to say.

There was a loud triple knock on the door.

Vera Juliana Lyons, blinded by sleep and in need of a bed, fixed her eyes on the cover of an old dictionary resting on the top corner of the trestle desk. It was beat-up and crimson red. It smelled of wet wood and seemed to weigh three thousand pounds. A life raft. She was drowning. She hung onto it with cold white knuckles.

There was an impressive silence in the Mystery Machine, and Vera became aware of the Music two floors below, hard-driving drum and piano rock 'n' roll, and then she heard the staccato clicks of high-heeled shoes on the other side of the door as they faded down the steps and were swallowed up by the song.

She had been holding her breath and didn't know—that's why her armpits were damp and her foot was tapping a steady 6/8 beat. She reached for the dictionary and began to scan the pages. When she was eight-and-one-quarter years old, Vera decided to actually start reading books instead of having Bremen read them to her. She'd leaf through the book and play the dictionary game with him, where she'd pick words that were unpronounceable and see if he knew them, or random words, or words with an attractive sound to the syllables, only half-digesting the definitions, soon sprinting back through the leaves as fast as her mind could run.

goad n. A pointed instrument used to stimulate a beast to move faster. –vt To prick; to incite; to instigate; to urge forward or rouse by any thing pungent, severe, irritating or inflaming.

ephemera n. [L. from Gr. daily; a day.] 1 A fever of one day's continuance only. 2 The Day-fly; strictly, a fly that lives one day only. There are several species.

intonation n. 1 The manner of sounding or tuning the notes of a musical scale. 2 In speaking, the modulation of the voice in expression.

fucus n. [L. See Feign] 1 A paint or dye; also, false show. 2 plu. fucuses. In botany, a genus of Algae.

Tonight, Vera Lyons had climbed the stairs at the end of the second floor hallway and shut herself up in the turret of the house before any guests arrived for the Funeral. The room was circular and well ventilated, fifteen feet in diameter, with seagreen walls that went up to her father's shoulders. The conical top was made from nine large oak beams, angled in at 45° and joined together in one point above. Bremen tacked a nylon cord and hung a lamp there. It was a porcelain man with winged feet and a winged helmet, carrying a spiral staff with a light socket at the top, and an on-off string you pulled at the bottom. *The Fool lights the way* was all she could remember him saying of it. The lampshade was cotton-white and always seemed to illuminate—she loved that word—the room with a different quality of light depending on the time of day and the angle of the sun through the window. Her fingers suddenly went stiff and ached like an old woman. Her eyes fluttered up from the pages. She set down the book, cracked her knuckles, each one sending an echo around the room, and felt exhausted.

At the south pole of the Mystery Machine there was a wooden rocking chair, and a low Jacquard woven couch with a repeating black and gold bird pattern, their wings primed for flight. Merlin had shredded it over the years. At the north pole there was the attic window and her trestle desk, with an IMAX globe to the east, near the door. At three intercardinal points about the room were small boxy bookcases with a single aloe plant on top of each. A Persian knock-off rug lay in the center. The Hope Chest, a family heirloom, was parked in the west.

"Why do you call it the Mystery Machine?"

Vera Lyons was nine and a half, playing Astronomer, sitting on the rug, examining samples of a meteorite that exploded two weeks previous in a fifty-mile streak over Mifflin County. She had begged and begged to explore the debris zone. Along with those space rock samples, she had two thickly illustrated books—one on minerals, the other on crystals—bought at the Geology Museum gift shop and dog-eared to the max, in addition to the abundant field notes she took on their trip to Blue Mound last weekend. The borders of the rug were littered with tomes on celestial mechanics that Bremen believed were too technical. Vera protested and won out and didn't come close to understanding them, but at least now she knew words like *gradient* and *parallax* and a whole lot more about gravity and light.

Bremen had been playing his bass when she asked the question. He stopped with a rude twang, aggravated, just enough for Vera to feel self-conscious. She hated that feeling. Then Bremen switched to a broad smile that meant he was probably laughing at you on the inside. Vera hated that, too.

"Would you rather I call it a classroom? Or an attic? Hey, V. Let's go play in the attic. Man, I'm bored. Where can we go? I know! The classroom!"

"It's not funny."

"What do you think a mystery is, kid? No dictionary. Give me a definition."

Vera took her time, staring into empty space with her tongue sneaking out of the corner of her mouth, a telltale sign she was thinking hard. Bremen shuffled through his scales. Vera cleared her throat. He paused.

"A mystery," she said, the vibrations of his last tetrachord hanging in the air, "is something you know a little about, but not everything. And you never will. That's why it's a mystery. Even though you know something, the whole thing is unknown." She paused and studied the debris on the rug. "It's like how no one really knows where the moon comes from."

"Yet."

"Yet?"

"The Mystery Machine is a place where mysteries are solved—then created again." He plunked a simple 4/4 blues beat on the bass and improvised with a drunken growl.

There are problems and solutions
Back and forth like revolutions
Mystery's what's in between
A never-ending learning machine

It was frosty up here, the air like stale marshmallows buried in the cupboard. The last thing she had eaten was raspberry yogurt for breakfast. She wore a sheer violet dress with thin shoulder straps, bought expressly for the occasion, and her favorite creamy white stockings. Her hair was pulled back in a ponytail and held in place with a bushy black band. It sharpened every soft feature on her face—chin, cheeks, and forehead—so she looked older than her twelve years suggested.

She tiptoed to the door of the Mystery Machine and listened. Nobody seemed to be breathing, or holding their breath, on the other side of the door.

She took her brother's journal out from under the couch and removed a bundle of five sheets from within, pressing them flat on the desk. She grabbed a pencil and gripped it between her thumb and middle finger. She re-read the last sentence she had written on the second page and scribbled it out. The tip of her pencil hovered over a clean spot. She scribbled out a different sentence. Then nothing, except blinks, for a solid minute. Vera dropped the pencil and skimmed through his journal. Music arrived from across the universe. Phaeton was scheduled to arrive tonight, bringing the Geminids, and at least she could look forward to a waning crescent and pray for a clear sky to watch the show. She leaned back in the chair and looked up into the lamp and stared open-eyed at the Fool until her head began to throb with the heartbeat in her everywhere. She pressed her fingers to her temples, letting her palms drift over her eyes. She slowly closed into herself like a flower at night and cried, a neat, soft cry, and wondered what time it was, bright red wet face, forgetting the most basic rule of the room: no clocks are allowed in the Mystery Machine.

Vera Lyons hovered above the Hope Chest. She confronted it. She confronted the night and what Bremen wanted. She wiped her face with the outside of her hand and sniffed away any lingering dread.

The chest was carved from pure Northwoods pine and, despite living through one hundred and seventy-one winters, retained its youth through applied sealant and summer love. It belonged to Vera's great-great-great grandfather, an explorer, a mediocre but dedicated one, Charles Lyons, Jr., who boasted of surviving two tours with Catherwood and Stephens in the Yucatan. The first one was awful and the second was worse, but Charles had grown spiteful and moody among the degenerate traders of Lake Michigan—he needed something new. He was born in 1819 in a brick house in Annapolis, a runaway at twelve, consciously moving westward, believing without a shred of doubt that Destiny was a woman with large breasts that would meet him on the prairie and guide him into her foxfur bed. In the end, he soured at all the rotten pelts he'd seen sold for high prices. Charles would later revise his opinion on the Territories, especially the freshly formed state of Wisconsin and a certain spot with rolling hills and deep valleys in the driftless southwest, but at that stage in his indehiscent life he was a bored young man who wanted no part of family or state. Where is the borderless realm? There was cruelty and squalor and shine in equal measure greeting him in every port down the Mississippi, everyone fighting to fit into some tiny carved out piece of Earth, so he bought a ticket on a sugar ship into the Gulf to escape the war searing through Mexico and Texas and the four drunk slave owners he robbed at knifepoint in New Orleans, and after a storm and two windy nights he set his dizzy feet down in Coatzacoalcos, bumped into the explorers within a week, just as he spent the last of his money on a top shelf meal at a flophouse, and joined their expedition out of desperation, instantly admiring their intelligence and adventure and wicked sense of humor, the way they maintained a palpable sense of certainty even while tramping through an overgrowth of Green Hell, horses and mules and native couriers in tow, only rough rocky sleep and an eternal insect buzz, every morning wetter, more gaunt, more lame, more afraid, until one day, Charles Lyons, Jr., half-dead, hallucinating badly, carrying forty pounds of gear and a chinked machete, hacked through a wall of fibrous palm plants with Catherwood and Stephens at his elbows—at least, what he thought were Catherwood and Stephens, since the pair had transformed into sparkling figures of emerald light—and reached those mighty temples and terraces thought by all reasonable men back home to be accessible only at madness or death, with tree trunks splitting up the foundation stones, decorated tombs, alien signs, ghost weather of the life-changing kind. But Vera couldn't remember her great-great-great grandfather's name. Fear washed through her like cold waves of brine. If she'd ever have kids she'd want them, and her kids' kids, and so on, to know Bremen, to have the name of Bremen on the tip of their tongues if the occasion called for it, and in response to these thoughts her big toe was shot through with real pain. She hit it so many times on the Hope Chest when she played in the Mystery Machine, and Bremen would hold the toe between his hands and remind her to breathe, and after a while of breathing and her toe between his hands she was playing again, no problem.

Vera cracked her neck like a bendy straw, turning it side to side as far as it would go. It made her lightheaded. She put a hand on the chest for balance and shook herself straight. Determined now, she lifted the lid.

It was filled to the brim. She removed an oversized sketchpad, a set of sixteen Prang Watercolors, and an aluminum lunch box rattling with colored pencils, calligraphy pens, inkbottles, hunks of charcoal, scotch tape, Elmer's glue, nickel-plated scissors. She tossed aside the homeschooling paperwork from the Wisconsin Department of Public Instruction. Bremen never bothered to fill it out. Time to burn the Aristoplay games—Punk Science, Music Maestro—she would never play them again. There were brochures from state parks and museums and roadside attractions, a plastic watering can, a plant food bottle with a broken eyedropper, and piles of little spiral-bound flip-top notebooks. Some contained Bremen's written records of her progress. Some were filled with lists. She used to love making lists. It meant there was something to do. She was full of pride after finishing a list. She even created non-functional lists about what topics she wanted to study, paleontology or invisibility, or what clothes she wanted to buy, or places she never wanted to go, things she never wanted to do, things she wanted to do but couldn't, things she could do but didn't want to. Bremen scanned the lists and talked with her for hours and hours about the real reasons behind what she wanted to do and why she wanted to do it.

The spiral-bound notebooks were dated on the front according to month and year. Vera opened May–June 2012 out of curiosity.

May 5th

I cleared away the strawberries pancakes from the table and asked what she wanted to learn this summer. She ran on and on and I didn't even try to shut her up. Here's what we whittled it down to: flowers, bones, music, electricity, planets, babies, South America, Ireland, lakes, and the sun. She blows my mind. If I need any more

clues I'll just read this again. I have to, have to, have to remind
myself that I don't need to know how to teach her everything. I
just need to know how—

That's not what she was looking for. Her focus had slipped.
Concentration is an act of limitation. Bremen lesson. She couldn't
afford distraction. Vera dug to the bottom of the chest. Ah, there
it was, underneath high-school textbooks of chemistry and physics,
Bremen's red-ribbon bound stack of twenty white note cards, 8 x 10,
Roman numeraled. It was his collection of quotes he didn't want to
forget, written down in his splotchy half-print half-script that never
tried to be legible.

For her eighth birthday, Bremen took Vera to a traveling exhibit
of Persian Art at the Chazen, and the only thing that stuck with her
were these hand-written, hand-bound books of Sufi poetry, not that
she understood a word of Arabic. She wanted to write like that.

"That's calligraphy," he said and warned her of the difficulties
involved. She nodded and forgot them.

"You can't even read."

"Yes I can. I just like hearing your voice."

Bremen was at the desk in the Mystery Machine, months later,
composing his collection of quotes. He often wrote them over and
over, as an exercise, as an act of solidarity with her, because she was
supposed to be practicing her inscription techniques.

Vera, sprawled on the rug, could not keep her script line level. She
believed her sight was excellent and refused to use a ruler. In a fit of
frustration, she threw the calligraphy pen on the rug, splattering ink.
She protested in the way she had grown fond of protesting, on her

knees and crying out in a shrill and defiant tone everyone believed she copied from Merlin, after hearing his insistent meow, which meant *let me outside right now or I'll scratch out your eye and eat it in front of you.*

"This is so stupid."

"I told you what to expect. Keep working."

"I don't want to."

Bremen did not lift his head from the desk. Vera did not stand from her knees. Sixty years from now, if she was still alive, she would be deaf and have blank spots of memory, but she would never (*Say it*, she thought, and she said it out loud in the Mystery Machine, "Never.") lose that tightness in her throat and the heat behind her ears whenever she and Bremen shared a moment of high tension. These memories opened up an emotional space so present and precarious and of immense size. Vera had a consistent image of herself in relation to her brother: she stood on an arid plateau at the edge of a pit into hell, the one she saw in the National Geographic issue of "The Most Evil Places on Earth." She stood at the precipice, bruised and hungry, exhausted from trudging thousands of miles to escape the endless armies of barbarian hoards which Bremen commanded and which had pushed her to the edge of the pit. Vera had two choices—face Bremen or learn to fly. She never faced him, and the image never went beyond her arms turning to wings and the sensation of gliding over flames.

"Calligraphy is about patience and discipline." He swung around in the chair and switch to a condescending tone. "You want to learn how to write nice? Go to some Finishing School where they teach little girls how to be little wind-up toys. I'll talk to mom and dad. They'd probably be glad to get you out of my clutches."

"As long as I get to live there."

"Just promise me one thing."

She crossed her arms, smirking. He smirked back.

"Remember you are going to fail, Vera. We try. We fail. I do. Mom does. Dad does. Think Merlin catches mice every time he hunts? You loved the Arabic writing. You were inspired and wanted to learn about that, attempt to try and write like that. You got the tools. You started on your way."

The ink smears. The unreadable lines. He was polished glass she looked right through.

"Calligraphy's not so much your thing. You figured that out. Good. Good for you. We'll do something easier. But you should still enjoy the discipline of working at something because it's interesting and important. To *you*. Optimally, this feeling of it being important should grow."

"Optimally?"

"It means the best results you can get under the conditions."

"What conditions?"

"The situation. The time and place you find yourself in." He shrugged. "Your life."

Vera took a breather and Bremen took a set break and turned back around in the chair. "What is real school like?"

"It's hard to explain." He put two fingers to his head and thought. She let him. "Let's do that. Let's play 'school'."

"Just tell me."

"Better if we play it. You'll understand faster."

"Maybe later?"

"You're torturing me. What can I convince you to do so you'll leave me alone and I can get back to my quotes?"

"Go outside and ride my bike."

His arm would lift and offer her the open air. She always took it.

Vera untied the ribbon and sat cross-legged on the rug with the cards in a pile on her lap. They were dusty and frayed. She ran her fingers along the top edge of the first card where the sharp angle became mushy like overripe fruit. Decay. She loved that word, too. She parted the pile to card number seven and decided to read with more patience, it was snowing again, Phaeton was approaching its perihelion, there was only the dull beat of the Music below, and she shouldn't be thinking about the time anyway.

The secret is the balance of two ingredients that sound, on the face of it, unappealing: sugar and acidity. Sugar without acid would be flat; acid without sugar would be sharp. But in good years the two are so finely counterpoised that they have the inevitability of great art.

At the time, publicity would have seemed like taking credit for the authorship of prayer.

That which was ultimately responsible for the state of the prisoner's inner self was not so much the enumerated psychophysical causes as it was the result of their own decision. Between stimulus and response there is a space, and in that space, our freedom.

Not the crude anguish of physical demise but the incomparable pangs of the mysterious mental maneuver needed to pass from one state of being to the other.

You were born and kicked off a precipice. And nothing can stop you from falling. There are a lot of rocks falling down with you, with trees growing on them, small pieces of land. You can cling to one of these rocks as you like, as it goes down with you, for safety. But it is not safe. Nothing is safe. Everything is falling apart, in a state of change. And there's no way of stopping it. And when you're really resigned to that, when you really accept that, there is nothing left to be afraid of.

I am cold. I don't want to be cold. If I close the window I will not be cold. I'll close the window.

Tune your hearing to the finer registers and you will notice the sharp chords of aggregate masses, the deep rhythm of liquid streams, the overtones of gas volumes, harmonics of light as it shines through a window as plainly as the choir that's chanting in church.

The evolution of all organisms tends to the ever more refined expressions/extensions of touch. We have eyes because our animal ancestors felt the effect of sunlight on their skins.

Suppose you were at the entrance to an unlighted room, perishing of hunger. Suppose the door was inscribed with a cryptic description of the contents of the room, and you drew the correct inference that all manner of good things to eat were on a table inside. Could you eat the inference?

Speaking with your own voice carries the force of personal intent.

*Speaking with a greater voice applies that force to individual con-
ditions in a more timeless and transformative way. A magic act in
world ruled by magic.*

Vera felt a crawl of hunger through her ribs. She longed for
Arianna's bread. There were muffled sounds of cheering and holler-
ing. Everyone was enjoying the Music. All those people downstairs.
Bremen had a wide net of friends and she'd seen some of them once or
twice or three times, but couldn't put her mind around even one name
floating in her head like a bank of clouds that obscure even their own
shapes. There'd be his students in large circles and laughing. There'd
be people he's played music with. People that have seen him play. A
total stranger might show up, a mystery in a suit or a dress, coming
here by mistake or on purpose, unknown to everyone, except that mystery would know Bremen. What could she possibly say? They all knew
him. Knew him. Knew. Vera closed her eyes and hoped the house, the
guests, the city block, Madison, the hand of Wisconsin, the lines of
the continent, the globe of the world, the sun and the planets would
all painfully twist and distort as the solar system vanished into the
nothingness of a black hole, and maybe now she would have a little,
just a little bit, of peace. A drum kick and another song began. None
of that was going to happen. She let the image go and thought herself
stupid for thinking the universe would save her. She opened her eyes
and there, without asking, in front of her face, was an idea.

Vera Lyons stood up and didn't care about the note cards that
slipped off her lap and scattered on the rug. She methodically
searched, one by one, through his record-keeping notebooks for
August–November 2014. In the index of a physics textbook she found

the entry for electromagnetism and marked the relevant sections. Vera arranged these materials on the desk with his journal and then sat on the chair—back straight, shoulders firm, as Bremen instructed her to do whenever she wanted to concentrate. She took a clean page and started writing, furiously, not a dash of self-consciousness, with a perfect integration of thought, hand, and pencil, so that even when her wrist cramped up and she shook it out and returned to the page, the action was seamless, for on this most pale and sticky of honey winter nights Vera was a star in the heart of the Mystery Machine, absorbing the energy of memory, subjecting it to the pressures of attention, and bringing about the combustion of creative rays, an outer projection of an interior heat, unable to kill the smile spreading across her lips.

Two heavy knocks on the door interrupted her writing.

Vera lifted the pencil halfway between 'becau—.'

Her mother opened the door to the Mystery Machine, but did not enter the room. Donna Lyons wore a strapless lime green dress, embroidered with orange and blue roses at her hip. Her hair was swirled up in a bun and, in a peculiar touch, was held in place by two special chopsticks. She was barefoot, and looked not at her daughter, but at her son, aged thirteen, wallet-sized, curved by time, the old photo leaning up against some books on the second shelf of the case across from the door. He was in the arm of a tree, the evergreen in their backyard, an alto sax around his neck, hair swooping down his forehead, his blue shirt brighter than the glint of the summer sun off the leaves. It was difficult to see him from that far away but Donna didn't squint.

Vera stared at her mother without, surprisingly, a shred of anger. The Fool was brightening the silk lines of her shoulders and neck, the wrinkles around her eyes seemed to erase themselves, the green dress fit her like skin, and she was, Vera was hard-pressed to deny, glowing, like some stronger lamp inside was shining through her pores. Her mother was more beautiful now than ever before. She never once thought of her mother as beautiful.

Donna slid the door half-shut but didn't drift further into the room. The Music rose like smoke from the living room with the storybook babble of guests.

Vera Lyons re-read what she had written. It wasn't necessarily true. She made something up by combining his journal entry and the physics textbook with a memory from last July when it was over 100° F. During that time, Bremen had taken her to Aztalan State Park because Vera wanted to volunteer on a real live archeological excavation. Any museum, be it natural history or fine art, ruined her mood. She couldn't touch anything. She needed to unearth ancient artifacts, a broken skull, a shard of pottery, a sharpened knifepoint, or the shell of an unknown animal and actually hold it in her hands. But Vera grew nervous on the car ride to Aztalan. She had never volunteered for anything before. "You're a shoo-in," Bremen said. Their father had donated thousands of dollars of construction materials to fix the stockades, pathways, and steps surrounding the two main Platform mounds. There was talk of a plaque of appreciation.

"How could his daughter not get some love?"

He parked his Prism near the Marker Mounds. When Vera stepped out of the car and into direct sunlight, she almost fainted. It was so hot and humid. The sun was a pinpoint and alone in the sky. She had to hold Bremen's hand across the gravel parking lot even though it was sweaty and the two of them kept slipping out of each other's grasp.

They followed the park trail and reached the cover of oak woods where it was barely cooler in the shade. Even the bugs were grounded by the heat. The trail turned south along Crawfish River, a lazy tributary of Rock River. Vera couldn't even look at the water—it was shimmering that fiercely and blinding her ability to think. Bremen paused to read each of the tablets posted along the trail. The plaques addressed different aspects of Aztalan life: their social organization, religious beliefs, diet, tools, agriculture, and recreation. "Hey V, did you know they gambled back then, too? And ate mussels? I wonder if they made beer."

Vera imagined climbing up the mounds and digging around inside. That summer she had struggled with, and gave up on, three technical books on archeological theory, a word still too big to hold in her closed fist. She cut-out and pasted up in her room the best glossy photos of geographic Sites of Interest around the Great Lakes and compared maps of the Middle American landscape pre- and post-Ice Age in the Historical Society library at UW-Madison. She also read a series of fringe science investigations about various temples in Egypt, Thailand, Peru, and Mexico and how they all aligned with constellations. At Bremen's insistence, they attended a talk on dreamcatchers at the American Indian cultural center by a Menominee elder who claimed to be one-hundred and seven. That couldn't be true. He looked way younger than that.

"If you are seriously thinking about pursuing Archaeology, you know, for real," Bremen suggested one day in the Mystery Machine, "then you should get some first-hand practical experience."

"Where can I do that?"

"What am I, your butler? Have I taught you nothing? You figure that out."

After a week of research, she picked Aztalan. By Wisconsin standards, it was the best bet.

The heat waves were visible and the trail seemed to flow in currents as if they were wading through a stream. It was a slow climb up the mound, their sweat-damp shirts sticking to them like crazy-glue. At the top there came the slightest and most refreshing cool breeze. Vera shielded her eyes with both hands to block the sun's harsh glare and get a better sense of the view. She pictured a thriving community where men hammered on stone tools and skinned deer and women smoked fish and beat clothes against the rocks. Children played chunkey on the open prairie. She could smell and hear these things from the wind as it whispered along the sculpted mounds of the silent sweltering earth. The cry of a chicken from a nearby farm, or a thousand years ago, pierced the air, and Vera knew without a doubt that this was where she wanted to be and this was what she wanted to do.

"Let's go," she said.

"We're here," Bremen said.

"To volunteer, stupid."

Bremen pointed to an efficient one-story wood cabin to the west, a Visitor and Information Center. "It's all yours, V."

Vera raced down the mound and called for Bremen to race with her, sprinting westward on the trail, not a second to lose. She reached the glass doors in no time and flung them open with enough strength to break the hinges. The air-conditioning blasted her on entry. She had been running at top speed in a hundred degree heat, and the artificial air brought her temp down too fast. She was fire and ice, dizzy and sick, and fell back against the wall and slid to the ground. The intensity of the feeling lasted only a few seconds before her vision cleared and her balance returned. Bremen walked through the door.

"What's up?"

"I'm fine." More like a fragile piece of glass that any tap would shatter.

There was nobody at the Information Desk. Vera leaned on the counter, still reeling with the residual effects of her run across the prairie. Bremen rang the shiny silver bell that reminded her of a dentist's office. Vera could feel each little individual droplet of sweat roll down her skin and freeze in place. The nausea burbled up in her throat and she didn't want to puke or faint, but that was all she could concentrate on. An old woman appeared from behind a curtain. Bremen and the old woman spoke, lips moved, but Vera couldn't hear what they were saying. It was like those silent slapstick movies where fragments of the conversation flashed up on the black screen of her mind: an age policy, a garden, a donation, an effigy—

"Go on. Show 'em, kid," Bremen said.

Vera glared at him, confused, show them what? The change in his face was dramatic and harsh.

"Do you want to clean up garbage? Be a janitor?" Bremen said. She had no idea why he was annoyed.

"Now the girl wouldn't be a janitor," the old woman said. She spoke with a drawl and accented her words with broad arm-waving strokes. "I told you twice we have paid staff for that. We only need volunteers to help with the Visitor Center during—"

"And that's all she can do?"

"I suppose we can see if she's able to work the cash register."

"V? Anything? You can be a janitor or checkout girl. Or weren't you listening."

A silence arose, Bremen vs. Vera. Eye-to-brash-and-unflinching-eye. It was a major battle that could've lasted centuries. Vera knew she would win, she faced him for the first time with that certainty, and so she won. Bremen backed down, made a half-hearted and mumbling apology to the woman, who took it like a scalp. Then she glanced at Vera, maybe with pity, maybe contempt, and said, with a touch of scorn only slightly less scorching then the July heat, "Best of luck with your endeavors."

They hiked back to the Prism in silence. Once inside he cranked the air and flipped the radio on to a classical station, which Vera quickly switched off. She rolled down her window even though it was hotter outside then inside. When they reached the highway and were going a comfortable seventy-five Bremen killed the air and rolled down the rest of the windows. Their battle extended most of the car ride home, but lost power as the miles wore on, eventually devolving into skirmishes along the outer perimeter, and when Bremen offered an olive branch, his voice, Vera didn't understand, she could find no trace of meanness in his voice.

"I should've looked into it myself."

"Looked into what?"

He checked over his shoulder to change lanes and then looked at her. "You really weren't listening?"

"If I heard then I wouldn't be asking."

"All they wanted was seasonal volunteers for the Visitor's Center. Emptying trash bins. Stocking the shelves with books and videos and t-shirts. There is an excavation planned in August with graduate students from UW-Milwaukee, but you wouldn't be able to volunteer with them." He gave her a silly grin. "Unless you just show up and break the illusion. I'd escort you myself."

"What are you talking about?"

"You know more about Archaeology than that woman in the Visitor's Center. I know you do. You know more about Archaeology than most undergraduate college students. I know you do. You have very little practical experience in the field. So what? You're twelve years old, so—"

"Almost thirteen."

"So when I say show 'em, you show 'em what you know. Demonstrate your knowledge. That's the only thing that might lead to a shovel in your hands. Or you kneeling in dirt somewhere in Guatemala. But a cash register only leads to another cash register."

"What do I show them?"

"What you can do."

"What can I do?"

"You can do anything you commit yourself entirely to."

Vera dangled her arm from the window. She stuck out her head and stuck out her tongue and tasted the air on fire. Bremen flipped the blinker and turned off the highway and she drew herself back into the car.

"Can I come to your place for a while?"

"I'm meeting Mo for dinner before my gig tonight."

"When can I come to one of your gigs?"

"They would never let a kid in a bar."

"I'm not a kid."

"I wouldn't dream of calling you one."

"Does Mo like me?" Vera thought out loud, with the only person who made her comfortable enough to do this.

"Dumb question," Bremen said.

"But does she have *illusions* about me?"

Bremen shifted his body in the seat and glanced at Vera with more than your average amount of reservation. He smiled weakly and shook his head, to himself, a move Vera was familiar with, and knew it meant she did or said something unexpected. She could push him.

"Everybody does. Has illusions, I mean."

"So it wasn't a dumb question."

She wanted his head to be a match she could strike from distance, and he must've felt it, because he laughed, a snort, and used a forearm to wipe away the sweat at his brow.

"Point to something in the car," he said.

Vera pointed to the steering wheel.

"That's an illusion," he said.

"The steering wheel is an illusion?"

"Point to something outside the car."

Vera pointed to a stoplight that switched from green to yellow as they passed, and Bremen accelerated and beat it and the pressure forced the seatbelt deeper into her shoulder.

"Illusion."

"That Dairy Queen with a line out the door?"

"Illusion."

"That guy waiting for the bus."

"Illusion."

"The bus."

"Illusion."

"Just shut up. It's not funny."

"Colors, the weather, the woman at Aztalan, Aztalan itself, TV, the brain, nations, books, death. Remember the definition of illusion, kid? It's not something that's not real, but something that isn't what it seems to be."

Vera took her sweet, sun-drenched time, with the world streaming by her window, the wind hot in her hair.

"So everything—is something—that isn't what it seems to be?"

He beamed. "Sweet Jesus. I love you, kid."

"It's quarter to eight," Donna Lyons said, breaking the memory like a dry stick over her knee. She took a few tentative steps forward, no fast moves. "A lot of Bremen's friends would like to see you. They've been asking me."

"What do you say?"

"That you're up here."

"And then what do they say?"

"They stop asking."

Vera flooded the Mystery Machine in volcanic sediment, fossilized it, fossilized herself so she didn't have to move or speak or do anything anymore. Donna floated into the center of the room and Vera spun the IMAX globe on its bronze axis, stopping it in the Atlantic. She imagined Bremen's body somewhere on the bottom of that ocean, hopefully feeding a family of fish, a strong crab, eel maybe, not a shark, it wouldn't share. Did he really think death was an illusion, out there on the boat? Did he just sit there like a statue while it was sinking fast? She couldn't believe he would let himself die without a fight. So when he was in that boat and it was going down and the water was filling his lungs and he could still think, was he thinking, then, that death was an illusion? When he was dying? How was death not what it seemed to be? Or her mother? Or the Mystery Machine? Vera squinted down at the globe, at the islands and the blue gaps between them. Fish don't eat bones. When picked clean they would be lifted like feathers and carried away by the current and eventually wash up on, Vera got specific, Inaccessible Island in the South Atlantic. Then it's settled. She had a vision of the future, saw it with a clarity that calmed her: she would someday lead an archeological expedition to study the ancient human settlers of that island, their tools and culture and migration patterns. One night she'd leave base camp, scramble down the sea cliffs to the beach, wade knee-deep into the rocky bay and scan the tides, and there, lodged in the soft sand and covered with a film of algae slimy to the touch, there she would find a human bone. And she would know. By the weight and the sheen and the sculpt she would know.

"What's he have to say?" Donna said, picking up one of the note cards from the floor.

"What's he have to say?" Vera repeated, lost at sea.

Donna stared at the back of her only daughter's head, her only daughter who was looking at a globe. "You've got his stuff out," she said coolly. "What's he saying?"

Vera had a talent for stonewalling, nurtured by Bremen. He never trained her to fill an empty space with words, or be embarrassed by awkward silences, or anxious with the need to show off, three things, Bremen said, that made up 95% of the reasons why anybody ever seemed to say anything. Vera didn't know if this was true. She did know that she enjoyed the frustration on other people's faces when she stopped a line of questioning with a blank look and an iron lock around her lips. No one had yet broken her.

Donna, familiar with this routine, huffed once in her traditional sign of deference and began to collect the note cards on the floor, slotting the numbers in their proper sequence. She tapped the re-ordered pile on her thighs and patted them even with her hands, re-wrapping it with the ribbon and placing the stack in the Hope Chest. She stepped back to appraise the old thing.

"This wasn't in his Will. He couldn't have forgotten." Donna laughed. "Or he did? That would be something."

She dropped into the rocking chair with a yawn, batting it away like a farmer does a night moth. She smoothed down her dress, twice. She rocked in 3/4 time and scratched a nearly transparent six-inch white scar, thin as a cat whisker, which began at the left side of her throat and angled down her neck until it met the clavicle, where it nicked off.

"Do you want anything to eat? We've got those cream cheese rolls you like?"

"I'm not hungry." Vera's stomach rumbled so loud that Donna heard it from across the room. Both avoided eye contact.

Vera attempted to convince herself she wasn't hungry, envisioned it with every cell of her body, and after a few moments the pangs ebbed away. What else could she ignore and would it go away that easy? The sound of the yellow buzz. The memories of guilt and fear. The gravitational pressure of her mom. Her brother's face behind her eyes. The endless interruptions from the world outside. If only she could ignore the whole world outside, hitch a ride on Phaethon and be dropped off on Pluto. Vera picked up her brother's journal. His words had turned into meaningless shapes of random length she couldn't even call letters, the words blending unrecognizably together like the voices and music below.

"We should go downstairs," Donna ventured.

"What's wrong with you?"

Donna stopped rocking and touched her chopsticks, gingerly, as if an indoor wind had disturbed them. Nothing was out of place. "I don't know. I've been feeling better this past week."

"Why don't you go to a doctor?"

"There's nothing wrong with my body."

"Are you going back to work?"

Donna lifted her head to the light and smiled. She began to rock again and lowered her eyes to Vera. "No."

"How come?"

"I can't."

Out of nowhere, on the next rock forward, Donna popped out of the chair and made a beeline for the desk. She stood over Vera who, caught off guard, used an arm to try and conceal her eulogy work, but Donna only rifled through the material Vera had gathered on the desk, a delight behind her lips, reading here and there, enjoying whatever it was she laid her eyes on. Vera didn't know what that could possibly be. Donna's arm brushed against Vera's bare shoulder to create a miniature lightning bolt and a beautiful little snap. Both ignored the shock. Vera seized her pencil. Donna turned and smashed right into the Hope Chest with her big toe.

"Fuck," Donna swore without thinking. She limped to the couch. "God that hurts." She sucked the breath between her teeth and squeezed her foot with both hands. It was genuine pain.

Vera reached for a new piece of paper. She tapped the pencil a few times on the page and began to write the eulogy again, more methodically than before, erasing here and there and pausing to think about kids in actual high school classrooms, adults living in skyscrapers, the inevitable collision of their galaxy with Andromeda, eight billion metal filings scattered on a magnetized disc, and she remembered a phrase in his journal she didn't know the meaning of: *fuck the barriers of Geometry and Time.*

Below, in another life, another song ended. She wished it were raining instead of snowing. It was not. It was snowing. Another cheer, not as audacious, rose up. Vera put down the pencil with a strange feeling: she wanted to keep writing but couldn't write anymore.

Donna had not changed position on the couch, and because Vera wanted to know right there and then she asked, in that monotone she perfected to conceal her true feelings, "Mom, what does 'fuck' mean?"

The opening notes of the next song were laced with electric harmonica. Donna lifted her head and shot back, "What do you think it means?"

"It's not in the dictionary."

"I don't know what it means."

"But you just said it."

Donna breathed so deeply that Vera thought the couch would collapse and fold in on itself, go crashing through the two floors that her father had built before she was born and drop on the dancers in the living room, crushing the funeral in its tracks. She hoped it would happen.

"Is there a reason you can't give real school a try?" Donna asked.

"How is it *real* school?" Vera snarled.

"As opposed to Bremen's—what would you call it—the way he

educated you?"

"Did you hate him because he never listened to you or because he always proved you wrong?"

"He made you believe you're better than other people. You're not."

"He trusted me."

"To do what?"

"To do things myself. He would never send me to school if I didn't want to go."

"You can't teach yourself everything. You need the expertise of people who have more experience and knowledge than you."

"Yes I can and no I don't."

"You honestly think that?"

"You don't know what I think."

"You're crazy if you think there is anybody on this earth that cares as much or has as much time to devote to you as Bremen did."

"I'm crazy?"

"You relied on him too much."

"*Real* school is the stupidest thing anybody's ever made me do. I'm never going back."

"So it's like prison for you? That right?"

"You're not going back to work."

"Ayla and Helene? You have friends that go to school."

"They're not my friends."

"I forgot. You hate everybody."

"I don't hate everybody."

"Who don't you hate?"

"Dad. Merlin."

"So no eulogy?"

"I hate you."

"You have no idea what the world is like."

"Yes I do."

"Tell me what the world is like."

Vera had been gradually rising on her toes, but shrank in response to her mother's challenge and eyed one of the aloe plants, sagging with the weight of its leaves. She had an overwhelming urge to water it. Donna re-focused on her toe and massaged. Both were content to say nothing further, for the heat and stress of the conversation had reached its natural limit, and a point of dissipation and release was needed before the next burn. Vera was at a greater loss then when she started. She didn't know what the ground she was standing on was made of, what her mother and father wanted, what her brother wanted, who had last watered the aloe plant or fed Merlin or what her eulogy was supposed to mean, and at that moment Vera didn't know anything, *anything*, that was certain and true. A rush of white heat knotted up the delicate part of her throat and she knew, very soon, she was going to cry. Look at the dictionary. It's red. Look at the globe. It's big. Her fingernails were dirtier than she thought. She was still in love with her dress. Look at the pencil. It's that purple-blue color you find in the core of a nebula. Look at your words. She wrote her *i*'s without dotting them. The harmonica in the song downstairs, plugged-in and overblown, was vibrating on its last drawn-out bar, like a super-melodious death rattle, and that was it, game over, the pressure of the night reached maximum capacity, Vera imploded, and the Mystery Machine expanded into one of those massive medieval cathedrals she had seen in her father's old photos of Vienna, and Vera was at the pulpit with nothing to say as the steeple bells rang and resounded through cobblestone streets in the golden morning haze while funeral guests sat like stones in the pews stretching back to infinity with every mossed and flinty eye locked on her in the silence she was expected to fill, and fill with heavenly singing. She recoiled, eyes moist.

"I can't do this."

"Stop it," Donna said. She rose from the couch and winced. She checked her chopsticks that hadn't moved an inch. "This is what he's asked you to do."

"But why not you or dad or Mo or any one of his friends?" She wiped her cheeks and her nose with her forearm, and wiped her forearm on her dress.

"You want to know *why* he picked you?" Donna wobbled, but remained standing.

Vera sensed the answer and feared it. She wished this person were not her mother and that tomorrow she'd wake up in Nashville or Tampa Bay or Boise or any other city besides Madison. She didn't feel the tears clinging to her chin like droplets at the end of icicles. Everything falls.

"You really think I know why your brother...? Why he wanted to homeschool you, why he wanted to have this insane funeral, why he wanted me to organize it or your father to serve drinks?"

Vera, thoroughly drained, kept standing. Her mother raised a hand to the eulogy fanned out on the trestle desk.

"All I really know, is that he trusted you to speak for him."

"It's not finished."

"I'm not worried."

Donna's face was unexpectedly tender, full of acceptance, a flickering of love that was unlike anything Vera had witnessed in the past six weeks. It didn't match with the pain Vera knew was throbbing through that toe, or any face in the ocean of her memory. Mirrored in her mother's eyes, she saw herself as young and proud and beautiful. Vera never once thought of herself as beautiful. She didn't hate her friends and she would never run away from home. She didn't know what the world was like and she did love her mother, but would never admit it. She thought she knew all the reasons why. Her hands ached, and that ache flowed to her chest and it hurt, this crush upon her heart, and she was drawn to the door, to its warm amber glow, to the voices and music of the funeral. The only relief from the pain, the only thing that made it flow back to where it came from, was the thought that her mother wasn't worried, and strangely she no longer carried a Steinway on her shoulders or had concrete bracelets clamped to her wrists. If she wanted to, she could fly.

Vera wiped her face clean from all its salty troubles. She removed the black band holding her ponytail in place, shook her head, gathered the hair anew, and cinched it back up. She collected the loose sheets of paper on the desk and folded them in half, twice, reaching under her dress and sliding the square into the waistband of her stockings, right at the hip. More rumblings in her stomach, gentle and insistent, like Merlin when he wants to be petted.

"I could eat something now," she said. "Is there any sweet potato pie left?"

"If they didn't finish it off. Blueberry, too."

There was no warning. Vera rushed at her and they hugged, a hard suffocating hug, parting easy. Donna reached for the cord and shut off the light. Vera swung an arm around her mother's waist, to ease some of the burden, and her mother put a hand on Vera's back, to balance the different weight of their bodies, and they left the Mystery Machine in a choppy rhythm, at their own pace, not bothering to close the door.

THIRD MOVEMENT

TABLE 1

Arianna Amilano Ancelotti was not your typical banker's daughter. She scorned the joyrides in her father's brand-new 1927 Maserati, his only mistress. She was allergic to all the luxuries that kept her mother's skin pale. She unchained her bike from a water pipe in the underground garage of her family's apartment building, and peddled down the narrow streets into Piazza Castella, near the twin bronze statues and the mansion they guarded, on through via Po and along the river proper, past the Library and the National Museum of Cinema, riding no-handed when she could. Never thought twice about the Shroud. Never thought once about Hell. She struggled like only a picky eater could to stomach the lamb on her plate when a bowl of cut-up tomatoes with sea salt would've done the trick times ten, and she wouldn't even have to wade through the ritual of refusal. She liked airy, unrestricted clothes. Early on she decided that her mother and father should leave her to herself, and in a peculiar, out-of-tune-with-the-times blessing, they did. She didn't like lemonade, and if life gave her lemons she had the habit of sculpting the fruit into pleasing shapes and bartering the shapes for what she really wanted, cherry soda. She hated her family's tenth floor penthouse, but loved her messy bedroom for the way it encouraged and embraced her solitude, as she imagined a ghost would befriend another ghost. She was rarely depressed for seventeen years, even with the rising world madness on all sides, which she didn't so much as walk around as swim through. And then: late summer, dusk, rainstorm recently passed, in a small valley with Dolcetto planted densely on the hillsides—Arianna Amilano Ancelotti woke up on a train, somehow taking a long time to recall the fact that, yes, she was Arianna Amilano Ancelotti, yes, she was traveling south, yes, she was eventually bound for Sardinia because, as she had told her parents, she was finally finished with *liceo classico* and wanted to go somewhere new and far away, why not Sardinia? Her parents said *Benne* and arranged a monthly stipend. Such amazing things do happen in life. Alone in that train car, smelling the stale and pervasive stink of the millions who had ridden before her, for the first time in her life she was spooked, in a panic, every muscle tense as hunted prey. She missed her parents, missed her bedroom, missed Torino and its sounds. The train car was traveling towards unbearable pain and the void of death. Her body would rot in anonymous ground. She got off at the next stop. Acqui Terme. The choice was a simple matter of life and death. A matter completely new to her. She drank from the sulfur waters in the *centro*, reserved a two-bedroom loft overlooking a famous fountain, took a rest for six months, found a job sweeping up a deli and learned to bake bread from scratch, marveled at how tawny the old men wore their skin, hopped a train to Roma, stayed four years, studied literature and architecture, became pedantic and ugly, quit school, moved back to Torino, lived there seventeen years, blossomed, held on with clean teeth throughout the war, working as a typist for a museum curator, as a consultant for an architectural firm, told by a warm and sturdy lieutenant of her parents' assassination by bullet and bullet, inherited more money then she ever comfortably wanted, failed to keep a journal, cringed at the nose of Barolo, mature or not, loved American screwball comedies, loved children who couldn't help staring at you, drifted aimlessly between men that, in all truth, could not keep up with her passions, let alone the paradox of her body, bony and soft, visited an aunt for a year in Paolo, despised it, was too hot, uprooted on a whim to Acqui Terme, settled six years, drank the sulfur waters every day, swept her feet along the floor of her old deli, met a group of well-connected contractors and landed a job overseeing the renovation of an important fountain damaged by the war, played with the rubble in her hands, felt healed, happily took a train back to Torino and along that same vine-rich valley she met a tall American, a financial consultant with a Sicilian accent and intimate knowledge of Cary Grant, crashed so funny into the cliffside of love, married, relocated to Chicago, stayed forty-two years, learned English, had a son, jogged in the park, was almost assaulted, jogged in a gym, cooked for relief, sipped Vermentino in the evening on the deck where the fireflies were legion, threw plates at her husband, forgave her husband, rode him in the basement on a lawn chair while their son was napping, taught Gadda and Pavese at community college, taught Italian at a private high school, cheered at lacrosse games, let the white hair grow from her temples, drove her son to Loyola, contemplated affairs, stalked museums, made love to her husband under the sheets in the bedroom, was ejected from orbit and onto a cold planet by a minor stroke, traveled to Acqui Terme, stayed eleven months, saw herself in the young girls and young men in the parks along the riverways, looking so good in the ripples and waves of their lives that could have, may have, possibly had been hers, because the deli was now a scooter shop, again felt healed, flew back to Chicago, met the soon-to-be-wife of her son, an all-bred Midwesterner with straight legs, bright eyes, and a devout belief in the kitchen, answered a phone call, heard of a heart attack, cremated her husband, slipped off the couch while straining to catch a bird that had flown inside, broke three ribs, moved, for the very last time, to Madison, Wisconsin, living with her son and his wife and two children, Rona and Élan, sparklers night after night, and she would rise especially early on Wednesdays and Saturdays, show the kids how to bake bread the old way in the small shed out back converted to a bakery per her directions, selling the loaves at the farmer's market near the capital square that reminded her of the more alluring spaces in her bicycle youth, which she hadn't ridden in decades, the point at which Bremen found her bread, died for it, asked about the method, unlocking old tales with a disarming ease, keeping in touch with her even after the market season ended, the bread was that good, and when Donna Lyons telephoned her last week and asked for an order for a hundred and fifty people, and gave the reason, Arianna Amilano Ancelotti, with all the nerve of her ninety-one years, pried opened that secret recipe box she had bolted just to the left of her heart, where she hid her recipes of Hell and the Shroud, of water that is white light, of Castor and Pollux and what it was they really guarded, and she woke early today, Thursday, baked her knuckles raw, delivered the bread in her son's minivan, not staying, no, not staying, but as a gift, one Donna knew how to accept graciously, with zero fanfare, she gave her seven pounds of insalade caprese in a big plastic tub, which Donna was now, in the serving room, next to the large wicker basket of bread, spooning into more convenient bowls, glass bowls, vintage, rarely used, with simple little etchings of dolphins at play in the sea.

———

"My collection of Dan Marino playing cards, rare back issues of Spectrum Music magazine, and that fourteen caret gold Muramatsu flute I found at a Pensacola flea market can all be sold at auction. The proceeds are to be given to my schoolboy friend, Luke Green, wherever he may be. Alive, I hope. In order for him to keep anything that results from," and here the estate attorney, Thomas R. Jones, a thin man with a thin mustache, turned from page twenty-four to twenty-five of Bremen Lyons' Last Will and Testament, "the sale of these objects, he must pledge, in written contract, to use the money to fund a trip to a country of his choice in South America, but he must not stay in any large city, such as one with a population exceeding 37,000. Preferably I would like him to stay as close and as intimate to the Rainforest as possible, but this is not a prerequisite to the proceeds."

Donna Lyons always knew her son had an abnormal relationship with death—he was six years old when he began making plans for his own. It was August, and too humid to do anything but turn on every fan in the house, drink Kool-Aid, and watch Blaze flip through the TV. He cycled through the channels three times before landing on a wide aerial shot of the Great Pyramids and the Sphinx.

It was your classic globetrotting NOVA documentary, *Story after Story: Death around the World,* but Donna couldn't keep from squirming. The documentary was insightful, treating each belief with respect, and for a child, *her* child, this was tantamount to approval and encouragement, exciting him to think about these things in a considered way. He wasn't ready. He would not have the life experience or the discretion to see how extreme these rituals really were. The documentary had raw footage of Buddhist Excarnations, where fellow monks hack up a dead brother's body and feed the pieces to vultures. They showed never-before-seen rituals of the Aghori living in the charnel houses of India, sleeping next to smoldering pyres, and eating rotten human flesh for the veneration of Kali, the destroyer of all things.

Donna spoke up. "Change the channel."

Bremen didn't bat an eye and Blaze just shrugged. It continued. There was an examination of detailed frescos capturing the Calatians as they mix their Beloved's ash with wine and drink the concoction; Romans who leaned in close, cupped their hands, caught and inhaled the dying's last breath; an analysis of native songs by the Iroquois and Pueblo which aimed to chant the soul to safety in the afterlife. Donna tried for the umpteenth time, "I really think we should change the channel," but Bremen had bonded to the screen and Blaze no longer held the remote in his hands. They saved the best segment for last. The Turning of the Bones. Every seven years in Madagascar family members show up far and wide, traveling entire days on foot, on bicycles, on trucks, for a great party, the greatest party: a dead relative is exhumed, the burial shroud unwrapped, the body proudly displayed, the body rewrapped, reburied, and for two days the people sang and drank and danced and laughed and cried and danced and sang and drank, the relatives huddling over the rags, thanking its spirit for protection and blessings, thanking the spirit, thanking the spirit. Donna made an executive decision. She scuttled Bremen up to his room in less than a minute. The next evening, he colored with concentration at the kitchen table.

"What is that?" Donna asked, pushing away a group of crayola pencils from the picture. It was a big red sun that filled most of the page, with small blue stick figures inside the sun, encircling a large yellow stick figure, lying horizontal in the center.

"My party." He didn't look up from coloring.

"Your party for what?" As if she had granted permission.

"Like when I come up from the ground."

"All my camping equipment can be sent to *Campers Anonymous*, a non-profit organization located in Chicago. If it is no longer operational, give the equipment to Gretta Attice, a girl I hitchhiked with in Peru, many years ago, and whom I haven't talked to since '08. These things happen. I'm sorry, Gretta. I should've kept in touch. Remember that night in Lima with the switchblade and roses? If she cannot be found or is not alive, donate my camping gear to a local homeless shelter."

Thomas R. Jones coughed and took a drink of water. He rubbed the bridge of his nose with his thumb and forefinger. He loosened his cream-and-navy blue argyle tie, and made a quick note with a black pen on his legal pad. Donna could see that he had no emotional attachment, but there was resentment, there was exhaustion, and she resonated with that mental state, unexpectedly full of compassion for Tom Jones and the energy he did not have. How ridiculous and pathetic this must all seem to him!

Then it began. Donna was now accustomed, as much as humanly possible, to the feeling. She didn't scream. She didn't faint. She remembered this morning in the kitchen, and that gave her the strength to get through this thing, whatever it was.

It started with a tingling pressure in her carotid artery, where her scar began, and it spread throughout her body like an algal bloom, to the aorta, the subclavian, the thoracic, the femoral major, until she could feel her whole body pulse with a vigorous heartbeat that threatened to crack her wide open. When Tom Jones commenced reading the Will, Donna saw flares of carnelian light shoot out of his head and ripple down his shoulders.

"I have a lot of post cards. I don't know what to do with these items. It somehow feels wrong to throw them away, and yet, they are worthless. They are blank postcards I bought to remind me of a definite time and place. All their meaning is pretty much bound up inside my chest cavity."

Donna Lyons did not directly stare at the light emanating from Tom Jones. Instead, she gazed intently at the empty spaces around his body, at the brownish-red light wheeling about him in fluid clouds. She squinted, narrowed her vision, and a piece of Tom Jones resolved into focus—a blackness the size of a quail egg had burrowed itself into his left lung like a tick behind the ear of a dog. With a delicate recalibration, she viewed the black egg full-on, and there was an immediate sense of entering into the pain of Tom Jones, exposing herself to the fast flickering impressions of his secret universe: an empty baby crib; a leaky kitchen faucet; his wife sitting on a lawn chair drinking pink lemonade and gin with the weeds swaying high against the chain-link fence that divided their land from the prairie field she faced, while he slept in a truck parked in their driveway. They no longer desired to live in a distant Dane county suburb with limited residents.

"Let's call the post-cards up for grabs. First come first serve. Suggestions: burn them; use them as coasters; send them back to where they came from, with a message on the other side."

It was a cold day, the sky low and suffocating. The law firm of Deacon, Jones, & Carlson was located on the main drag of East Washington, two blocks from the Capital Square. The reception room had a view of the Dome. Refreshments were complimentary. A tone of reassurance radiated from the mauve-colored hallways. Donna wondered how Bremen even found this place. Tom Jones' office was spacious, elegant, and accommodating. One full wall was devoted to morbidly obese legal volumes, and the other to his framed academic credentials. Solid red curtains, covering the office's floor-to-ceiling windows, gently shimmered from well-hidden heating vents.

He walked around his slim oak desk to receive Blaze, Vera, Mo, Terry, and Donna, appropriately somber. Five chairs were set up in a singe row in front of Tom Jones' desk. After an awkward interval—nobody knew where to sit—Vera took the far left seat, Mo the far right, Blaze next to Vera, Terry next to Mo, and Donna, last woman standing, plopped down in the middle. Donna felt claustrophobic as the reading began, so she scooted her chair back a few feet, breaking the row, out of line with the others, but the creeping sense of enclosure, of compression, remained. She asked Donna the Luminous for help.

Help arrived.

Her visual field expanded beyond the peripherals. Her mind was lifted into direct perceptions. This is what allowed her to see Mo as a hot yellow sphere of fire, as a woman so in love with her son that she was angry with him for dying. To see Blaze, leaning his head against the back of his chair like a weary traveler in an airport, consumed by green guilt and confusion, clueless about where to step next. To see Terry (best posture of them all) crumble into despair when the Will mentioned that Bremen's Afrobeat records were to be given to a former student of his, Anastasia Something. A dark blue cloud engulfed Terry's head and took up residence like fungus on a plant. Vera was slouching, crossing her ankles, she shouldn't be doing that, but her daughter was so frightened by the death of her brother that she believed it was better to act as if she had no more family left. And Tom Jones? He was a mirror, reflecting back to Donna who she clearly was: an exhausted, hysterical woman, one who lost certain foundations in her life and was buried in the collapse that followed. She was trying to claw her way out, find some sort of path back to herself, and if she took the wrong way, let's not think about that. Donna Lyons was on the Verge. She could almost touch her fearlessness. The past did not push her forward—the future pulled her towards an event of unknowable magnitude.

This was the best way she could explain it to herself.

WHEN DONNA LYONS FIRST saw an aura, she blacked out in her office and awoke ten minutes later to an unforgettable headache. The pain in her skull was so immense she thought she must've knocked it on her desk. A ring of doctors and nurses hovered above her. She called for Blaze, and he appeared, was somehow already there, and with a ferocity he often saved for the Construction Site, he scattered the doctors and nurses and drove her home. They sat in a very sick silence in the living room, waiting for Vera, and then Vera walked through the front door. The rest of Donna's memory of that day has been erased, like censored secret memos.

When it became clear to the Hospital that something radical had happened to their best Senior Administrator, rumors started to swirl thick as cigar smoke that she wasn't coming back, that she'd be replaced by a brill-creamed BSD just out of Brown Medical Management. Her co-workers assumed it was because of the phone call, because of the news about her son. It was extremely easy for Donna to allow this interpretation to stand as the truth. So she allowed it.

After the phone call from USCG Sector Charleston Command Senior Chief Philip Joyce, she had to go home and lie down, but did not want to share with anyone, anyone, the reason why, not to spare them the gloom or embarrassment, no, it was because she hated the thought of people feeling sorry for her, and this was the last place of all places she wanted sympathy, even if it was real. She decided to jump out her fourth floor office window. She rationalized the snow-banks softening her fall. Her legs were dangling in the air and her arms were poised to push off when her secretary entered the office unannounced with a quire in one hand, a red ballpoint in the other, and her bloodless lips running on stenographic mode.

"For this Friday we've got twenty-seven OR patients on schedule and just five FTE's so I assume—" She dropped the pen and put her hand to her mouth.

Donna turned back inside and slid off the window frame, guilty. Then she saw it, a blue fire around her secretary's head, rising off her like heat waves from a radiator. Donna blinked once, twice, three times the charm, but the flame pulsed and persisted. She was spellbound, inching closer to the source, and once within reaching distance she began to paw at the blue flame as if it was solid.

Of course it wasn't.

TABLE 2

MORE RECENTLY, MORE INTENSELY in the past few weeks, his mother had become *La Sucia,* the Dirty Woman. It was true she slept with men, and men, sometimes, paid her, and it was true she enticed them near the river pools, by surprise, appearing out of night when the mist lifted off the canopy and you caught a rare glimpse of the moon in a patchy sky. And it was true she sometimes drugged and snatched from a man whatever important and worthless things were in his pockets, and it was true she would kill a neighbor's chickens without permission, and she would stab a stray dog with swollen testicles, if it tried to take her scraps. But she was a real human being and her name was Roberta, it was not just a story, he kept telling himself that. She had toenails to clip and a favorite color—that dank shade of brown on a tree trunk after a storm. In the bars sprawled along the shores of La Ceiba, some of the men on whom she had descended would first tell of a voice smooth as river stones, of a body that bends tight like a jungle stream, and all that wetness. Then the teller would go tight-lipped and glassy-eyed, and a guy in the back of the little crowd would snap his fingers, and in the midst of a banana sea breeze cooling the sweat on his neck, another beer would be set down by an anonymous hand, so on with the rest of the goddamn story.

La Sucia carried her just-born son to Rio Cangrejal on the east edge of town, south of the ruckus of Barrio La Barra, where he was probably born amid calls for Rum and Gringos ripe for robbing. She knelt with him at the rocky shoreline of the river, looking left, looking right. She held him under the water. An old ragged drunk, a Garifuna, a lifetime of doors slammed in his face, had stumbled out to that very same place at that very same time. He saw what she was doing, snatched the boy from the water, and with fists like mountain stones, beat Roberta to death. The police, unable (and unwilling?) to see the full picture, hung the drunk, as they had been waiting to do. The child was registered to an orphanage and put up for adoption. That child, Louie Russert thought, huddled up in a Packers leather jacket, smoking a blunt of Granddaddy Purp on the front porch and watching it snow, the flakes falling slow and quiet like honey falls from a spoon, that child was me.

A trunk lumbered down the street, breaking up his thoughts, sprinkling a salt solution out its ass that will rust cars like cigarettes age people. Louie checked his cell phone. 4:27 pm. The sun dropped its dagger on the vinyl of night, and the snow was crisper, almost crystal. It would get cold as hell tonight. His blunt was down to its nib, and the resin made his fingertips sticky. He took one last pull and smartly tapped it out on the porch railing, tossing it in a broken clay flowerpot half-filled with frozen dirt, and ran up the stairs into his apartment.

Desmond Dekker spun on the player, "Nincompoop," and Louie thought it was summer and he was absurdly overdressed, but his Honduran soccer jersey and boot-cut Levi's were perfect for the upcoming occasion.

He dropped a liberal dose of Visine in his eyes, smelled his hands—tar and ash and bud—and washed them, twice. He brushed his teeth and looked in the mirror. Still there, shithead. He rolled a pinner on the desk in his room and stuck it behind his ear, wiping his hands on his jeans then spotted the guitar—a six-string Gibson Blues King Vintage Sunburst, acoustic-electric, which Bremen had left him—leaned up against the wall, beset by dirty laundry. The guitar and Louie. Louie and the guitar. The two could have been looking at each other from across a bridge, each about to undertake separate journeys to novel lands.

His roommate, Reed Cline, clomped up the stairs and busted down the front door and shouted, "Yo, Louie? You home?"

Reed was into weightlifting, split-routines and supersets, didn't really smoke, studied too little, worshipped woman too much, didn't give a shit about anything political, but he could cook a mean Duck Ragout and did his dishes after dinner, a real responsible man.

"Louie! You here?" Reed had the habit of starting and maintaining conversations through the walls of the apartment. How was Louie going to leave the house without having to see Reed or be seen by him?

Louie took the Gibson Sunburst in his hands. The fret was coated by a layer of fine dust. The tortoiseshell pick was unfamiliar with his touch—he hadn't slept with a girl in months. When he held the small guitar to his body he was surprised (because he did not remember) at the fragility of its spruce and mahogany frame. His life consisted of reading a lot of books, listening to lots of music, watching lots of movies, smoking lots of weed, and working a shit job at a deli inside a corner grocery store after dropping out of college, because he didn't go to classes and would quit any job that gave him responsibility over even one person. He plucked a few chords, deep full sounds, yet without precision and out of tune. He closed his eyes and bowed his head and set the guitar on the bed, telling himself he would play in the morning.

"Louie, man, what are you up to tonight?" Reed shouted through the walls.

FRANK'S DELI WAS ACTUALLY a grocery/liquor store on the corner of Paterson and Eagle, a true historical relic built in 1926 and owned by a fourth-generation Slovakian family. It had a screwball layout, with ten-foot high shelves and slim aisles that prohibited two-way traffic. It resembled the passageways of an unkempt hedge maze, like the isthmus itself, and Louie loved working here. The job was easy. The owners didn't get in your shit if you didn't get in theirs.

The parking lot was empty and unplowed. Louie reversed his Taurus up to the back alley door. When he hit the brakes, the rear wheels locked and the car skidded into the building. No damage that would matter.

Inside the meat cooler were eight large saran-wrapped circular trays. Four were cheese trays: a selection of Brie, blue, cheddar, and Spanish. Four were mixed fruit: exotic melons and berries, grapes and cantaloupe and kiwi. One by one he carried them out to his car as if transporting artistic pieces of priceless cultural value. The final tray of cheese was in his hands when the Deli's new cashier popped his head through the cooler doors.

"We got a special kind of—" turning over his shoulder and addressing somebody in the store. "What is it?"

Louie heard a female voice, sharp and certain and delicate as a killer strand of Sativa. "Drambuie."

"Drambuie," echoed the cashier.

"We have it."

The woman was preternatural, her dark brown hair coiffed like an aging movie star from the 70s, looking snazzy in a red fur shawl that couldn't have been warm enough tonight, especially with the sparkling silver dress she was sporting underneath. She had a cured-olive glow to her skin that may or may not have been the product of genetics, Louie couldn't tell, and her face—real blood and cold blushing her cheeks, the lightest pink shade of lipstick, eyelashes thin and long and individual—had to be near fifty.

"Drambuie?" Louie said. "Let me show you."

She followed obediently.

He became aware of the Sure Fire Mega Mix that played over the store speakers, which was the official music station of Frank's Deli. It was a rotating selection of songs, whatever-was-popular or whatever-used-to-be-popular, the selection determined by a not-yet-fully-self-aware computer fed trillions of statistical data bites a second, sifting it through multi-dimensional algorithms devoted to profit, and then demonically generating a never-ending broadcast which is pumped out from some clandestine warship that never docks, only circles the globe and inserts itself in the airwaves with the most pathetic messages that can amass in three to four minutes, that was the job (as Louie imagined it) of an aural virus like the Sure Fire Mega Mix—to infect the already harmonious human being with dissonance. He had, for the better part of his time at Frank's, been successful at canceling out the station from his conscious awareness, but now he heard, could not stop hearing, "The Promise" by When In Rome. The woman's high-heeled shoes clicked behind him in syncopation with the cheesy beat.

The entire back wall of the store was stocked with over two hundred different bottles of liquor. The woman was awestruck, teetering back and forth, showing her tipsy hand. There was one Drambuie left, far to the northwest. Louie retrieved a tiny stepladder in the corner.

"Hope you don't need two."

The woman didn't answer. She was staring at the wall, eyes rapidly scanning. "Do you have Absinthe?" she said.

"Right there," pointing to the middle shelf, slightly to the left.

"What do you carry?" she said urgently.

Louie glanced at the Absinthe bottle within her sight lights. "You mean what kind of Absinthe?"

"What Absinthe do you carry?"

"Pernod and Lucid."

She absorbed this information carefully, and her next sentence was low, as if she was transmitting a secret few should hear, and if they did, would they even understand? "And Suze, do you have Suze?"

Louie, if he were sober, would have wordlessly retrieved the bottle and held it an inch from her face. He couldn't remember the last time he was sober at work, but he tried, and as he tried, he split off like a branch from the main tree and hovered above the situation, looking down at this woman, this boy, this store, these bottles, these lyrics, and totally on cue he remembered there was a funeral tonight, and he had a serious role in it. Someone was dead, someone he knew, and here he was treating a stranger like the shithead he never stopped being. The Fruit and Cheese trays waltzed through his mind like a demented couple dancing in an old folks' home. His face was death under a white sheet. His face wore a toe tag.

"We have Suze." Louie reached for the bottle, an arm's length away, but the woman suddenly snatched it first.

"That will do," she said. "I didn't mean to bother you."

"It's fine," Louie said.

"One can't always know what will do—until it does."

"I think so."

She clutched the bottle to her chest. "You are uneasy. Why?"

"I—don't think so?"

"Yes, you are," not angry at all.

"About what?"

"To me? You want to apologize to me?"

"I was only trying to help you get what bottle you wanted."

The woman moved toward him, looking over his shoulder and around his head. She sniffed—was it a stuffy nose or holding back tears?—and with the second knuckle on her left index finger, she wiped the outer crease of her right eye.

"And you did," she said. "You helped me."

She lowered her head and held herself there for a moment. "I thank you."

Louie believed if he offered his hand, she would kiss it. The woman straightened and stepped back to appraise him, soon pursing into a smile, as if finally solving a puzzle she had worked on for months.

"I have known you since non-becoming, but I was not aware of this current manifestation." She took a few wobbly steps backwards, never breaking eye contact, brushing against a floor display of all-natural potato chips and almost knocking down a shelf of hot peanuts, but righting herself, not a hint of damaged pride, and then she walked away.

"Until the next life," coyly over her shoulder.

Louie Russert hopped on John Nolan Drive, skirting the southeast end of frozen Lake Monona, dotted with the dedicated shacks of ice-fishers. He merged east onto the Beltline and knew it was a comfortable twenty-five minutes to Bremen's house if he cut north up Stoughton, less cops, the isthmus might be crawling with them.

The snow fell as before, but the woman at the store had unnerved him. She struck a rarely-resonant chord. His mother, his real mother, was a note he didn't want played by anyone but himself. He removed the joint from his ear and flicked the thumbwheel on his lighter and a flame appeared. He passed two cars—one on its side, one flipped over on its roof, hazard lights blinking. They had recently crashed in the ditch in the center of the highway. He lifted his foot off the gas and thought about stopping, but far in his rearview there appeared, cresting a rise, three sets of cherries and blueberries, so he put the joint behind his ear and sped up, thinking that he wouldn't be doing these things if he hadn't been adopted from Honduras. What, then, would he be doing? Would he be standing with his teachers as the COBRA squad launches canister after canister of tear gas into their circle? Would he be cheering with the thousands in the fútbol stands, feeling that sense of purpose and certainty, surrounded by an ocean of his own people, an ocean that cannot be contained or controlled? Would he actually touch the daily dirt and humidity, and maybe, just maybe, realize what it's like to live in a place that's mostly about fear and regret? These were well-trodden thoughts with clear vistas. Same view as: Why even bother? Why go? He would not be used to the weather. He didn't have any of the big words in Honduras, *friends, family, commitment*. His Spanish was gleaned from the announcers on TV. Besides, it was the same here as it was there, all the corruption and despair and injustice makes you think anything you do is of no use. How do you go on here? How could you go on there?

Louie took a right on Nelson, a left on Bailey, wanting to drive the back roads, but the plows hadn't reached this area yet. He rounded a corner that was wider than it appeared and a fishtail began. He eased off the gas, turned into the skid, lost control, and the Taurus made two smooth 360's before it jerked to a stop in the middle of the road, facing the correct direction. No cars were oncoming. Fruit and Cheese were unharmed. Louie took a big stabilizing breath, shaking his head in disbelief. He gripped the steering wheel, crept the car forward, slow and alert, scanning the scene, nothing dangerous, then poof, forgetting any danger, forgetting the fishtail, speeding up, transforming the snowy road into nothing remotely specific, only the seductive and powerful idea of a New World, a world where Wisconsin and Honduras overlapped in his imagination and shared the borders of frozen lakes and rainforests and the smell of hand-pounded tortillas and Friday fish fries, where everybody cheered for the Packers and Marathón, where government records carried no weight because the only thing that mattered was that everywhere a human being went a human being remained a human being. Louie concentrated on this universal characteristic everyone shared, on driving as strong as possible in this basic humanity, so that when he gazed out his breath-fogged window, *plain as day tho it's night,* even the dead of the world climbed out of the snow and waved to him like the good friends they were. He waved back.

Hey, shithead, where's that joint?

DONNA. "YOU MUST BE Louie."

He tried to look down at the cheese tray and not at the scar on her neck. "This is the first one."

"Follow me."

The kitchen was the size of his living room and smelled of plucked-from-the-tree apple pie. The hallway was crammed with family portraits he never once posed for. He walked into an enormous living room, empty except for a small glass table pushed against a wall. A white laptop, closed, rested upon it. Two gigantic black speakers loomed on either side. Hazy voices and bodies moved about the house but he saw no one.

Donna opened a set of double doors to the serving room. Directly opposite the entrance was a large bay window where succulents and air plants and Wandering Jews hung from the ceiling. Three miniature electric water fountains bubbled away on the bench seat. Four lacquered tables displayed the funeral food. The first, going left to right, served bread and salad. The second was bare. The third had sushi, crab cakes, and snap peas. The fourth, some entrancing pies.

Donna. "You can put them on the second table."

Louie moved in a stilted fashion, too stoned to do anything but watch '80s action movies or read about anarchy. He was having a mild freak-out and Louie Russert never has mild freak-outs: they are always full-blown. Each time he returned to the serving room Donna was standing in the exact same spot in front of the window, watching his every movement, and the second Louie set down the last tray on his designated table, she said, "The food looks fantastic. I really appreciate you doing this. It means a great deal."

"It's cool."

Acorn brown for Louie, granite blue for Donna—each of them roamed their respective eyes over the completed vista of the Four Tables.

"How long did Bremen give you guitar lessons?"

"About two and a half years."

"Why did you stop?"

"Couldn't afford it anymore. He told me he do it for free, said I had talent. But I guess I just didn't feel like it."

"I know what that's like."

They pretended to be absorbed at the sight of the food. In the air was twenty pounds of uneasy pause.

"So—do you still play guitar?"

"I'm trying to play more often."

"Louie, I'm sorry to ask. But—is that a joint in your ear?"

He quickly palmed the pinner in his hand. His face was hot enough to spark it. "Shit. I totally forgot. I didn't—"

"It's fine," Donna reassured him. "You don't have to worry." She lowered her voice like uncool parents were in the next room. "You can go smoke out back. Before a lot of people start showing up."

Where does the weight go when relieved? To the source of the weight, which is the light.

Last week, stressed and sober (his dealer was waiting on a shipment from Boulder) and strumming his way through a jazz exercise on Bremen's guitar, he thought about his mother, La Sucia, and that the ability to pluck the strings with his fingers and follow the notes with his eyes was a miracle beyond his comprehension, that the dead man's guitar somehow embodied his soul, and there was an unsettling acceptance for the mother he would never know and the life he often thought he was wasting. Donna's voice, her unremarkable words, her scar and sincerity, echoed this feeling, intensified it like a Fender 40 Watt Amp, and so Louie smiled at her as goofy as possible to keep from letting the tears, in their nascent stages, form and fall.

"Would you want to smoke this with me?"

There is something Donna Eleanor Lyons does when she sacrifices a pleasurable impulse with a knowingly satisfied outcome for an uncertain future responsibility: she holds her breath.

"I can't. There's just," surveying the Four Tables. "There's just so much to do." Louie nodded and put the joint back in his ear. Donna breathed normal.

"Did Bremen ever smoke with you?" she asked.

"No, I wish I could have though." For a moment he glanced at her and in that moment she glanced back.

And now, thank the Supreme Neutral Center, there is a special pause, around Donna's lips and Louie's brow, a pause at the perfect place in the composition, after a dash of grace notes or a grating bass chord. It's a pause that occurs after an argument thoughtfully resolved, between spouses or siblings, to avoid bloodshed or banishment. A pause in the aftermath of a stranger doing something decent for another stranger, whether it's picking up a MetroCard dropped on the subway steps, or agreeing, when sharing a noon whiskey at a dive bar, with a grievance wholly justified. It had the intended effect.

Donna pointed to a quarter-wheel of cheese, creamy custard yellow. "What's that one?"

"It's Camembert, a French cheese. Like Brie."

Donna said dreamily, "I do like Brie."

Louie couldn't contain himself. "There's this stupid joke Bremen told me once."

Donna couldn't either, electricity in her eyes. "What?"

"How do you get a bear down from a tree?"

"How?"

Louie, crooking his finger and cooing to his pet, "Cam-on-bear. Cam-on-bear."

"I DO NOT CONSIDER Merlin to be a possession. I never registered him with any humane society or pet control center. Microchip free. He never had any serious diseases or injuries that required surgery. He is seventeen years old and in excellent health. I let him roam outside often, but not when—"

Donna Lyons was a board-runner for the Recovery/Outpatient division of Community Memorial when they found Merlin (or, if you like, he found them). She reviewed the minutes of EOM fiscal meetings to get a sense of the responsibilities, enjoying the overwork and how it stimulated her body to the limit of its powers and pushed any conspicuous inner voice to the background. She was often late to every engagement outside of the hospital. It was near ten pm when she finally picked up Bremen from his Friday night guitar lessons south of the UW-Madison campus. Stressed and hungry, Donna drove home straight through the heart of the isthmus, but it was Halloween weekend and the Capital Square was clogged by hundreds of costumed partygoers criss-crossing the sidewalks and streets.

Bremen rolled down his window at the red light on Washington and Fairchild, curious about the crowd. Something knocked against the side of the car, and a petite redheaded girl appeared at his window, huge black pupils pulsing, *Miss Universe,* said the sash across her glittering pink mini-dress. In a Disney princess voice, she told Bremen he was beautiful, reaching through the window, brushing his face with her fingers, that he was the most precious thing she had ever seen, the most beautiful thing she had ever seen, she hoped he would never die—roll up the window—please never, ever die—roll up the window!—it would be awful if you die.

At home, Bremen asked Donna what was it supposed to be like when you die. She didn't have anything prepared. She said—it doesn't matter what she said, because that was when they heard a series of prolonged and strident meows from outside and upon opening the back door they saw him right there on the steps, a lean orange tabby with white strips and visible ribs, expectant and poised like the Pharaoh's personal kitten, ratty with burrs and licking his chops.

"—I lived on a busy street. My wish is that he reside with my father, mother, and sister. I understand this may not be to everyone's preference, but he is old, his time is short, and we must think of Merlin's happiness, not our own."

Tom Jones took off his glasses, dropping them with a tired clack on his desk. He gazed out upon the gathered. Nobody paid him the slightest bit of attention, except Donna. Their eyes met. The collar on his ordinary Oxford button-up was two-fingers too big, the suit hanging off Tom Jones like he was nineteen and had borrowed it from his father for his first job interview. The thinness seemed like an irregular function of his metabolism. Beamed from the black egg inside Tom Jones, Donna received a transmission, a knowledge gained and understood biochemically (there wasn't anything in her head you could properly call thoughts), sensing and feeling what Tom Jones sensed and felt as he evolved from the loss of a thing so much loved to the inability to transfer that love elsewhere.

This is why Donna put her hand to her throat, why her eyes watered up and reflected the light of a Northwoods lake. The initial pains of a migraine began to ping in her temples.

"I think we should take a short break," Tom Jones said, flipping through the pages. "We have about an hour left."

Mo, irritated, as if watching a good movie somebody unexpectedly paused, "Why are we stopping?"

"I'm asking if anyone wants a break?"

"Like, right now?"

Tom Jones blinked a few times and spoke down to the desk. "Does anybody have to use the restroom?"

"Let's just keep going," Blaze said.

His posture had not changed—he was still slumped in the chair—but his head had managed to lift itself off the backrest. You could hear a police siren far away like someone whispering in the next room. Blaze Lyons adjusted his shoulders and hips and physically centered himself in the chair. "The less we draw this out the better. Let's keep rolling."

"Yeah," Terry and Vera said, in unison. They leaned forward to eye each other from across the row, stunned, as was everyone, at how both enunciated the word with the same tone, pitch, and duration. Shame there was no laughter.

Tom Jones, silently, put his glasses back on. He cast an ambivalent glance in Donna's precise direction, and she felt the pain of the migraine subside and the electricity in her limbs fritter away. She did not let herself be read.

Everyone resumed their previous positions.

It played on.

Donna did her best not to think about what the Will made her think about: a cat, a man she's slept with for thirty years, her daughter. Presumptuous denial is not your weapon. You cannot live in irrational dreams. You cannot escape into erroneous images. Turn over your thoughts and inspect them as you would a diamond for flaws. Transmute by the sword and transmute by the scale. Life is aware of your awakening and will assist you. Don't you remember? This is not the first time. That was the voice Donna had been hearing off and on for about two weeks, closely connected with her headaches and the lights, and it continued to transmit at a frequency only she could hear. Inside her, the many impressions of Tom Jones merged into the definite shape of a story, a story of a small black egg that caused him breathing problems at night, and how it was created by his infant son who died in his crib. A story of his wife, Loren, hollowed out from within by the grief, a story of Dane County prosecuting them for the height of weeds in their yard. It was a story of Tom Jones and the unresolved trauma that sapped key energy from his cells, siphoning off the elemental force of his life. He was literally wasting away before her eyes.

Donna Lyons used to be a suspicious and doubtful person. She used to hold things so close to the chest they grafted without effort onto her skin. At every point in her life, from school to home to work and in between, she was conditioned in ways subtle and gross to accept the idea that her own interpretations of life were unreliable, her own thoughts were not to be trusted, and she had to rely on outside objective opinion for correct knowledge and direction, and that she would never know, and could never trust, the truth and reality of her own perceptions.

She's changed.

THE MORNING AFTER A blue flame appeared around her secretary's head, Donna awoke with ten-thousand ice picks breaking up her brain, each one tasering like riot cops whenever it hit. She squirmed in bed and smothered her head in Sobakawa pillows. She called to Blaze, repeatedly, and he seemed to take an hour to materialize. She was sweating, a ton, and drained of motive power. Water touched her lips. Lukewarm, she tasted an ugly chemical taint, and spit it out like the poison it was. Against the judgment of her tongue, she opened her eyes.

Here is what she saw: dim yellow light pulsing in her peripherals, and dark morphing figures in the background that settled into silhouettes she could almost recognize. Blaze, or the outline that resembled him, came towards her and opened his arms. There was a violent white flash and despite the phenomenal pain she had a vision of Blaze as a child, sitting on a blanket with his mother and father in Capital Park, traumatized by the Fourth of July fireworks, crying like only a helpless little boy could, feeling in the explosions the wordless truth that his mother, rough and curly hair, was going to die, and his father, massive burly hands, was going to die, and he himself, small toes and tummy, was going to die.

Blaze and Vera were in the bedroom, at the foot of the bed, speaking with each other. Donna heard the words *condition* and *weight* and *hospital*.

She spoke, maybe even shouted. "So that's why you don't like fireworks?"

She didn't see their reaction. By then, everything had faded to a nice uniform black.

SHE REGAINED CONSCIOUSNESS SOME other night. Merlin stretched and yawned and slitted his eyes at her from the edge of the bed. When Donna made a slight move to rise he jumped off and raced out of the room.

The house wasn't breathing. There was no pain and no light. Everything in the bedroom was switched off and she had a strong compulsion to keep it that way. She saw a familiar glowing, soft fuzzy peach, coming from the bathroom. Someone left the light on. She moved towards it, but didn't walk. There was a magnet in her stomach attracted to a magnet in the bathroom and the potential of this attraction increased the spin of her atoms past the speed of light, decreasing the force of gravity on her body and boosting the levity of every cell. She was weightless, being pulled down the hallway like a song pulled from the soul of a sharecropper, after his rejection by the mean-old Ms. McGhee on the banks of an creek two miles from the train station. The tips of her toes brushed along the hardwood floor, insisting on her weightlessness. Donna obeyed.

Shaving cream and black whiskers were stuck high on the sides of the sink. The faucet dripped. An unfolded straight razor lay on the counter, wiped clean. It had a carbon steel blade, a dark brown and beige handle made of Ram's horn. Donna sliced off a lock of hair. She studied the spilt ends and entertained the possibility of cutting it all off and transforming into a new person—she didn't want to be Donna Lyons anymore. But that'd be a shallow gesture, a cosmetic crutch, would no more make her a new person then if she put on a wig, or got breast implants, had a heart transparent, a sex change. Donna ran her thumb along the smooth handle and sharp blade and came to the totally obvious conclusion that nothing but death could make her a new person. Everything else was posturing and cowardice. The clarity of this thought overwhelmed her, made her overflow with gratitude at having it. She put the razor to her neck.

Donna Lyons was determined, but inexperienced. When she pushed the carbon tip into her flesh there was a stinging pain of self-preservation, and instead of drawing the blade across her neck she drew it down in panic and missed the carotid. She still fainted. There was still plenty of blood. Vera found her, sleepy crust in her eyes, having down come from the turret to use the bathroom. She walked into a living nightmare, so you couldn't blame her screams for scaring the shit out of Blaze, who was downstairs in the kitchen searing a steak. After shaving that night, he realized he hadn't eaten for three days straight.

BRIGHT YELLOW SUN SHIMMERED along the edges of the window curtains. That's all Donna knew, in bed, underneath multiple comforters. She lifted the blankets and smelled something dank and stale. She hauled herself to the shower. She ripped the bandage off her neck and didn't feel the sting. The cut was slim and superficial and looked worse than it actually was. She wouldn't need stitches. In the shower, which never seemed to get hot enough, Donna thought about the hospital, if it had caved in on itself without her. Probably not. She air-dried in front of the full-length bedroom mirror, skin pink and red from the scalding water, foreseeing a scar that would always be visible. She was certain that if she returned to work she would be unhappy in ways so terrible and desolate that a host of migraines began to assemble behind her eyes. So she wouldn't go. Perhaps never again. Donna Lyons began to grow, keeping proportion, but growing out of the boundaries of the mirror, growing out of the roof of the house. She rose up through the snow-dusted trees and beyond. The neighborhood stretched north and merged with flat farmland. The west was clotted with highways and apartment blocks and car parks and the capital dome between the blue beacons of Mendota and Monona. Donna soon surpassed thick clouds and thin clouds. The buildings became bugs, and the details of terra—rivers, cities, forests—gave way to geometric abstraction. She grew upwards and upwards to a deeper and deeper blue. The Moon was as vivid as a war-torn street. She could barely face the Sun. She spied the red spheres of Jupiter and Mars, caught a flash of Saturn's rings, growing and growing, grown too big for the Earth. She was unable to keep both feet on the ball. She lost her balance, reached feebly towards substance, and tumbled through black without time and sound.

TABLE 3

WILD SALMON HAVE RUN their birthright stream, spawned, died, been smoked, and now rest in tender pieces with homegrown cucumbers and onions, swathed in Amish devout-in-their-daily-prayers-to-God cream cheese, everything nestled in a cold rice and seaweed roll, alongside Volcanoes and Spiders and Rainbows and Dynamites in austere sleek white serving trays, dotted, wabi-sabi style, by green blobs of wasabi. Next to the trays are white marble bottles filled with Nama Shoya that was aged in cedar barrels, the same wood as the chopsticks, each pair tied with a bow of red string, all fanned out at the front of the table, the utensils to remain unbroken until 6:03 p.m., so sayeth the Will. Crabcakes and snap peas, with equally abiding origins, shared the same space.

You could say Sado Haroki did not much care for his customers, that he did not attempt to please their egos or aesthetic principles, comp them or consider them his peers. You could say Sado Haroki thought he had no peers.

One night, a group of Oyama's cooks and servers, including Bremen, joined Sado after the sushi restaurant closed. They polished off six bottles of White Tiger Sake and were discussing rival restaurants in the area when Pratima, the Indian hostess with sandstorm eyes Bremen never misplaced in his memory, brought to Sado's attention the fact that there existed much more famous and well-regarded sushi chefs with restaurants in Vegas and Manhattan and Rio and Sydney and here he was, in Wisconsin of all places, not even Chicago, here in this crumbling brick shithouse, with low ceilings, electric candles, very limited seating, cracks in the bathrooms walls covered by generic Buddhist art, where the water pipes freeze every winter, and we're not even on State Street, not even—and here Sado cut her off with a brutal chop of his hand.

"If a child with a desire to cook keeps this desire until he is a man, and if this child has talent, for the ease of this conversation we will call it natural, and if the child works hard to nurture this natural talent, then through his work and, for the ease of this conversation we will call it luck, through his work and luck he will succeed—he will have a well-regarded restaurant in a well-regarded city. He will be considered a great natural talent."

When Sado Haroki wanted to make sure people were listening, really listening, to *him*, he did three things, in this order: examined them with such concentration that the unfortunates in his sight lines covered themselves with their hands from the fear of nakedness; then he laughed; then he would wipe his mouth with the back of his hand, or, if he had a drink, he drank. So he drank.

"This desire that has led him to success may also lead him to consider, for the ease of this conversation we will call it pressures, consider pressures *not his own*. What does that do but take him away from himself? From the desire he had as a child? Dead the natural talent. Dead the luck. You work for other pressures. And then you die.

"I don't want to die. I am immortal. So this is," and his gesture included everything within the restaurant, "enough. This will be fine for my eternity. We don't frame our awards and nail them to the walls, Pratima. We don't take out ads in *The Isthmus* or *Capital Times*. We don't have a website. Oyama is all word-of-mouth. And you should be thanking me. We are in no danger of closing doors."

Sado took a victory slam and climbed the chair and balanced on the back legs for fun. He could've touched the ceiling. He dropped the bottle of White Tiger from up high. A decent smash. Bremen talked him down with the argument that if he fell and hurt himself, which was bound to happen, who would be chef in his place?

And that is all you need to know about Sado. That, and when Donna Lyons came in to pick up the sushi plates. Bremen hadn't worked at Oyama for a few years, but even as he received a funeral invitation in the mail, as he talked over the catering order with Donna on the phone, as he slapped avocado on the Philadelphia and dusted the California with flying fish roe, Sado Haroki was bizarrely depressed, as if he hadn't ever experienced death before, as if his mother and father and two sisters hadn't died terrible deaths. His fingers cramped up in the middle of a roll so he took a break and chain-smoked three

Marlboro Reds, wondering why it was hopelessness that hit him now instead of indifference.

Bremen was a decent employee by Sado's tough standards—never late, never rushed, never unsure about the job, never promised a customer anything, never refused to look Sado in the eye. Yet his memories were dominated with incidents of Bremen challenging his authority as no employee had ever done, on trivial things like servers switching from pens to pencils, or whether the restaurant needed a bell on the front door, things that in reality, Sado's reality, were not trivial at all. They had strong emotional significance. He didn't want a bell or the servers to use pencils for many, many good reasons he didn't feel the desire to share.

Sado Haroki's internal summary of Bremen Lyons: who the hell did this kid think he was?

A new blonde hostess, her first hectic night, rushed into the kitchen—"Never. Rush."—to let Sado know Donna Lyons had arrived for her order. Sado waved at his dishwasher with a sashimi knife, which was the signal to take the sushi and snap peas and crab cakes to the customer's car. Five minutes later the newbie cleared her throat by the pick-up window. Donna was asking for him.

Sado walked out of the kitchen pretending to be on his cell-phone, avoiding eye contact, and when close to her he removed the phone from his ear and said, as detached as an old bearded fool who has wandered the red-stone mountains for decades, "Yes?"

Donna smiled. "Mr. Haroki, I know you are a busy man. I appreciate the time you've taken to prepare our food. But would you let me know when you are not so busy? I would like to give you a proper thank you."

"I will," Sado pressing the phone back to his ear.

Shame simple as a spear. He left Oyama before dinner rush was done, which was unprecedented. At home, his wife expressed worry and he did worry. Selectively. He stewed on three fingers of JW Green, neat. He thought of looking in on his daughters, decided no, he would wake them, he did not want to wake them with his breath. He stewed on two more fingers. His wife was out on the porch smoking a cigarette in her puffy white parka, watching the yellow and red lights zoom back and forth along the beltline. She flipped her hood up. Sado went to the dark bedroom and slid open his closet door. Donna Lyons sensed an imbalance. It was not in the food. She slowly scanned the third table set-up, nodding to herself as if what was wrong was in front of her face the whole time, and barely nudged a Volcano tray so that its bottom left corner was perfectly even with its right. There.

Here, the two respectable hands of Thomas R. Jones, thrumming with warmth, covered one of hers. It was genuine.

"There is a matter of some importance we must discuss. Concerning your son's Will? You could stay for another," removing one hand from hers and checking a black Movado with scratches on its face, "fifteen minutes?"

Thomas R. Jones had the hands of a musician. They were not faultless and they were not agile, but his hands knew with precision and intuition and intimacy all the little secrets of his instrument. When someone is in rhythm with you they are more apt to listen and obey.

"Let me tell my husband," Donna said.

Terry left to warm up his car. Vera and Mo stood together and stared out the lobby window at the snow-dusted Capital Dome, looking like a ghostly womb for the birth of something unimaginable. Blaze waited in an oversized leather chair, reminding her of Bremen after a visit to the dentist: bored, upset, impatient to go home, absorbed by what was filling the empty space, his thoughts, thoughts Donna wished she knew the details of.

"Something needs to be ironed out in the Will," she told him.

Blaze gave up his car keys without exploration or distress.

"Drive safe."

He joined Vera and Mo and all three left in sync, nobody looking back.

The office had been rearranged. There was one chair, directly across from Tom Jones, situated behind his desk. He offered it to Donna, she took it, and took in the flutter of candle flame around his head, coughing in and out of her vision.

"It's unfortunate I was unable to speak with you until today," opened Tom Jones. "I attempted to get into contact with you personally, but your husband said you had not been feeling well, that you had to take a sabbatical from work, and that any talk with a 'lawyer' would be too much additional stress. Not a problem. You are here now. And it seems as if you are capable of exercising sound judgment in these matters." He made a flourish with his hand that could've meant he was illustrating for a jury the most self-evident thing in the world.

Donna Lyons was not interested in his judgments. She was not interested in her son's Will.

"Do you have any children?"

There was a brief stumble, like slipping up the steps, before Tom

Jones could reply. "No. No, I do not." He looked at Donna as if she was an entirely new person, someone to be watched and tracked for possible signs of aggression. He slid out a desk drawer and produced a blue folder.

"This is your son's addendum to his Last Will and Testament."

"You never had a child?"

Tom Jones physically deflated, but he spoke strong and clear, like the lawyer the world told him he was.

"Mrs. Lyons, I am very sorry for your loss. I can't imagine how difficult it would be to lose your only son. But, I assure you, there is nothing in my personal life that would be of any help or consolation to you at this moment." He buoyed himself and lifted an arm, extending a blue folder to Donna.

"Please."

Donna felt sizzling sparks run down her shoulders and arms, saw a flash of light like the sun when it strikes you sideways.

"Please."

Hey Mom,

The Symphony has been written, not by me, but there it is. Every Instrument has a part to fulfill in the Performance. That is the most important thing: that we Perform according to the Music. The Conductor won't listen if the player says I'm too tired or I've been sad or I'm so happy I could die, or if they suffer from eczema, leukemia, clinical depression. That is not the Conductor's concern. His only concern is the part the particular musician must play in the overall composition. If we can't play the Music when the Music calls for it, then that is our problem. The Music is perfect. The Music is—

Donna broke away and shut her eyes. Someone was pushing in her eyeballs with iron thumbs, a hard dense pain. Her sockets were cracking from the pressure, and yet, when Tom Jones spoke, she could see, in the eigengrau behind her eyes, the outline of his body alight with a bright orange fire.

"Mrs. Lyons, your son has nominated you to be the Executor of his Will. Do you know what this means?"

"I'm not—what?"

"You carry out the provisions in your son's Will."

Donna couldn't form a coherent response.

Tom Jones breathed in and out with adjudicative pace. "There are certain liabilities and responsibilities you should consider as you make your decision. Big things, like opening probate and tracking down the beneficiaries. And little things, like getting copies of the death certificate and filing letters of testamen—"

She opened her eyes, but didn't listen to the words. As Tom Jones spoke, the fire of his aura rippled around his head, it sparked from his fingertips when he gestured with his hands, and this told her all she needed to know. The spoon. The kitchen table. The sunrise. The ground. The grapefruit. The headaches. Tom Jones needed a kindred soul, needed to talk about his long dead son to a receptive and resonant being, a person with no motive, no expectation. That was Donna, who didn't believe it to be beyond any of them.

"—is unfortunately not possible as—as there is no body—but his Funeral does not require one. The blue folder in your hands contains his provisions on the matter. Again, as executor, you would be responsible for carrying these provisions out. Now, my job, when hired by your son, was to read his Last Will and Testament to the relevant parties, and inform you, his mother, of his wish for you to be his Executor. You may decline. However, Bremen has specifically asked me to inform you that if you do decline, his entire Will, the one we just spent the better part of three and a half hours going over, becomes null and void, according to his wishes. As a legal consequence he will have died intestate. Can you see now why it was unfortunate I could not contact you before today?"

"You've lost a lot of weight."

"Have you been listening, Mrs. Lyons?"

There was an absence of guiding principles, operating, as she was, on wavelengths unfamiliar. "Since your son's death."

Tom Jones is quite a prepared human being. If any mistake or deviation from his plans occur, no matter the situation or personnel, he will go on the offensive. It is his default attitude. It is ingrained within him. He cannot help it. Tom Jones placed his elbows on the desk and pressed his fingertips together in the shape of a power pyramid, generating intense heat, about to cross-examine a hostile witness, completely forgetting the position each was actually in.

"Pay close attention, Mrs. Lyons." He sniffed for pause and effect. "Everything, especially your son's money and his possessions, including his handling of—"

"What was his name?"

"Name?"

"Your son's name."

"You are deliberating misrepresenting everything I'm saying."

"Loren is your wife. Don't you think she still loves you?"

"My wife…" was all that could escape from Tom Jones.

"You must still love her. Don't you?" Donna sat straight in the chair, her hands resting on her thighs, looking at him and not around him.

Tom Jones steadied himself, for he had received many blows. He stared into a reflective blur that shined on his desk, and within that distorted light, he asked. "How do you know her goddamn name?"

———

WHERE WAS SHE—OH YEAH, it was after midnight and she was third in line at the Open Pantry on Randall and Regent. In her arms: a bar of milk chocolate, raw honey, a bag of walnuts, a bundle of bananas, bacon, eggs, and pancake mix. Nothing that she needed, but the only memory was waking up with hunger pains ripping through her stomach, and Merlin mewing like a chainsaw in her face, reeking of fresh litter, and now here she was, standing in the checkout lie behind a computerized brunette arm and arm with her sentient beef slab as they argued over two, no three, no two bottles of Veuve, and a homeless-looking man trying to redeem a leaky bag filled with crushed beer cans, so she couldn't just leave empty-handed, could she?

The register beeped. Doors opened and closed. Words fluttered and died. Bodies moved and rested.

Suddenly she was in the parking lot. Her car was not. She held a grocery bag in one hand, her keys in the other, shivering. She went back inside the store. "I—I can't find my car. I was sure I parked it in the lot. But it's not there. It's not there!"

The cashier had been in the middle of testing a six-letter word in *The Isthmus* crossword puzzle (3 Across: Spanish Dance; Ravel's Triumph). She slowly put down her pen, slowly tore her gaze away from the paper, slowly took off her glasses. They hung from her neck by thick nylon cords.

"You parked it out front?"

"I parked it!" Donna dug in the plastic brown bag with nothing she needed in it.

At least one person remained calm. "What's your name, honey?"

"Honey? I have honey. My car is not out there!"

The woman's nametag said, "Ruth! Two Years of Service!" She was short-limbed and round with a transparent gray halo of hair. She looked Donna kindly in the eyes, freely giving her attention to the problems of a stranger, a hostile pushy stranger, and so became a goddess of compassion on par with, with—Donna didn't know any goddesses of compassion.

"I don't know any goddesses of compassion," Donna said.

"I don't either," Ruth said with suspicion.

"Do you have a son?" Donna asked.

"Is this about your car?" Ruth said.

"Do you have a husband?"

"Is there someone I can call for you?"

Hot white light flashed in her eyes, like old camera bulbs going off in her face. A reel of images unspooled in the blindness that followed. Ruth with brumous blue eyes. Ruth hiding from her brothers in the closet. Ruth suffering from asthma in the dry Wisconsin fields.

It just kept going. One after the other in a patient and furious montage like Donna had tapped into a TV broadcast and couldn't change the channel.

"I just need to change the channel," Donna shouted.

"There's no radio playin."

Donna dropped her grocery bag, backed out the doors, and ran down Regent, three blocks in a flat out sprint, cutting diagonally across four lanes of traffic and through a parking lot shared by Bujinkan Dojo and Hong Kong Cafe, through the back alley of a student apartment complex, huddling behind a green trash bin with neon graffiti on the sides.

A chill closed in. It was the cold. It was very cold. So cold there was no smell, right next to a dumpster. She stayed there, crouched like an insect, until the moon dropped from sight in the sky. There was no glow emerging from the opposite horizon.

It seemed every single person on the street was drunk. Her feet were icy stumps that hurt with every thudding step. Donna considered holing up with a healthy Hendricks martini in the corner booth of a bar, anything to get out of the cold. She wrapped her arms around herself and kept her head down against the snow that would sometimes whip up and stick to her face.

She raised her eyes, searching for Hilton or Hyatt signs, but this is what she saw: a giant billboard for St. Mary's Hospital, her hospital, where she was Department Head of Surgery and Recovery, with a view of Lake Wingra from her office window. It must be new; she had never seen the ad before. The hospital's name was written in friendly black letters with a big red heart replacing the period in St., and the bottom tip of the heart aligned with the central pillars of the 'H' in

Hospital. Along the bottom of the billboard was the slogan of the hospital and its close affiliate, the Thomlan Group, and its multi-state corporate partner, VVP Health Care:

Through our exceptional health care services,
we reveal the healing presence of God.

Donna Lyons never thought about God in the context of her work. She had absolutely no contact with patients. Certainly there was no presence of—Him? Her? Donna could go either way—in the decisions she made. Her job was to keep a focused financial outlook by eliminating needless revenue drain. She cut staff on low census days, reduced the length of patient recovery time, docked pay if a doctor failed to perform the necessary amount of surgeries, along with many other costly decisions that were nonetheless crucial if the hospital was to function at maximum efficiency, and so, actually, she did, sometimes, on very busy and exceptionally clear-headed days, think of herself as a God, though with limited power in a limited domain, compelled to report her final budget line to a God higher up, which would report to a higher God, and that God to one higher still, on up the chain, this line of order used to justify the pure human cost, ten dollars for a band-aid, the labyrinth of people you see. The sign was ridiculous. There was nothing exceptional and no God. Healing, maybe. The red and black letters of St. Mary's Hospital seeped into the creamy background. She was dizzy. Wheezing. The slogan started to vibrate. Her head became a paint can in an industrial shaker. Donna bent to her knees and wretched nothing but air. She couldn't tell if what was happening was outside in the world or inside of her mind.

She pulled her coat tighter and stood up and looked at the billboard.

There was a lightning bolt. It struck her in the forehead and knocked her to the ground. Two boys who had been waiting for a bus saw her collapse and ran over. Donna heard tinny voices and the pounding of the sea from very far away, like seeing the Rockies from an airplane. The boys were asking her name. They were asking *are you ok?* They each held one of her hands. She couldn't say her name. She wasn't ok. Her head was in so much pain.

"Just tell me where I am," Donna cried over a squadron of horns in traffic.

The young boys brought her to her feet. They were on the corner of Dayton and Marion. The boys had honest faces of concern and bodies that fed her jade green light. And then she was speaking to them, telling them everything, about her only son that had died seven days ago, about her car that was parked on Milton Street, about how she was sleeping more than she ever had in her whole life and not eating much and waking up so hungry but never wanting to eat. She told them how impossible it was to speak with anybody about the headaches she was having, the voice she was hearing, the green light she had just seen streaming from their faces. She told them how quickly she dressed that night, how silently she tiptoed down the stairs, past her husband in the kitchen smelling of garlic and lamb, and her daughter watching an animated documentary about spiders on her tablet. She stole the keys off the bureau by the front door and when backing out of the driveway she knocked over a purple ten-speed bike, what was it doing there anyway it's the middle of winter, and sped away from the crime scene with snow blowing off the roof of the car in crystalline drifts, a receding figure chasing her in the rearview mirror, waving its arms, shouting something she wouldn't be able to hear anyway, idiot, sprinting down the blue-moon shadowed street, if that's what you'd call sprinting.

TABLE 4

Joy Clark Reicioto unlocked the door of A Clean Plate, crossed the threshold, and locked the door behind her. It was an inviting place on North Henry just off State Street, with cute round tables and comfy chairs and two front glass windows etched with steaming Eplegaarden apple pies. Five barstools lined the counter space by the cash register. The kitchen was semi-visible and quaintly ultramodern. Hanging on exposed brick walls were medium-sized prints of clever and charming pie quotes from Sokolov, Joe Hill, and Swift, but dominating the shop were two film frames, blown-up from 35mm to three by five feet: on the east wall was a double of Laurel and Hardy from the climatic sequence in *The Battle of the Century;* and on the west wall was a score of messy politicians and military brass throwing it down in the War Room in a deleted scene from *Dr. Strangelove.*

It was dark outside, snowbound at six in the morning. Joy threw off her coat. She took the mixing bowl and flour from the freezer, removing the peanut oil, the key to her tender-flaky taste, from the coldest part of the fridge.

She worked on the big wide butcher-block table, adding salt, adding splashes of peanut oil at intuitive intervals, adding a teaspoon or water here and there, relaxing the gluten. Joy worked the dough, knowing when to stop by how it congealed in her hands, as if by sorcery, not chemistry. It was all about the hands, but she wasn't paying close enough attention today, kneading with too much force, adding too much water, and before she realized her mistake there was a tough glutenized rock in her mixing bowl, useless as a mouth with no tongue.

It was strange, but Joy felt she understood—completely and correctly, all fear and trembling neutralized—why men go to war and shoot other men in the face, why women were beaten in apartments and raped in alleys, genocide, lynching, the slaughter of innocents on a sacred slab of stone, and in a rage against that understanding, Joy pitched the mixing bowl across the kitchen, where it shattered against the far wall, and then grabbed her marble rolling pin from the freezer and bashed a yellow mop bucket over and over until her hands were numb and stinging from the repeated blows.

Joy cleared the sweaty hair from her face. She could've knocked out Tyson in his prime, at least, the murder in her eyes could. Why did Joy love to break bowls? Why was there such a gratifying pleasure when they smashed against the wall? She rested her elbows on the table and thought, for the first time since she could remember, about herself.

She'd quit her stable job as a legal secretary at a top defense firm downtown, a job which made her despondent and edgy, and so her marriage and daughter as well. It wasn't anything she wanted anyway. Joy spent two years planning A Clean Plate. She worked nine-hour days, six days a week on the regular. She was beginning to make hard profit. The store was inching its way into the cornerstone of the neighborhood. Sales were crawling up. None of this she regretted. Her husband, Andreas, now wanted sex both night and day. She no longer caught him looking at her with that resigned judgment, and he said, actually said, two weeks ago, perfectly timed at her most unguarded and physically vulnerable moment, eating her trite-but-true-can't-sleep-snack of vanilla ice cream and a slice of apple pie, studying once again the net sales spreadsheet on her laptop, "You know, you probably made the right choice with this thing."

There was a frantic search for an answer—to the question of why she had these violent urges, why she loved to break bowls—and when nothing appeared Joy couldn't help but trivialized her thoughts as being hollow and melodramatic, like the clichéd cop shows Andreas watched, where seasoned detectives raced against the clock to discover the whereabouts of a mastermind killer before he (she?) struck again. But no solid evidence actually appeared, no witnesses leaked secret clues, sadistic taunts arrived by phone, shriveled tongues arrived by mail, a child's corpse was found on a bridge, Joy's sense of being time-poor escalated, and the fear began, that familiar fear of the world and all its hunger rushing to her table with rumbling stomachs and when they found empty plates—it was Joy they would eat.

She sent a mass text to all employees on today's schedule: *Store closed today dont worry everythings fine open up tomoroww.* She started over, tossing one handful of flour at a time on the table so she could watch the powder float and separate and settle.

Was there something finite hitting something infinite? Or was it the other way around. Was the infinite coming up against the finite? The finite everybody thought was the infinite? You know what would be nice now? A piece of pie. Joy remembered the first time she grasped the law governing food and attitude, and it was the same way all the great bakers and chefs grasp it, the same way every person who cooks their own meals grasps it, because there may be ten thousand lessons burning, but only one law is the flame.

Joy ran through her childhood checklist.

—Baking soda, from the back of the fridge

—Milk, out-of-date

—Eggs and flour, borrowed from a neighbor

—Margarine, cheaper than butter

—Sugar, none found

—Syrup, old

—Sick mother

—Dirty house

—Busy father

"It's important to try and be happy when you cook," her father said while juggling a checkbook, a phone, and her little brother over the stove. His pancakes were amazing. Her flour was suspended in the air like the last fading note of a nocturne. She hated to cede to her father's logic, but it bore out in practice. His formula was straightforward and experimentally repeatable. If you make a pie angry, it will be an angry pie. Emotion cannot be separated from action at the chemical level. This is the law. If you make a pie with love, it will be a lovely pie.

Joy didn't recall Bremen by name but when Donna Lyons showed her a picture—there it was. A very confident and generous guy, dark hair, dark eyes. He paid cash and hit the tip jar and cleaned his plate and always got that table directly below Peter Sellers and George C. Scott.

She stopped tossing the flour. It was not that she contemplated suicide, it was just that she wanted to know what it might be like if she was dead right now. If she accidentally fell on a knife, or was shot by a robber, or slipped on the floor and cracked her head open on a corner of the table. Her family, and friends, and the countless peripheral figures that swirled around her life would continue to survive. Everyone would miss her, of course, but more important for Joy were the people who didn't know her or miss her, the people that were starving and needed to eat, and if she was dead all the pies would go unmade, and the person who suddenly meant the most to her now was the one who would never get another slice. If you have the power, you can't let anyone go hungry. She was rooted to the spot, a warm salted sadness falling from her chin and landing on the table, soaking up the flour. She didn't know why she felt this way, and there would be no investigation.

Joy washed her hands and patted them dry.

Hours of baking passed by with a single snap of her fingers. On the crowded butcher-block table there were five sweet potato, five apple, five blueberry, five caramel pecan, and four lemon meringue pies that had passed her physical and psychological inspection. It was 3:34 pm, and she hadn't checked her phone once. There were missed calls from Andreas and the staff, multiple texts, nothing she responded to.

Joy was transported to another kitchen, not her own, speaking with Donna Lyons.

"When does this…funeral start?"

"In a few hours. I'll just heat up the pies when we get close. For now, let's put them in the fridge," Donna said, performing her administrative duties with panache, picking up a lemon meringue with each hand and opening the fridge with her right foot.

"I'm sorry, I'm sorry. Wait—"

Donna Lyons froze in place, balanced on one foot, holding up the pies.

"I need a piece of paper and a pen."

"Of course."

Joy wrote down her directions. They were very detailed, including precise reheat temperature and length of reheat time for each individual pie, directions on how to cut a correctly proportioned slice, directions for visual arrangement and tasting patterns, repeating some directions two, three times, as she was writing them, and in her super-emphatic-sometimes-insulting tone, and then hearing herself and shutting up in the middle of sentence.

"I'd be glad to defer the responsibilities to you," Donna said, in perfect stride.

Joy wouldn't be able to stand much longer. "Are you sure? I'll come back."

Guests had been arriving at a steady clip, and the chorus of voices rose and blended with the deepening night like the extended tuning of an orchestra before the Grand Performance. Get a seat. Nobody will save one for you. In three minutes Donna will kick off the festivities with "Man, Oh Man" by The Persuasions, the opening track of the official playlist of Bremen's Funeral. Joy had not returned. Donna was alone in the serving room, slicing the last hot blueberry pie, and the moment her knife sank into the crust the pie released a pungent blue smell, rich and concentrated, a smell that seeped into her lungs, sending its deep blue signal to all her cells, unleashing reactions of comfort and warmth and a sense-memory of bread and jelly during one raging thundersnow night with the power out and her own mother feeding her with a wooden fork by candlelight. She wanted to go back there through the sweetness of time. A piece of crust smeared with a glob of blueberry filling had broken off from one of the pies. It lay at the edge of the table, and she can't, she just can't help herself—Donna, don't!—brushing the crumbs into her hand and bringing it to her lips, the candied fruit and layers of airy crust collapsing in her mouth with a harmony simple, direct, and pure.

That is so fucking good.

BAD ORANGE AIR WAS circulating, the kind that billowed from rusty steel drums around the bombed-out amphitheater of a city park, the fires out back behind the slaughtering barn, the fire and the moonlight along the Rue de la Huchette.

"Mrs. Lyons, let me explain things so there will be no more questions. I have no son. I was briefly married a very, very long time ago. Do you see a ring on this finger? Do you see pictures of a family anywhere in my office?" Tom Jones shook his head once, only once. "They don't exist."

Not a speck of dirt lay on his shoulder but Tom Jones swiped it clean with one deliberate stroke. He coughed. It was as long as he would wait for a response.

"You either sign here and become Executor of your son's Will," he unveiled a thick piece of paper with raised lettering and pushed it toward Donna so she could see her name typed in fat block letters below a line passionate about her permission, "or you decline. And then Bremen dies intestate, the case is filed in probate, and the court locates a public administrator who works on behalf of the State."

"But Loren was your wife. How could you stop loving her?"

Tom Jones tucked his chin against his chest and hardened into limestone, except for his hands, his fingers, drumming on his desk like a pianist playing some brooding Rachmaninoff masterpiece of vengeance, and when he talked, he talked to his shoes digging in the carpet of his office where he sacrificed at the altar of himself most of his adult life.

"How do you know her goddamn name?"

An explanation could not be found in any of the mental modes she was familiar with. Yet she knew. That's how she knows. She wanted desperately to give this answer and give it without fear, through a pure account of reason, or little statements of logic that led one after the other to a sound conclusion, but there was only gin in her veins and the view through Loren's eyes, a view of a twisted chain-linked fence and a vast apple-blotted plain that rolled into a sunset the colors of which she couldn't describe to Tom Jones, looking up from his desk and into her face with all the hate of a morning star for the sky where it was born.

"How do you know her goddamn name?"

Donna wanted to cleave that expression off his face. Blood, the great refresher. She wanted to look away. But then what kind of person would she be? Never. Look. Away.

"Did you divorce?"

"This is—pointless."

"Because of your son's death?"

Tom Jones, finally, stood from his chair. There was a harmonizing power in the action. It aligned him with certain parts of himself he didn't believe to be real. He was rippling with the wisps of smoke from an extinguished fire, everything once bright around him now dimming to a light unreadable.

"I've made an atrocious mistake. I've pressed this on you at a difficult time. Please reschedule with my secretary."

He offered her the door, but it was such a long journey.

Donna Lyons wanted to stop thinking and feeling. That wasn't going to happen. A hard pinging started up in the back of her head, gaining power and speed like an approaching freight train. It was only simple things that stood in her way: Thomas R. Jones, the pen, the line, so she signed, even though something like heat waves wafted off the paper. Won't Tom Jones at least put a hand on her shoulder and tell her that what she was doing was what she was supposed to be doing? Donna flinched when she wrote the last *s* and the letter was jagged and unlike the others.

From Thomas R. Jones there was not a second of pause, not the slightest glitch in his array, and the moment Donna lifted the pen from the page he slid the document over to his side, executing a perfect 180° by rotating his wrist and crooking his elbow—possession transferred. He did not sit.

"My secretary will refer you to a very good tax attorney who can help with some of the more detailed passages of the process."

Tom Jones stared at his pen—capped, gleaming black—so intently you'd think it would glide across the desk and up into the air and fit snugly in his breast pocket. If his secretary walked in at this moment she'd be forgiven for thinking that something awkwardly erotic just happened. Not that Tom Jones or Donna Lyons could even describe, in their language, what that was. He stared at the paper with her signature, symbolizing her complete authorization and the termination of his professional liabilities.

"One last thing," he said, lips curled in a mean imitation of a smile.

Donna sat in her husband's little truck with the windows and windshield frosted up. Where was she going to go? Home? She tried to massage the pain out of her eyes. She was shivering, shivering and couldn't stop, didn't want to stop. The sun appeared briefly through a crack of stony clouds and shined full force through the icy windshield. There is nothing like sitting in a crystal. The light went away. The light came back. The light went away.

Tapping the buried strength she had left, Donna put the key in the ignition and cranked the heat, and when she was warm enough she stepped from the car and slammed the door so hard it rocked back and forth on its wheels. She re-entered the building and rode the crowded elevator up five floors, striding past the secretary yakking on her headset, kicking Tom Jones' door off its hinges, taking one-two-three steps and shattering his jaw with a wicked hook that would probably break her hand. He spit out two teeth and a mouthful of blood and she kicked him in the ribs, twice. Fuck Tom Jones. Fuck his dead son and his wife. She was only trying to help. More shivering, from the cold, and a holding back, a holding back, a holding back, and you can't keep that up forever. Donna screamed. She screamed so loud and so long that she was no longer cold. Tears are warm. Pain is warm. She slumped, conquered in the car seat, unable to find the energy to actually start the car. She heard a voice in her head and on the other side of the window, but no voice she wanted to hear. She rubbed the scar on her neck and noticed the blue folder on the passenger seat. That's the voice. The sun came out again, like a baby never bored with hide-and-seek, and she opened to a random page, blinking—it's hard to read inside a crystal. The heading at the top said PROGRAM* and the asterisk at the bottom explained how it was to be printed with jet-black ink on his Father's orange paper.

> Greetings Family and Friends and Long Lost Pals and Students and Colleagues and, who knows, even Total Strangers. Welcome to my Funeral. Please take off your shoes. Silence your cell phones. The bathroom is down the main hall, second door on the left. So I was born but now I died. Do you hear that music in your ears? Can you feel the warmth radiating off the body next to you? Okay then. Have a fantastic time. Share your memories. And if you don't have fun my ghost will haunt you like opium smoke and I will possess your soul until you exorcise me with a laughing fit. Oh, and pet Merlin. He's the cat that's rubbing on your leg. He likes it under the chin.

The sun vanished in the clouds.

Tom Jones threatened her in cold blood. "Get out of my office, and if I ever see you again, I will rip your heart out of your goddamn throat."

FIVE TWENTY-NINE AM. THE Wisconsin winter night still maintained its dominance of the sky. Donna was in the kitchen eating a grapefruit with a knife and a spoon. For the record: she felt amazing, which was really something considering the last two weeks. This was an important chance.

Headaches were a thing she used to understand. She knew the general and predictable causes: after too much sunshine, too much perfume, too much driving, peaches, after a movie in the summer afternoon and stepping out of the cool cinema into the hot world, when she was pregnant with Bremen (not Vera), and if she drank more than two dry Junipero martinis with blue cheese stuffed olives. The pain was not mysterious either. It wasn't paralyzing or sharp, but a wide cloudiness, a thunder-heavy storm cell that drifted from the front of her head to the back. Duration: anywhere from twenty minutes to half a day. If called upon, if something had to be done, at work or at home, she could pop five Advil and marshal the last reserves of locomotion and do the job and shield her body from the inconvenience. Sleep was never a problem.

Headaches were a thing she no longer understood. They weren't appearing the way they were supposed to. Since the water of the world decided to bury Bremen beneath its blue, she's had fourteen headaches, one every day, both alone and around others, enclosed by quiet or noise, in darkness or light. She couldn't pinpoint any causes, but the pain was intense and sentient, as if it knew the weak spots in her gray folds and stabbed at them without restraint. Her vision would blur and streak with superimposition. She'd lose coordination of her body and her arms and legs would sting and burn like her nerves flowed with magma. She might sweat. She might puke. It was the worst pain of her life (she was epidural-ed for both Deliveries), even though it lasted no more than five or ten minutes. Her senses had become by turns godly delicate and dumbly mute. Sleep was still not a problem.

She cut a slice of grapefruit and put the piece in her mouth with her middle finger and thumb. The coldness, the sharp acidity made her pucker. She scratched the scab along her neck and collarbone. She had been awake for thirty-five minutes.

Donna Lyons knew enough about the brain to know that it processed sensory information coming from the world outside, and by this information and by its own internal interconnections, the brain created a perceptual experience of the world, an interpretation. There's a river. I see a river. Yet there's always the possibility of the information coming in to be misperceived and misinterpreted. There's a dog. I see the number sixty-four. Enlarge a tumor, swallow a pill, clot a vessel, make a thought one-pointed, run a little volt through a dime-sized section in the parietal and the doctors and nurses in the hospital might dissolve, and you could be back in the bathtub with soap in your hair and your mother telling you to stop splashing. There's a fence. I see a wine bottle.

This was how she rationalized the light, or lights. It was a misinterpretation. She was missing the mark somehow.

Donna highly doubted epilepsy or schizophrenia (no genetic history), or any type of cerebral cancer (other symptoms would've been occurring). When the lights appeared by themselves, which was harmless but alarming, she gave it no attention, and noticed no details. When the lights merged with the headaches, however, the pain was so all-consuming that she was forced to focus on what was probably not in her field of vision anyway: layers of light, textures of light, rippling over surfaces, congealing in whirlpools, pulling itself apart like taffy.

The most recent and beginning-to-be-typical example: yesterday she was on the couch watching TV—a reality show about Bear

Hunters, why?—when a jabbing pain started at the base of her neck. She couldn't rub it out; that made it worse. She shut off the TV and a solid pink light, a saturated dust mote, appeared in the northwest quadrant of her sight and streamed with her as she stood up. Her ears popped and a leather belt wrapped itself around her head and tightened quickly, notch after notch, the entire circumference of her skull buckling from the pressure, she could feel it in the bones of her face. She collapsed to the floor. Any movement enhanced the pain. Her eyes were locked on a plant hanging from the ceiling—an Asparagus Fern grown too big for its clay pot. A bunch of new stems had developed, curled into themselves like flags around a pole, ready to unfurl. A faint yellow light ebbed and flowed over the green spines and needle-like leaves on every branch, one of which had a cluster of red berries, and at the center of the biggest berry was a vortex of reful- gent red light, spinning clockwise. She zoomed closer and the vortex contained a number (she shouldn't be expected to count) of smaller vortexes within, evenly proportioned, each spinning counterclockwise, generating a power in their polar relations, a quaking at the quantum level, these invisible vessels of knowledge. She lost consciousness with all that spinning and didn't find it for the rest of the day, never know- ing it was Vera, returning from an astronomy session at the library, who found her and called Blaze on his cell. She was too small to carry Donna somewhere safe and today they were scheduled to read the Will and Donna wanted to be there, she had to be there.

Slow down. We have space. You are being tempered.

She set aside, for the moment, the recent lapses in consciousness. The keys were the headaches and the lights and, more explicitly, the thoughts.

Slow down. Take a breath.

Donna took a breath—inhaled and exhaled—then three more. All her movements felt brand new in the darkness of the kitchen. The grapefruit was a citrus shock, priming her system. Her skin tingled like she just stepped out of a summer lake and was sitting on the sand with the wind chill and drying.

Now sit up straight.

Donna set the knife and spoon on the counter with a muted click and put her hands in her lap, flexed, remained taut on the chair. She itched her neck again, helpless against the impulse.

Just sit.

She did, finding a crossroads of grout in the Persian blue tiles of the countertop. That centered her sight.

The thoughts in her head were detached, firm, and logical, further illustrating or commenting upon what she was seeing or feeling at the moment, whether explaining the effects of fireworks on Blaze, or unraveling the true nature of St. Mary's Hospital, or describing how the polarized spin of the red berry allowed for efficient transfer of energy into the seed. These thoughts were expressed in a voice without gender or age and in a quality Donna didn't believe she possessed and shouldn't be expected to replicate. It's why she never spoke them. *Your discomfort is a stage, a necessary consequence of the creative process, which proceeds through progressive development. The brain does not think thoughts—it is an instrument that provides the conditions for thought to be expressed. Structure establishes quality. Structure is continuously determined. Structure is compromised by complacency and stagnation. Your thoughts are discordant. It's the same chord over and over and over. A string, many strings, are broken* on your instrument. This is a re-tuning. This will permit you to hit certain notes. It is an operation familiar to all peoples at every time and every place, by all manner of delivery systems, by all manner of triggers. Death is but one. Your son, the headaches, the lights—is but one. This means going from less capacity to more, and the moment of transmission is compact and comes all at once and cannot be broken down by the intellect, although the intellect is freely invited to try. Resign to be at the mercy of the process.

Donna shook her head ferociously and said, "This is not me."

This is you.

This is not me.

This is you.

Is this really me?

When you sit long enough without doing anything you begin to feel something. That something is who you are. This is you, full of fear.

Donna Lyons cut another slice of grapefruit. It was triangular and bright with fine white hairs, unbelievably sour and fresh. The neighborhood was asleep. She could hear the haul of eighteen-wheelers on the inhuman interstate. Merlin purred with Vera in the turret. Blaze snored in Bremen's bed. There was the barest hint of dawn's breath in the sky and she didn't have a headache or feel like she was going to have one. The thoughts had a snap and clarity that carried all the way through to the back of her head. She closed her eyes.

How disgustingly in denial she must look. She was incapable of dipping a big toe in her own emotional ocean, to pose questions of motivation and behavior beyond the surface level of apparent memory and fact, for any upsetting intimations were re-routed by programs installed for such defensive operations, because of the fear of an uncertain, and perhaps destructive, effect on the whole system. From this fear an immediate example arose in Donna, embodying the scope of the process: she no longer knew, or contained the memory of knowing, exactly how she fell in love and why she married Blaze. The reasons she would voice, if asked, revolved around themes—Young Love, Financial Security, Doing the Right Thing—so vacant and bland that to take them seriously a laugh had to join her delivery, and this dual emptiness, the lack of memory and the lack of meaning, caused her more self-hatred that can be presently expressed. *Why* did she do *this* thing instead of *that* thing? *What* for? She supposed her situation was similar to the fear first-time skydivers have, at least, the ones who have taken it up on a dare or followed through on a misguided gift, either way, the door of a Cessna 182 is wide open and you're deaf from the wind and blaring engine, goggles soldered to your face, toes looking down 12,000 feet, the pilot and crew giving you strained smiles and sarcastic thumbs-up (jump already) while the instructor strapped to your back is screaming his head off with encouragement you don't want, and at this point you wonder, the entire body in revolt, what exactly are you doing up here? Even if you don't find the reasons, you jump. That's what it takes to follow the descent of your own thoughts. Only there is no expert double leading you down. There is no parachute to pull. You will always land hard. You will die. You will be reborn.

Donna jumped out of the plane. Her son was dead.

Say it out loud.

"My son is dead."

Those four words, arranged in that particular combination and then vocalized, to herself, at last, unlocked the magnitude of the flash of her life, and she felt very much like she was falling, falling through the blue postlude of the world and passing all the things she never fully enjoyed or understood, falling towards some kind of commencement of the imagination with the world refashioned and revitalized and waiting for her to arrive. There is always a high tide and a low tide, a relative and absolute in the activity of Suns, Saturns, Sapiens, Snakes, Shrubs, Sapphires, and Sounds. In these degrees, the reality of death is movement along the scale, where position determines both situation and ability. The windows of manifestation are small. This is why you feel a separation of the house from the foundation. Why you feel a shattering sense of time and opportunity lost or wasted.

Bullshit. What she had done with her forty-nine years was nothing short of miraculous. This was what she told herself. That was her story. Living the unbearable childhood of an only child, who left the tiny town it came from, Donna Lyons transformed herself into one of the driven, cruising through the Wisconsin School of Business in three years with a major in Management, amassing a stellar résumé of contacts and internships, even through a young and unexpected pregnancy, keeping her nose above the grindstone and her foot as heavy on the accelerator as it would go, having thirty, fifty, a hundred people under her administrative thumb, aiming for the achievements of a magnate for no particular reason other than the accomplishment, such are the driven. She matured into an aloof woman, attractive in her aloofness, a skirt never above the knees, dressing exclusively in solid browns and grays and blacks, and dominated a profession (Hospital Administration) mostly made of men by fighting through the intimidation and resentment of mostly other women, and never once, never once, engaging in petty office politics on any level, remaining utterly impersonal, which is what it took to keep corporate sponsors happy and one of the biggest hospitals in Wisconsin running at maximum efficiency, what it took to move her parents into a nursing home, a hospice, the graveyard she grew up around, what it took to survive another unwanted pregnancy, a caring but disingenuous husband, an inherited cabin on Lake Buckatobin. Donna Lyons once convinced a skeptical executive to sign off on a $22 million dollar robotics deal for minimally invasive procedures (high volume, high turnover, high profit), and she's caught and gutted and filleted monster perch, and she can process a thousand patients a week and draft future budget expenditures and stick to them like velcro, her, a farm girl from Viroqua who fed all the stray cats.

You feel something. You don't want to feel it. And you do what you have to in order not to feel it. These are memorized programs of cover and evasion, set patterns of clearly defined and limited reality.

This is my life.

This is your idea of your life.

This is my life.

Your idea is your life.

What is my life?

You think and you feel. You feel. And then you think. There is a rhythm to it. The pendulum never rests but you don't need to go with every swoop. It is possible to watch from a higher position.

Donna had been sitting motionless for some time. The red bars on the clock stove were swimming and she couldn't read the numbers. A pool of white-pink light leaked out of the horizon and shimmered at the edges. The tiles on the countertop rippled like the surface of a wind-blown stream. And then she realized her eyes were closed.

Donna felt the weight of the lids, but she could still see. In the initial awe, she almost opened them—was this happening? Your own experience is all the proof you need. It was a thought Donna normally wouldn't have agreed with, would be suspicious about accepting—now its logic seemed infallible.

If she could see through her eyelids, if light could pass through flesh, her mind could pass through the idea of Donna Eleanor Lyons, and at this corresponding thought (which she most definitely would not have agreed with), and in her special state of receptivity, an onslaught of other thoughts presented themselves, with no other desire than to be acknowledged by the thinker. This was the ground rushing up. She spoke to the space of the kitchen as if it was her best friend who would never hurt, never lie, never betray her.

"I don't like most people. I don't like people very much at all. I refuse to sign any cards at the office. Birthdays or funerals. I don't want to acknowledge any anxiety about my age. Vera makes me feel guilty. When I come home from work I wish I didn't have to talk to her. I didn't want another child. I don't think I've ever asked her what she wants to do with her life. I tell myself it's genetics, that I'm just like my dad. That's not true. I'm like him, but only because I chose to be. It overwhelms me to be around stupid people, and I think most people are stupid. I'm much more capable than everyone else. I complain about people. I belittle them. I fire them. I believe that no one ever listens unless their life is on the line. So I put people's lives on the line, on purpose, to test them, and if they fail, I make sure they know it. Blaze makes me angry. I see him as a failure. Every day he fails in the goals he wants to accomplish."

She kept at it, this verbalized vivisection, but a moment came when Donna wanted to stop the procedure, stop talking. She both stopped and continued, bifurcating. There was no struggle. She could see through her eyelids, floating above her chair, patient and pellucid, and after a moment she tapped herself on the shoulder and stopped talking out loud.

The atmosphere in the kitchen was charged like an electric fence, but Donna was unable, currently, to extend it for very long, and when she returned to thinking the first thought that appeared was of a desire to control her thinking. If she could control her thoughts, stop and start and direct trajectories, it was possible she could organize and manage them more effectively, and then boom, it happened, as easily as day overtakes night and night overtakes day, the real thought from the real voice, the thought that made the chaos of the past two weeks fall into the hard ground of sense: Donna Eleanor Lyons would have to be remade.

A door opened upstairs. Then it closed. After a minute, the toilet flushed, and the door opened again.

She was no longer aware of such things—the yawning house, Blaze dressing for the day, Merlin clawing at the turret door. She was making the thought one-pointed, *Donna Eleanor Lyons will be remade*, and that gossamer aura above, Donna the Luminous, pledged to use all of her available power to achieve this aim, agreeing to act as a constant watchful presence that would accompany her physical body as she moved through the space of the day, meeting the people she had to meet, doing the things she had to do. It would only observe and collect, and in the time that is no time it would impart to her its knowing direction for the process of regeneration. In the bleak prairie fields outside, the wind was turning everything to ice. She almost opened her eyes. And she knew why. It was because of the exposure. The process, if she really went through with it, would offer her no protection. She would be naked before every single person in the world. It would destroy what they always remembered and believed her to be. The potential fallout was terrifying: how would people react, personally and professionally? How would she handle that reaction? How would—the gauzy hand of Donna the Luminous tapped her shoulder.

There was great pleasure in the silence that followed, in the electric envelope of air she was able to sit in a little bit longer, an indescribable sensation of boundless space within the boundaries of her body, like watching earthrise from the surface of the moon. She was in bloom, rarefied, gravity gone, the cold dawn sun bouncing off the clean kitchen tile, the husk of the grapefruit and the citrus pumping through her blood.

Now—what was she going to think?

FOURTH MOVEMENT

 The Funeral was in full swing.

TERRY LYONS WAS DANCING with two girls when his Maker's ran dry. A hard-driving bluegrass song stomped its way through the funeral speakers. The girls were short and softly tanned. Bremen's students. He had forgotten their names. One had a purple birthmark on her shoulder, white-blonde hair. One had a ruby gem in her nose and a husky voice. They had come in a mixed group of ten and he approached them immediately, introduced himself as Bremen's cousin, thirty-one, a freelance photographer. He charmed the circle with stories of Bremen's not-often-revealed-past: stealing his car back from a shady mechanic; camping in national parks without any permits; the time he broke his thumb getting thrown from a bus. Terry enjoyed telling the stories. It seemed everyone enjoyed listening. The girls didn't mind when he slipped between them on the living room dance floor. He wondered again why he wasn't giving the eulogy.

"THERE'S NO WAY I'M coming over there."

"Can't we just talk, Isabel?"

"We are talking."

"Can't you just come over and be with me?"

"That's not what you want."

"It is."

"No, Terry, what you want is a harem of cocktail waitresses and a bottomless glass of whiskey."

"You're the best thing in my life."

"I'll call the cops again."

"I love you."

"Do you remember when my father died?"

"I do."

"Do you remember how I just wanted to be alone?"

"I do."

"You should take some time off work."

"I'm swamped."

"Sorry about that. I really am."

"Come over."

The line went dead and Terry threw his cell phone across the apartment and it smashed to pieces against the wall and he didn't even care about the contacts he would lose, pouring another couple fingers of his prized Colonel Taylor and turning on ESPN.

"That's not what I asked. I asked what do you, personally, think about a system, a social and political system, which invests more money in incarcerating its population than educating it. I'll assume you haven't even thought about the question that deeply. You're busy. That's part of it. They overwork you." Jeremiah Sezla sat back in his chair.

"Jesus Christ, kid. How old are you?" asked Terry.

"You've got my file."

"And what did you do?"

"You've got my file."

"I want to hear you say it."

"Part of me was looking forward to this. As an opportunity to see how things worked from the inside. It's one thing to read about the for-profit prison industrial complex, the corporate and political corruption, but when you're in that system, there's a human face. And that's you, but it's not a good face."

"Guess what? You're not in the private prison system."

"What I mean is that you're not a bad person, but that you can't be a reasonable human being in this system. You can't think for yourself. You're a robot."

"Alright. Enough."

"Robot's just spit out whatever is fed to them."

"Shut the fuck up or I'll revoke your probation right fucking now. How's that?"

And this was just the first time Terry had met Jeremiah Sezla, in his modest office at 517 E. Louisiana Ave., The United States Probation Bureau, Eastern District of Wisconsin, and afer Terry's threat, a thorny silence filled the room, echoed exactly a year later, if a little earlier in the morning, when Blaze Lyons knocked on Terry's apartment door, a door his brother had never knocked on before, and shared Bremen's watery, unexplainable fate.

The first meeting started some sort of spin, which the second, like a slap across the face, only accelerated.

THE BLUEGRASS SONG WHOOSHED through a bottleneck and picked up the pace. The crowd grew and condensed at the same time, forcing the girls further into him. Ruby and Blonde, as if on cue, both swayed and smiled in his direction. He smiled back, that smile, the one Bremen called hollow, irrepressible, and barely containing your shamelessness, Terry. That was seven months ago, at Vera's big one-two, when he scored the digits of a single mom with a tight ass in white pants whose kid spilled Orange Crush and vanilla cake on his khakis. They were smoking on the back porch. Bremen was barefoot in the late summer night, grinning, looking at the numbers on the napkin Terry held up in the tiki-torch light, with mosquitoes eating his ankles and those incessant cicadas under the he-could-not-remember-what-kind-of sky.

WHEN SPREADSHEETS GET TOO deep, this is what happens, the sheer flow of information drowns your ability to navigate it.

He hadn't seen Reggie Henry Tompkins, ML-11-A237, for five months. His two boys, four and six, lank and restless with knotty hair you couldn't get a steel comb through, answered the door. Everyone had a threshold. When passed, the reactions were unpredictable. Four P.O.'s in Wisconsin have committed suicide in the last two years. Barbaric workloads, smaller budgets, and insulting pay led to a gradual exodus of quality caseworkers. Even his mighty superiors in Madison walked a knife-edge in hard rain. Every bureaucratic officer was one little tick away from a tragic explosion, and whoever was in the vicinity would just get sprayed with shrapnel. It was a vicious, sarcastic, condescending atmosphere he breathed about nine hours a day. Some sort of breathtaking transformation was occurring beneath the surface of this nation, moods were deteriorating, selfishness reigned, anger ran cold as absolute zero. So he understood the purpose of Stress Reduction Management meetings three times a month, the need for verbal steam vales, to complain to maintain sanity, and all the pitiful case files turned into dirty racist jokes. Terrence Calvin Lyons, though, never talked shit. It's no good even trying to make sense of senseless things.

Reggie's apartment smelled like a herd of cats had pissed in an ashtray the size of Cadillac. A layer of blue-gray mold was blooming on the corners of the ceiling, creeping in. The living room floor was covered with damp pillows, used paper towels, crusty clothes, and the only light (the windows were blanketed) came from a giant flat-screen HDTV, the nicest thing, by far, in the entire place. The kids had carved out a space to sleep in front of it, watching music videos on TRACE Urban. Reggie lay like a bloated corpse on the reclining chair, his mouth wide open, snoring. Terry checked for breathing. Still alive, too bad, now the paperwork will be a shitstorm. On the lamp stand next to the chair was a bag of white powder that was, yep, cocaine, but tempered, possibly by heroin, and Terry coated his gums with it to make sure he was not dreaming. Yeah, this was where he actually was. Reggie stirred as if swimming in his sleep. Terry handcuffed him to the nearby radiator, asked the kids to name their two favorite pizza toppings, and called Dominos for delivery. He didn't want to summon an ambulance or Social Services, but he did. Before they arrived, he shut off the TV, cleared a large space on the floor, and sat down next to the boys.

He didn't ask their names. He didn't want the memory. He tried not to give straight answers. They just wouldn't understand.

Dear Agent Lyons,

I'm not going to explain why, but I feel compelled to share my plans with you. They are not complicated. When my time is served, that is, if I'm granted parole when eligible, I'm going to find you and kill your wife and children. If you don't have a wife and children then I'll kill your girlfriend or your dog or your cat. And if you don't have a girlfriend, a dog, or a cat, then I'll rip up your plants or blow up your car or burn your house down, basically, and just so we can have a clean slate, I will destroy every object you have an emotional investment in. And if you don't have any of those objects, that is, if nothing in your immediate life can be taken from you, if you have some-how managed to alienate and separate yourself from the memory and feeling of the things that cause pain through loss, then I'll destroy everything you interact with in any meaningful way, starting with your trans-actional acquaintances and working on out to estranged friends and relatives. Their homes will be burned and I'll take you with me and we'll watch the fires together. I see your face as you read this. You laugh. But listen carefully, Agent Lyons, listen carefully. I have more time than you can imagine. I have thought this through. Every word has been very carefully thought through.

My Very Best,
Jim Hank

Dated July 26th, 2017. It'd been awhile since he'd gotten a letter from prison. Occupational hazards. He showed this one to Bremen, who calmly instructed Terry to burn it, don't open any future mail, and definitely don't answer them: don't give a psychopath any attention. But Terry saved this letter along with the rest of them, his collection of bizarre secret trophies, these talismans he believed were his safety and protection. Nobody in nine years and nineteen letters had ever hurt him. Yet. He was always saying 'yet'. He was trying to ban 'yet' from his vocabulary. Yet even now he was trying to remember who Jim Hank was and what he had done and what facility he was at and how long he had left on his sentence.

"WHICH ONE YOU WANT?" said Bennett, a veteran drinking buddy from Terry's time in college.

"Girl with the pink top and those sweet DSLs," Terry said.

"That's who I want."

"What's wrong with the other two?"

"Brunette chick has banging titties. Weird smile though. The other's got vibe like a nympho but I'm not into redheads."

"What's this bartender doing?"

"You got any of those purples?"

"Glovebox in the car. You want one now?"

"For the girls."

"Three Watermelon Sugars, a Double Maker's, and a Gin and Tonic, extra limes. Thirty-four fifty, sir."

Terry handed the bartender two twenties and nodded to keep the change.

"Gonan put on your rape face, huh?"

"I'm not a rapist, man. Just—they might be down for some fun."

And here Bennett and Terry stopped shouting at the top of their lungs, over a classic Lil John track, and gathered their drinks and weaved through the sweaty and congested meat-market bar to a corner booth where three girls who were under twenty-one waited with sexy pouts of impatience, as if there could be any other kind.

"Tell me again. Gently this time. So I don't cut my ears off."

"It's not just you. It's all of us, from the judges to the prosecutors to the department heads."

"How is this possible?"

"You know the deal CCA rammed through the State Senate."

"How could the facilities not be at max? I'm at max. I've got 164 cases. Violent and non-violent."

"They're not at max."

"Who's saying that?"

"You know who."

"Bullshit. It's impossible."

"Terry. I'm just doing my job."

"That's what I'm doing."

"And now you're going to have to do it a little differently."

"Do you have to do your job *differently?*"

"We all do."

"Do you have a quota to meet?"

"That's a retard question. You're not a retard. Are you?"

"You know what one of my cases said to me the other day?"

"Write a good report and I'll give you a blowjob?"

"It was a boy, no, adult now, eighteen."

"Even better."

"He said, 'I don't think you've considered the absolute insanity of the people engineering the vast majority of the world's problems.'"

"Engineering? Sounds like a wacko. What'd he do?"

"Assaulted a cop at the Capital Protests last March."

"Details."

"Cop was busting one of his friends who had been sleeping in the lobby. He tried to stop it. Nothing major."

"How long does he run?"

"Two more years."

"Going to revoke?"

"He's staying out of trouble in school. Home visits couldn't be better. Parents are supportive."

"But I *just* told you about the new guidelines, about the potential advancement if you're able to—"

"I can handle it."

"You can handle it?"

"Leave, please. I got reports to prepare for court this afternoon."

"Handle it. Otherwise—"

And here Mr. Randy Ginger, Chief P.O., ran his finger across his neck like a switchblade, smiling out of his fat sadistic face.

TERRY SUDDENLY SMELLED CITRUS, faint orange, pear? From the girls. Ruby and Blonde were close, it was warm, and they were sweating a little—sweet damp hair sticking to their necks and a shine on their foreheads and temples. They moved with a fluid grace Terry thought only belly-dancing girls in movies possessed. He made a mental note to remember this moment. Over drinks at Black Cat he'd tell Bremen about the two hot girls he danced with, *your students,* and Bremen would shake his head, sip his spicy porter, and talk lightly of the consequences of being a white thirtysomething statutory rapist in a population of other prisoners whose crimes the white thritysomething statutory rapist is awfully familiar with. Terry caught himself. He had been doing that lately. It was becoming a minor problem. Imagining Bremen was there with him, or that he would see him in the future, a future where they still talked and shared stories. There was no more Bremen. There was no more Bremen.

FIVE MONTHS BEFORE BREMEN drowned off the coast of South Carolina, Terry Lyons had a day full of revocations and near-revocations. A Marquette forward pissed positive for dope. A Mexican foreman stabbed his co-worker with a screwdriver. A girl in the best prep school in southeastern Wisconsin broke apart in his office: she was pregnant and using meth to kill the baby. It was already five forty-five, and the only reason Terry her gave a dire warning and didn't revoke her probation (but set a psych eval with a court-appointed shrink) was because of the pile of paperwork that was waiting if he did.

He sped home and stripped off his clothes, except for his boxers and socks, filled his tumbler with Maker's, then opened his laptop and typed Sexy Naughty Girls Tumblr into Google. The first site was fairly soft-core, a scroll of smooth, cute, gorgeous, interchangeable girls taking selfies in front of the mirror, mixed with sleek professional shots of models in traditional poses, biting their bottom lips or squeezing their breasts, and Terry would click on a picture he liked, opening it in a new window, then go to a different site, whatever that picture was linked to, scroll through again, and by this method he discovered sites and images he wouldn't have looked for on his own, aggressive and hardcore, but it was doing the trick, it was doing the trick, it was doing—he finished on a soft focus black-and-white picture of naked woman's taut upper torso, arms tied behind her back, nipples pierced with steel barbells, eyes bound by a leather blindfold, neck wrapped in a leather collar and attached to a silver chain that led, link by link, to the hand of a shadowy figure that towered over her off-screen.

THE TIME BETWEEN APPOINTMENTS and home visits and drafting court reports and nips of saving grace from his monogrammed flask—Bremen's present for Terry's 30th birthday—was spent in a haze of frenetic filing. Hard copies had to be kept in a workable order by transferring vitals of each case file to the computer, the workload tripling in the eight years since he started, a phenomenon people around here called *the unceasing shitstorm*, a phrase Terry loved and would occasionally use because of the strong apocalyptic qualities it contained. Who can stop an unceasing shitstorm? Jesus Christ? Please. He stumbled across the Post-Conviction Review Assessment questionnaire. In the lingo of the PCRA, four is strongly agree, three is agree, two is uncertain, one is disagree. Every offender was required to it fill out and then Terry sent it off to be analyzed. He received a score sheet and a lean psychological profile that was used to assess the level of supervision required, and to recommend specific rehabilitation programs. Terry took a swig from his flask and started answering the questions.

1. I will allow nothing to get in the way of me getting what I want	[4]	[3]	[▪2▪]	[1]
2. I find myself blaming society and external circumstances for many of the major problems I've had in life	[4]	[▪3▪]	[2]	[1]
3. When pressured by life's problems I've said "the hell with it" and followed this up by using drugs or engaging in destructive behavior	[4]	[3]	[2]	[▪1▪]
4. It's unsettling not knowing what the future holds	[4]	[▪3▪]	[2]	[1]
5. I occasionally think of things too horrible to talk about	[▪4▪]	[3]	[2]	[1]

A COUPLE DAYS AFTER his brother stopped by, Terry Lyons woke up sober. Rather than fixate on Irish coffee or Blood Marys, Terry forced himself to think about how common that was, how normal it was supposed to be, waking up sober, how many hundreds of millions of people were doing it all over the hemisphere, and how those people, today, this very morning, were still physically and mentally and emotionally disturbed in ways beyond his imagination and beyond anyone's help and beyond any of the problems Terry had right now, and he felt better, at least about himself.

"All I said—was that she has nice titties. Is that a goddamn crime?"

"No, it just makes you a dick, man."

"I can't help it if you're girl is interested in this."

"Dude, Terry, shut up, man."

"Get your friend out of here."

"This is between you and me."

"What's between me and you?"

"You. Can't. Handle. Your. Shit. You are weak. You're a weak person."

"Dude, I asked you nice. Don't push it."

"Fuck him up, Troy. We got you, bro."

"Troy. What a pretty name. They got you, bro. Since you can't do shit on your own."

"You say one more thing to me or my girlfriend and I'll break your face, ok?"

"I'm going to put a bullet hole in her forehead."

Troy popped Terry in the face, not hard, but hard enough to send him back a few feet, water his eyes, get that blood shooting to the brain, and Terry, as if the punch had aligned the proper gears, launched himself forward and wailed on Troy, and that's when Troy's friends rushed in and started swinging. Terry somehow found a glass bottle in his hand and broke it off on the bar and held the jagged half to someone's throat. "You can all come at me," he said, "but one of you is going to get really, really, really fucked up."

Troy and his friends backed away. You could hear the snaps and pops from "She's Got You" as it spun from the yellow-smoke stained jukebox, the sultry tune transformed by the violence and its aftermath into an ominous croon of unfulfilled revenge. Bennett dragged Terry outside and he puked against a wall. It was very cold and windy. The mucus froze to his nose. The powdered snow drifted along the concrete like sand over the face of the desert.

"What's wrong with you, man? You could've killed that guy," Bennett said.

"You're a pussy," Terry said.

"You're wasted."

"I didn't see you helping."

"Helping?"

"I didn't see you stepping in there, bitch."

Terry shoved him.

Bennett disappeared.

Numb from drink and cold, he walked in whatever direction he thought was home. He awoke in his car, the sun spearing his eyes, shivering like an army solider pulled from tank wreckage.

THE BLUEGRASS SONG ENDED with a screeching halt. Everybody cheered. Terry shook his glass. There were two melting cubes in a dirty gold puddle. It was very important to make another Maker's right now. Ruby balanced on tiptoe with her hand on his shoulder, looking over the crowd for someone or something while Blonde scanned the opposite direction with her bare glistening shoulders very close to his chest. The crowd exhaled and then there was space. Ruby stood flat on her feet. Blonde turned her neck around like a swan. Terry said they should kiss, and so they kissed. He brushed the hair from their necks as they tongued, as they grinded up against him.

"Mr. Grammaticologylisationalism Is the Boss" began. It is Terry's all-time favorite song. Bremen introduced them. Blonde and Ruby shrugged to each other. They hadn't found who they were looking for and started to dance by themselves.

Dear Agent Lyons,

They have a pretty big screening room at the prison. But I don't watch those movies. Most movies are shit. So I make my own. Here's what you do: get yourself in a small room that is completely and totally dark, and stay there, by yourself, for an extended period of time, say, twenty-three hours a day, and soon you'll start to see things—shapes, patterns, flashes of memory that can't "be real". You'll smell and hear things, too. I won't repeat what I've heard. But if you're in total darkness twenty-three hours a day for, let's say, twelve to sixteen months, you start to become familiar with the things you see in the dark. You can actually control how they appear and in what sequence. What I do is concentrate on a very detailed image, with accompanying dialogue and non-diegetic sound, of me and you and your dead children, or me and you in front of a burning house, and soon (creation being the mystery it is) that exact scene will begin to play itself out in front of me, through a different kind of projector, and the miracle (another attribute of creation) is, other scenes, scenes I did not specifically imagine (outgunning the police, a goodbye in Canada, a bloody rock in your hands), will grow out of that initial image, and I'll watch it evolve in the dark, my movie, shape it like the auteur I imagine myself to be—no, that I am—demanding another take, another, ruthless, always fine-tuning the scene until its perfect right there in front of my eyes. What will, in time, be the future for you is only the past for me. I have already seen it all.

My Very Best,
Jim Hank

"For the last time," said the Warden of Dodge Correctional Institution, "I've read them. And I'll repeat myself for your benefit: there is no record of Jim Hank serving time in solitary confinement."

"Then he's a fucking psychopath," Terry Lyons said.

"That may be. It's been twenty-eight months since his last full-on eval, which was decidedly above average, but I have to say, until your visit here today, Jim Hank has been, for six years, without question, an exemplary prisoner. No history of violence or mental instability. He volunteers for tough jobs, even in Med Ward. He spends time helping other inmates with art and education."

"This doesn't make any sense."

"You could ask him yourself."

"Ask him what?"

"Why he's writing you."

"Where is he?"

"Block K, Cell 114. I can have two of our guards esc—"

"No. I already know. It's because he's a fucking psychopath."

"It's really none of my business but—did you do this guy wrong?"

"With all due respect, Warden, you don't have a clue who he is. Fraud, extortion, manslaughter. He was directly implicated in the death of three people, one of them a teenager. I was his P.O. at the time and got shit from above because I didn't revoke his ass before he got busted."

"What's your intention?" the Warden asked.

"I want you to stop Jim Hank from writing me letters," Terry said.

"Ok."

"And I don't want him to know that it was me who made it stop."

"Ok."

"So—how are you going to do that?"

"We'll let him write, thinking they'll be mailed as before, but we'll confiscate them before they're sent out with the other prisoners' mail. I have not been given any inclination to monitor Jim Hank's activities, but I admit the letters are disconcerting, they shed a different light on his character. We'll be watching him more closely. Keep the letters as evidence. He's up for early parole in two years." He shook his head and smiled. "On your word alone, nobody would believe his threats against you, or that he ever made any."

"Warn me if something comes up?"

"We'll let you know how he's doing from time to time."

"Fuck it, send me the letters."

After refusing to explain his contradictions to the Warden, Terry got the hell out of Dodge Correctional Institution and drove east to the center of the isthmus and hit the third bar he saw walking down State Street. It was Saturday and happy hour so he drank beer. He ate soggy over-fried food. He switched to whiskey-waters around sundown. He played pool and darts with strangers that quickly turned into friends. "Who's buying shots?" Terry. 'Round midnight he attached himself to a cute girl with a blackbird tattooed on the underside of her forearm. Or she attached herself to him. He forgot, but remembered she had a nice body and a face he could wake up to without makeup. That night, he was the Terry Lyons he always wished himself to be: a dashing, charming, funny, intelligent, honest, thoughtful, and compassionate man, the embodiment of joy and spontaneity, full of passion and purpose, and it was easy, it was like magic how the girl invited him over her apartment, how they fell onto her couch making out, her peach tongue and breasts as soft and forgiving as pillows, and when she suggested they move to the bedroom he lifted her up and carried her in and threw her down on the bed. In the darkness, she told him she was pregnant.

Terry was wasted and thought it was the future and that he had been in a relationship with this woman, whose name he couldn't quite remember, a real and serious relationship, Blackbird, and that *he* had gotten her pregnant, it was *his* child, but he couldn't have a kid now, his job was unstable, there wasn't enough money, the goddamn world we live in, or you know what, he could do it, man-up like he's told thousands of other felons, let's have this child, show the world what a father can do, because he loved her, Blackbird, in no uncertain terms it was clear to Terry that she and the child she was carrying were his salvation, his chance for escape, the utter grace that entered into his life to change it, and he told her he didn't care, she didn't have to get an abortion, he'd love them both, wherever and whenever and forever.

She laughed. "It's not your kid, stupid. I'm only seven weeks along. I just wanted to tell you."

"Ok. You told me."

"Do you still want to?"

"Sure."

16. I am uncritical of my thoughts and ideas to the point that I ignore the problems and difficulties associated with these plans until it is too late	[4] [3] ▌2▐ [1]
17. It is unfair that I've been blamed for things I've done when bank presidents, lawyers, and politicians commit illegal and unethical acts every day	▌4▐ [3] [2] [1]
18. When not in control of a situation I feel weak and helpless and experience a desire to exert power over others	[4] [3] ▌2▐ [1]
19. Despite the wrongs that I have committed throughout my life, deep down I am basically a good person	[4] [3] ▌2▐ [1]

"YOU WERE HARASSING PEOPLE at the Brookfield Mall."

"I didn't harass anybody. In your world, handing out free information, information complied by physicists, architects—"

"Stop it, Jeremiah. And you think I'm dense."

"How can you even keep doing what you do?"

"It's my job. And a potentially long running one."

"That's one of the most depressing things I've ever heard, Mr. Lyons. What have you always wanted to do?"

"Take fucking pictures for National fucking Geographic. Who gives a shit? My life is none of your business."

"And yet mine is."

"That's exactly right. And the direction of your life is in my hands, these, see them? There are a thousand other hands around here that wouldn't hesitate to choke everything out of your life."

"Can't you admit that—"

"No—stop. You need to understand what I just said. You need to give me some respect. Any other probation officer you were assigned to would've revoked you by now, all of them, and you'd be in jail. I want you to realize that."

"Fine. I get it."

"With all the material you've sent me, with your 'activities' on public and private property, would you be innocent of, say, extreme ideological sympathies? Potential treasonous acts? Are you an imminent danger to public safety? Do you think that these complaints don't make a difference? You signed the Conditions for Supervision. You are playing on their turf. All these things you think you know."

"You can't revoke me just for sharing information. I know the process."

"Kid. You have no fucking *idea* of the process."

"Would you girls like anything to drink?"

Ruby and Blonde didn't hear, or pretended not to.

Fela's electric organ rolled into the song, wah-wahing in and out like vertigo.

"Would you girls like anything to drink?" Terry asked louder.

The girls turned inward on the living room dance floor. The crowd, responsive to the beat, began to coalesce and suck in the surrounding pockets of people. Terry Lyons took one last thirsty look and then muscled out of the mob and into the hall. It was shoulder to shoulder. A camera flash stung his eyes. Someone was laughing really loud in his ear. Terry laughed as well. It was contagious. He was having a fantastic time. The electric organ made him dizzy and euphoric. He didn't know anybody, but nobody did, right? This was the miracle sent from Bremen's heaven. I have natural voice, a special voice, a one-of-a-kind voice, a voice I should get on paper, I should get into poetry, become the hard-knock poet of working class life like, like—Terry didn't know any hard-knock poets of working class life but he loved the idea he could become one. He sipped his drink, which had nothing in it, and melted ice washed over his upper lip and whiskey-water dribbled down his chin.

The bar in the garage was just as packed as the dance floor, but the air was refreshed by an occasional blast from the side door of the garage where people shuffled in and out to smoke.

"Maker's?" asked his brother.

"Correct! And please call me 'sir'. Or you won't be tipped."

Blaze snatched the tumbler from Terry and swirled what remained of the cubes. He held it out in front of him as if staring down the barrel of a gun. "Are you sure you don't need any water?"

"Bartender! I believe the customer comes first. Tonight of all nights he comes first."

"Terry, how are you? It's been a while."

It was a nasally voice, belonging to a face which was flush from the cold outside. He gripped Terry's hand very tight, shook it very soft, and then yanked him into a bear hug.

"I've been good, real good, as good as can be," lips muffled by the shoulder pad of a silver suit jacket. Terry smelled menthol tobacco and wanted a cigarette. They separated.

"You think you could bum me a smoke?"

The man cocked his head in disappointed surprise, then took a pack from the breast pocket of his suit and tapped one out for Terry, who put it in his ear.

"So what have you been doing with yourself?" the man said, all good will returned, grinning with a row of crooked bottom teeth.

"Not a goddamn thing. You?"

"Sold the business. Retired. Jordy and I live in Colorado now. La Yunta. Nice quiet town. Flat. They've got an amazing private science institute there. It's really something. I volunteered to teach a couple classes."

"Great. I love it."

"Love what?"

"What?"

"What do you love?"

It was the Music, it was too loud. Terry lost his bearings. He smirked and put the cigarette in his mouth and asked for a light. When the man said, in a dark resonant voice like a comic book super-villain, *you cannot smoke here,* Terry forgot he was at a funeral and was about to tell this guy to back the fuck off, asking him what he loved, who the fuck was this guy? He felt eyes on them and swung his head around, scanning different faces at different depths. He caught a girl by the opposite wall watching them with an intensity as cool as mint in a Mojito. She didn't glance away like she was guilty or uncertain or anything but the one in charge.

He patted the man on the arm. "Right. I'll see you."

She didn't even stop looking as he approached. She was in all different shades of blue.

TERRY LYONS WENT TO see Bremen play three times. The first was jazzy FM shit and he blacked out. The second was pop-rock covers and he blacked out. The third was salsa-blues and he maintained a spectacular baseline, blacking out only in the Uber ride home. The bar was called The Kingdom. The ceiling was low as a cave, the beer decadent and expensive. The band was nothing special—guitar, harmonica, piano, drums, and bass. Bass was Bremen. The only hot girls were here with boyfriends. Bummer. Terry had a deep and detailed conversation about the political situation in Venezuela (of which he knew nothing) with a pale boy in a tight flannel shirt and a girl's perm. During applause, he thought about the future and how everyone will be one sex. Then Bremen was telling him about backbones. Terry didn't understand it in a technical sense, how the bass is a spine and you build the sound around it, but he agreed, and they toasted to backbones, and they drank.

Surfacing from the blackout at the front door of his apartment, he dropped his keys, banged his head on the doorknob. Terry swayed inside, kicked off his shoes, loosened his belt, collapsed in bed, and expected the Moon herself to descend through the shades and suck him off for a thousand years.

GINGER, CHIEF P.O., SENT him an email with a Vimeo link and password and the message: *what the fuck is this and why is it being send to me from the fucking mayor's press secretary's office?*

White-on-Black Title Card: Fall 2017 Public Hearing of the Milwaukee Police Department's Annual Operating Budget.

An old white man in a black suit was at a podium, a USA flag pinned to his chest. He was receiving a big applause. He yielded the floor.

Jeremiah Sezala stepped to the mic, shuffling some papers at the podium. Terry's stomach dropped like a satellite from space, heating up and going to pieces. The kid started with his foot on the accelerator. He didn't seem to know any other way.

First, he listed "only a fraction" of MPD's "outrageous" expenditures, which included armed Humvees and paramilitary weaponry for urban warfare, for which the Department cited "terrorism, both foreign and domestic" as justifications in the "sound and judicious" use of this federal, and public, money. Second, he compared MPD's view on terrorism to the hard facts of the actual danger of terrorism, "both foreign and domestic", happening in a city like Milwaukee, which had its fair share of violence, but nothing would justify the expenditures previously cited. Third, he attacked the "unquestioned ideological assumptions" behind such expenditures, assumptions "bound up and now solidified" with the ideas and symbols of safety and protection that "grew out of one day, were traceable to one event, and our perception of that event."

It was worse than Terry imagined. Boos rained down like a shower of meteors. The kid didn't blink. He was eventually escorted out— "And why are you all looking at me like that? A traumatized subject is a receptive subject, and into that traumatic state steps a false impression: that the government, your government, is there to heal and protect you from traumas such as the one you just experienced. If you believe this, then any information pointing to government complicity in such trauma can't be honestly accepted. That creates paralysis, creates obedience and docility without physical force. Watch the President when he speaks, the crowds as they cheer, yourselves as you vote."

Terry Lyons was in the shitstorm now.

"Hello."

"Hello yourself."

"Didn't we meet earlier? You came in that group?"

"I don't think so."

"I'm good at remembering faces. But I can't recall your name. I definitely should have." Terry was drunk but lucid, one of the greatest pleasures of hard alcohol.

"I was a student of his. A singer."

"Not anymore?"

"Not quite the same as before."

"But you still sing?"

"I sing."

"I'd love to hear you sometime."

Terry could tell, because he was finally peering into them, that she had pale aquamarine eyes with flames of yellow and orange at the edge of her irises. She returned his cocky stare with the unbridled and limitless power that only the youth, eternal youth, and regenerated youth possess.

"You two really do look alike."

"Who two?"

"You and Bremen."

"I've heard that before—we are cousins."

"Aren't you his uncle?"

Terry laughed at how stupid that sounded, laughed at this girl in different shades of blue, and he didn't want her to think he was somebody's uncle, let alone Bremen's.

"Bullshit. Who said?"

"Bremen said."

"He told you that?"

She nodded, and conveyed her superiority by plucking a thread from his shirt and pitching it over her shoulder like spilled salt. "Aren't you a parole officer or something?"

Terry took a phantom drink. Fela's trumpets sounded like a military procession of victory through the streets. "Who are you again?"

"You don't know me?"

He couldn't escape, he was locked in, seatbelt fastened, riding the groove of this recondite night, riding the whorls of the larger world that, in our time signature, was funneling down with fantastic speed into a bottleneck so tight, a darkness so dark, that there was only light in deeper darkness.

"Would you like anything to drink?"

"No."

```
33.  I find myself expressing
     tender feelings toward
     animals or little children       [ 4 ]  [ 3 ]  [ 2 ]  ▬▬
     in order to make myself
     feel better after engaging
     in irresponsible behavior
```

34. People have difficulty understanding me because I tend to jump around from subject to subject when talking	[4] [3] [2] [■]
35. When it's all said and done, society owes me	[■] [3] [2] [1]
36. I view the positive, helpful, and charitable things I have done for others as making up for the negative actions I have engaged in	[■] [3] [2] [1]

Dear Agent Lyons,

Prison guards make me wonder. Do they like prison? Nobody forced them to work here. Is there a desire to see suffering, or to inflict it? Is there a desire to wield power, or bear witness to it? To say, *I saw that* or *I did that?* And when I meditate on this point, the two young prison guards outside my solitary cell become a little more intelligible. I get them. I understand why they would want to see me suffer, why they might want to inflict suffering upon me. I know why they want to shave every day and lifts weights and get married and have daughters, not sons. They believe they have total control over me, and are using this control in a moral and compassionate way. This odd harmony, compassion within power, is probably what keeps them from swinging their clubs too hard on my head. I have come to the conclusion that it's best not to judge. Can this be something you can embrace? Every night before Lights Out I tell myself that I am Awake for this Prisonbreak. Are you awake, Agent Lyons? Should I set an alarm? Do you need a wake-up call? I would love to speak with you.

My Very Best,
Jim Hank

"Long story short, I gave it up and went back to interior architecture, it's my first love, and anyway it's only a three-year program."

"Interesting."

"And you? What do you do?"

"Photographer for National Geographic."

"Wow. I know it's probably stupid to ask this but—what do you take pictures of?"

"People."

"Sign this or you go to jail."

"I'm not signing anything." Jeremiah squirmed in his seat.

"Read it. Sign it. Or I revoke your probation now." Terry was sharp, though running on fumes.

"On what grounds?"

"Your contact with the police at that hearing for starters."

"I was never arrested."

"Consider this a last resort. This is the best I can do."

"Am I supposed to take that seriously?"

"Your probation has been enhanced to the maximum supervision level."

"I never violated the Conditions."

"Signature? Or jail cell?"

"I didn't do anything wrong."

"I would've thought, smart as you are, that you'd understand by now."

"Understand what?"

"That you don't have to do anything wrong to get in trouble. Drawing attention is reason enough. And also that I'm literally saving your ass, in ways you can't even fathom right now. But like I said, you don't have to sign. See what happens."

"I don't have a pen."

"I have thousands."

Terry Lyons asked for it. He did not beg. It was not his conscious desire. But he did ask.

It was Tuesday and his lips were crusty and white. Dry-heaving, he went for sink water in the kitchen, eyes don't you dare open, hunched in half like a mythical beast. He straightened his back and felt a spear go through the base of his spine, and the spasm of pain made him jump and knock his head against an open cupboard door.

He slammed it shut, repeatedly, then roared and ripped it off its hinges, and looked at it lying there stupid for a moment, all splinters, brackets, screws, his head throbbing like a big toe hit with a hammer, decided no, it was better if he just got a new one. He put the broken pieces outside his door and sat in a hot shower for forty-five minutes. Weeks later, a neighbor gathered the pieces in a garbage bag and took it to the dumpster behind the complex. She was sick of looking at them.

TERRY LEFT THE GARAGE and stumbled into the hallway, failing to navigate its current with the proper skill. He fought through several kids passing their phones back and forth and snapping pictures—he photobombed a few. He collided with older couples shuffling around with fluted drinks. They paused, recognizing him, expecting Terry to recognize them, expecting him to talk about this feeling—*we know each other, but how?* Why else did Bremen have this funeral? But Fela, the silky voice of Fela, slid into the song and above the crowd—

Terry felt the pressure to piss. He plowed his way forward, gathering a sense of purpose along the way, but the bathroom line was five deep, and not even Ginger could command him to hold it.

"Where are my shoes?" He was suddenly at the front door, pawing through the shoe racks.

"Take 'em," Mo said, holding up his faux leather boots like a murder weapon she wanted him to hide. "Don't mess up my system."

"They're goddamn shoes," swiping them from her.

"And there's over a hundred goddamn pairs of them. Where are you going?"

"To have a smoke."

"Since when do you smoke?"

Terry Lyons fumbled with his boots. Slippery laces. He teetered back and forth, set one boot on the floor, and jammed his foot into it.

"Christ, Terry. You're drunk."

"No, I'm not. These laces are knotted. It's cold as shit in here. Do you know what I did with the other bottle?"

"Bottle of *what?*"

"Does Donna? Where is she?"

"I have no idea."

His dumb clubfoot wouldn't fit. He threw the boot at the door. It made a booming echo and left a black scuff. That didn't stop the Music. Nothing did, nothing would. Mo quickly entwined her arm with his.

"God, Terry. Follow me."

Guests in the kitchen were situated in pockets of two's and three's. Mo anchored Terry in a chair at the island table and poured him a glass of water. She used her free hand to lift one of Terry's and bring it up to the glass, something you do for the blind, and she closed his hand around it, because he was blind. She talked to him in a real voice, one he imagined Bremen must've heard in all its registers of pleasure and pain—the air spun. Mo grabbed his chin made him look directly into her eyes, which were, Terry noticed, churning with the colors of green algae and brown soil.

"Do you—understand me?" she said.

"I got it," Terry slurred.

"Someone's at the door." A dramatic baritone from the hall. "Mo?"

"Drink that water. Eat some bread. Vera, will you watch him a second?"

Terry swiveled his head, the first stable movement he had made since entering the kitchen, and saw Vera at the end of the table with a slice of blueberry pie on a red plastic plate. She had the fork in her mouth, and slid it out slow. He could hear the metal scrape against her teeth. She chewed and nodded *yes* to Mo (who sprinted off) as if she was being asked to keep an eye on Merlin while he was asleep.

TERRY LYONS HAS THIS fantasy: being a husband and father. He sweeps Blackbird off her wings and supports her and her child, a girl. They marry, have a boy, and then another, who they name Bremen. As the kids grow up and the parents grow old, Terry continually works long hours and is under great stress, as before, but there is a transformation in the attitude he has to work and life. His desires are finally purified. He lives with remarkable stability. No force can break this state, not even when Blackbird is dying and she can't get around without a wheelchair, but their house had never been made for one, so in the mornings Terry carries her out of the bedroom and down a flight of steps where the wheelchair waits like a pair of uncomfortable shoes.

"You don't have to do this every morning," Blackbird says, raising her head from the pillow, making it look like she's got enough strength to move her own body. "I'm tired anyway."

He glances out the window near the bed. "It's beautiful outside. Let me take you for a spin."

Blackbird reaches up, which is no small feat, and brushes his hand with her fingers, because he never clipped her wings, ever. He turns to her.

"Just around the block," she smiles.

```
58. Looking back over my        [ 4 ]   ███   [ 2 ]   [ 1 ]
    life I can see now that
    I lacked direction and
    consistency of purpose
```

59. There have been times when I've made plans to do something with my family and then canceled these plans so that I could hang out with my friends or engage in selfish and irresponsible behavior	[4]	[3]	[2]	▣
60. I believe that I am a special person and that my situation deserves special consideration	[4]	▣	[2]	[1]
61. Strange and persistent odors, for which there is no explanation, come to me at certain times and for no apparent reason	[4]	[3]	[2]	▣

"YOU OKAY, UNCLE TERRY?"

"I need ice," groaning, in agony.

He took his time standing. He took his time charting three steps to the fridge and opening the freezer door. He reached for the ice tray and saw a waxy blood-red bottleneck buried in a corner beneath frozen bags of raspberries and broccoli. He didn't believe it. Even as he had it in his hands he didn't believe it.

His Maker's.

Some people, not knowing Terry, mistook the look on his face for a religious experience because of the profound reverence by which he made his drink. Terry carefully calibrated his ass to the seat of his chair. He cradled the drink, his finger tapping out the Afrobeat on the glass, head bobbing to the rhythm, eyes closed, in communion.

"Vera?"

She stopped in mid-chew, mouth full of pie.

"What are you going to say for the eulogy?"

She swallowed, throat bulging. "You should probably just read it."

"Sure," opening his eyes.

Vera Lyons produced a thick folded square of paper. She unfolded it and pointed to the starting place and said, "Here to the end. Not that long."

Terry tried to read, honest, but only letters were legible, not words and definitely not sentences, so he doubled down and moved his eyes along the page like a competent reader would, latching onto individual letters—g, i, m, l—as if they contained whole passages of prose. A word, solid and complete, abruptly floated off the page—Sunday—and he was overwhelmed by memories of Sunday, of football and brunch, of cartoons and church, Bloody Mary's and Mimosas, Blackbird and Vera, who was born on a Sunday, two pounds, two ounces. Terry did the math in his head: Vera was twelve and Bremen was twenty-seven; he was forty-one and Blaze was fifty-five. What if his brother had died when he was Vera's age? She licked her finger and swiped it across the plate to get every crumb. In that moment, Terry pretty much wanted to kill himself. He didn't look forward to the tests and trials of the future. Everything he remembered about who he was and wanted to be was gone. He missed it all. And he would never see it again. And he knew alternatives did not abound.

Terry handed back the eulogy.

"You didn't read it all," Vera said.

"I can't—finish right now."

"He should've picked someone else to write it."

Vera poked her fork at what remained of the pie, mashing the crust over and over, and Terry poked his finger into his glass of whiskey, hitting the ice cubes over and over.

"Why did he do this?" Vera said.

"I don't care." Terry wasn't strong enough to raise his five hundred pound head, let alone answer a straightforward question. "I have to piss." A side door in the kitchen led into the basement. Terry staggered off the chair.

"I don't think the toilet works. Dad didn't finish hooking up the plumbing."

Too late. Terry was already moving toward crescendo land.

"WELL—I CAN THINK OF one thing that's a problem with the 'Information Age'."

"Ubiquitous porn?"

"And that. But also that no one can tell what's what anymore."

"But really it's the 2 girls 1 cup thing, right? Another whiskey-water, please."

"I'm just saying that it's become difficult, if not impossible—I'll have another Mud Puppy—if not impossible, to perform the basic requirements which ensure the integrity of language and perception: the ability to make distinctions."

Dear Agent Lyons,

I've learned that most boys here lack any greater purpose or motivation. Most committed crimes because they had to, or because they liked the power and intoxication of it. But that's all. And that's not much, in my opinion. They've taught me some proper mechanics, but there is something missing in their approach. There's a whole other dimension they don't appreciate, which is what I want you to appreciate. It's the Indians I get it from, the Cherokee long ago who killed the deer, and they loved the deer, they revered the deer, they believed a spirit of personality was in the deer, and they still killed it, but they knew what it was, what it really was, and that's why when we meet, Agent Lyons, I want you to know that I know what you are: you are a spirit of personality and I will give thanks like a hunter as your heart is opened and blood fills your lungs and you breathe blood. I cannot wait for the day.

My Very Best,
Jim Hank

THE BASEMENT LIGHT WAS poor and cloudy like water from a city tap. Fela was still going strong. Terry could feel the beat, the dancers stomping on the floor above, those girls still grinding. He set the glass and whiskey bottle on the basement sink and fumbled with his belt, unzipped, and the first powerful stream missed the toilet completely and splashed on the floor. He readjusted, leaning his arm against the wall, letting his mind rise with the Music, thinking of boyhood vacations with his parents for the first time in decades. He shook himself, a few drops landing on the rim, and zipped up. Bremen would laugh when—don't even think about that. Don't ever think about that again.

"WHY DIDN'T I GET a call, Ginger? If there's any contact with the authorities I'm to know about it first."

"The mayor's office requested I stay abreast of the matter. All outside reports were rerouted to me personally. "

"What the ever-loving fuck?"

"No further contact with police. No protests. He violated those conditions. It's clean. I know you tried."

"Gee that means a whole lot of shit."

"Don't get your dick in a sailor's knot. It's not a good look for you."

"I got it."

"Convince me."

"I said I got it."

"You've never been one to be polite."

"I know."

Terry slammed down his office phone, put his head in his hands, knew if he actually saw Ginger in the next couple hours he'd probably break the fucker's jaw and five or six of his ribs, but it was only eleven after nine in the morning on a Wednesday, and Terry didn't know how to perform miracles in a shitstorm. He gulped his whiskey and coffee, made another one and gulped that and booted up his computer, a computer he wished would say *Good Morning* to him in a sweet Southern girl's voice (someday...), and revoked Jeremiah's probation and issued a warrant for his arrest, and he didn't even think about it until later that night, when the flames of the day had cooled off and he was sitting with his last dram of Colonel Taylor's in front of his HDTV watching the Packers vs. Giants, a game which would determine home field advantage throughout the playoffs, thinking that it's okay, Ginger intervened, he could do nothing about it, that was the job, it was Jeremiah who brought it on himself—everyone brings it on themselves—you can only carve out your own small space for refuge and protection against all the onslaughts of this world, because it's just another day in the Federal Military Government Complex, and here he was, raising his drink to a tidal wave.

TERRY LYONS WAS SLEEPING when a knock at the door woke him up. It was four am. He stumbled through the darkness. He felt for a cold brass knob. He opened the door. It was Mr. Apocalypse. Terry was confused. What was he doing here? Shouldn't he be somewhere more important, like a town on the US/Mexico border, or a village in Central Africa, or a megacity in China?

"My activities are personal and planetary," said Mr. Apocalypse, who despite his dark figure was surrounded by a thin corona of light. He put an arm around Terry and led him outside on the little balcony attached to Terry's apartment, so little only the two of them and a frozen plant Terry had forgotten to bring in for the winter could fit. The stars were bright and a thick layer of snow covered everything like child's blanket.

"Do you know why I'm here?" Mr. Apocalypse said.

"Probably not," Terry said.

"I'm here because there are laws, Terry, laws we must all follow, and not because they are imposed by beings like me, but because they are part of the essential nature of everything in existence." Mr. Apocalypse tightened his grip on Terry's shoulder. "What do you think of when you think of me?"

"I don't know," Terry said.

"Think," Mr. Apocalypse said. "Just list things that come to your mind."

"I think of pure evil. Pain and torture. Suffering, mass death, extinction."

"Who does these things? Do I do them?"

"Probably not," Terry said. "I don't really believe you exist. So I guess it's other people who do them, other people who inflict pain and suffering on everyone else. But you must help all that along. Like, you're the power source behind these things."

"Terry," Mr. Apocalypse said, "you're kind of half-right. People do horrible things. And they don't want other people to know. They try to keep their activities a secret. And they're good at that. But when the time is right, I disable their covert attitudes and increase their delusions. I press them into revealing things they ordinarily would've concealed. They expose themselves. The baseness of their character is proven beyond any doubt or illusion. Their activities are no longer secret. You see what they are doing. And you may take action. But that is not my area of dominion. My dominion is exposure. I assist in the unveiling and allow things to be clearly seen."

He gave Terry a hug and Terry's soul drifted away to death. When Mr. Apocalypse released him and left the little balcony, Terry broke down and cried from the happiness he felt at coming back to life, even as he thought it stupid that such a thing could make him happy, or cry. He hoped this was the end of his dream, but it wasn't. He told himself it was over, wake up. He commanded, "Wake up." It was only when the stars had disappeared in dawn and the wind iced his cheeks and a squirrel jumped from one branch to another, snow falling off the limbs in wet clumps, that he recognized he was already awake.

A HUMAN BLUR IN the mirror. He should quit drinking. If not quit, at least cut down. He wanted to love someone and he wanted someone to love him back because love departs from those who have forsaken love and love does not abide where love is not sought after and longed for more than any other thing. These thoughts—who is giving him these thoughts? They stayed with him as he uncorked the Maker's— glug, glug, glug in the toilet bowl—and whipped the empty bottle at the basement wall, the shatter reminding him of rain. It's been so long since it's rained. He tore up the cigarette over the toilet and watched the black flakes flutter into a brown maple lake. As reward, Terry did not pour out the fresh drink in his glass. He took a sip, the alcohol burning his upper lip, and swallowed strong and breathed fire through his teeth. Satisfied, he pressed the toilet handle. There was no flush. Again and again. Nothing.

He tried to wash his hands in the sink, spinning the knobs back and forth. They didn't work either.

FIFTH MOVEMENT

 You're tuned to the FELIS CATUS frequency . . . .

MAY YOUR WHISKERS ALWAYS be clean and sharp.

THE BIG BANG.

And God said.

The battle between Ormuz and Ariman.

Spontaneous creative cycles.

Ultimate sex with Shiva and Shakti.

Skies united and cloven asunder.

A floating island and the water beetle's soft mud.

You get one free singularity in your model building. We will put ours in the domain of pure shape and proportion, in the language of music and light.

Felis Catus lives in the Great White Void. It is a formless place, without dimension or time, a unity where all is at rest, at peace, enough, and very boring for Felis Catus, who has an eternally curious temper. So he contracts the Great White Void to a simple point, a selected area for action, an everlasting pivot and fulcrum from which to radiate and expand his curious temper above and below, right and left, front and behind, weaving together these extensions to create an individual composition, which is also the instrument that plays it.

The sky, the sex, the spoken word.

The bang, the battle, the beetle.

We are extensions from that simple point. We are not Felis Catus. We are not the Great White Void. Our purpose is practical. We are powers and potentialities. We are in the service of realizing his sheet music. Think of us, in a very sincere way, as the major notes of the major scale, because reality is a grand piano created and played by Felis Catus and the manifested universe and everything in it is an example of his complete mastery of its intricate harmonics. You know because you have played us. Do re mi fa so la ti. We assist his compositions through all of the corresponding scales as they undertake the sonorous passages that leads back to the Great White Void where they were first sounded.

Do you not hear the Music?

By him we shall make ourselves heard, and by us you shall hear Felis Catus. You shall hear us because you are no longer where you used to be. You shall hear him because you are now where you are: the Felis Catus frequency. Here, chemistry shares its chord structure with the color wheel. Anthills are the sharps and flats of minor cities. Personality is the keynote of it all. Geological time is 12/8. A family resonates with a nation. Atoms are octaves of stars.

Do

MERLIN HAS INITIATIVE. HE'LL start the action and work with the reaction. He often sleeps like a bread loaf, with all four legs and paws tucked in, his tail wrapped tight around his body, his head slightly bowed and nestled in the hollow of his chest. Try to rub his back when he's this way. The boy will snatch you up.

Merlin tastes the air for prey, moving like an arrow through the grass, the fine hairs on his coat picking up second by second changes in the wind, his paws catching the hums and thrums that reverb through the earth. This is how he hones in on a field mouse or a sparrow at the base of a tree, and once caught sight of, once surely seen, Merlin proceeds with full faith in his abilities, borne out of a significant pride in the feline body that is carrying them out.

He crouches in the long grass, content to move closer by millimeters, slithering along the ground, never taking his eyes off the target. He curls his tail for balance, twitches his whiskers and ears, not from anxiety, but to calibrate his body for the pounce, for avenues of pursuit, narrowing his field of attention, eliminating the impressions of an airplane droning overheard, sunlight bouncing off the leaves, a blaring lawnmower, two girls running through a sprinkler next door, Bremen calling his name and clanking his food bowl with a spoon, the black ants crawling over his couch-sharpened claws. He desires his prey, and when in a position of total focus, at the peak of his purpose, with all his normal and extra senses in alignment, he springs for the kill. He can't wait to tear into the soft easy flesh.

Out of anybody in the room, Merlin always has the most clear-cut awareness of what's really going on.

Blaze Lyons, the father, arrives home late from caulking the bathtub at a cardiologist's mansion and fixes himself a turkey sandwich. Bremen, the son, wakes early and strums a few warm-up chords on his bass. Donna, the mother, hops out of the shower and dresses before her body is dry, the socks sticking to her shins. Vera, the daughter, mutes the commercials during a documentary of the Sahara on NGC. In these moments, each member of the family feels something, a sense of being stared at.

Blaze stops eating his sandwich, Donna struggling with her sock, Bremen plunking his bass, Vera daydreaming on the couch, and they look around and catch sight of Merlin, sometimes in shadow, sometimes in plain sight, but always self-assured and unflappable, perfectly composed like a fugue by Frescobaldi. He has been watching them for quite some time. He'll start to clean himself and suck the family into watching the unhurried grace of his movements, only to suddenly stop, tongue sticking out, fur gone haywire, and turn his penetrative gaze back upon them.

While the family, each in their own way, questions their superior nature in this small silent moment, Merlin knows his.

RE

MERLIN LOVES SHOULDER RIDES. Here's how he gets them: he jumps on a counter, mews, waits for someone to walk over, looks eagerly in their eyes, hops on their shoulder, tightens his claws in the gentlest of grips, and they carry him around for as long as they can tolerate his maniacal purring and the wet nose he rubs into their ear.

Merlin once busted out of the house and into the thickets of a soppy spring morning. He didn't come back until the full moon, gigantic and orange like some cartoon exaggeration, began to rise in the sky. He was hobbling, his left leg lame. Donna didn't find any blood or swelling. Bremen fed him food pellets by hand. Blaze reasoned that if he didn't seem to be in too much pain they might as well give it a week and see what happens.

Then Vera came home from a long day at Mud Lake with her friends and saw Merlin limping across the living room. And in the adult way that only a child could act, she scooped him up and put him in his favorite place: on the couch arm closest to the window. And when he was hungry she scooped him up and put him by his food bowl. And when he was thirsty she scooped him up and put him in the bathtub and turned on the water to the ideal trickle so he could put his head under the stream and drink because he wouldn't drink water from a dish or bowl, always pawing at his reflection over and over; he would only drink water that flowed. For about a month, Vera carried him everywhere, from the attic to the basement, his upper half and front arms draped over her shoulder and his bottom cradled in her arms.

Merlin soon healed, but wasn't about to give up his shoulder rides. The experience of that first ride created a powerful link in his mind, binding him to a chain of memories that traveled together in a well-provisioned caravan across the deserts of space and time. It was the memory of kittenhood when his mother seized him by the scruff of his neck. It was the memory of a child's hand lifting him out of a cage. It was the memory of a medieval ship captain taking him into his personal cabin during a squall on the Mediterranean. It was the memory of a painter in Tangiers protecting him from a deranged chef, and a party of writers in a hotel in east Jerusalem singing his praise. It was the memory of a priest in Abydos who carried him to a silk pillow where milk and honey waited as a reward for keeping the temple clear of rodents. Behind the posturing of aloof independence there is a truth Merlin keeps to himself: he wants to be taken care of, to feel safe, to have a sanctuary from the terrible dangers of this world, which are Legion, and which would destroy him if given half a chance.

So he's trained the family, and Vera indulges him every day, Bremen when the mood strikes, Blaze when his hands are clean, Donna only if it's the weekend. For Merlin, the memory of shoulder rides is the memory of security is the memory of love is the memory of everything within him.

Mi

In his dreams there is a garden, a place of fecundity and play, with cypress trees and acacia shrubs enclosing the space. He sits, trimming his back claws with his teeth, on an elaborately carved stone bench with vines growing up the sides, their tendrils just playthings for him to swat at. There are roses, ferns, wheatgrass, lettuce, and delicious herbs that he can't wait to eat. A placid creek flows through the scene, and Merlin stands at the edge of the water, pawing at the minnows and goldfish that dart past in the shallows. He sprints for the sheer joy of sprinting. He eats spiders and beetles and rolls belly-up in pure yellow sunbeams. He chases stray leaves blowing in circles, rabbits down their holes, squirrels up their trees, and the chittering sound he makes when they run beyond his reach is duplicated in sleep when the family see him twitch his whiskers and paws. They think he's having a bad dream and shake his head to wake him up. Dazed, heavy-lidded, he stares at them like, "What'd you do that for?"

In the kitchen is an avocado-green door with a burnished wood handle. Merlin has observed the family pushing the handle down, pulling back, opening the door, dragging it behind them, and closing it shut. He wants to open and close the door himself and leave and return when he likes, but he can't replicate the rhythm of their movements, he's a cat, and so he mews in a high plaintive cry.

One balmy summer afternoon, Merlin took a catnap in Bremen's open and empty bass case (a favorite spot) and dreamt of his garden. But not his regular garden. Flanked on each side by a pair of trees, there is an avocado-green door with a burnished wood handle. Merlin studies the wood grain, the hinges, the handle, the four small windows in its top frame, the square borders, and the seeming weight of its body when he stretches against it. He sniffs around and approaches the bottom corner of the door, same side as the handle. He feels air moving through a space, green air, green space. He paws at that corner, claws at that space, and the door opens. He's awake.

There's no time like the present. Merlin hopped out of Bremen's bass case and sauntered to the kitchen door, the same door as in his dream. He clawed at the lining of the bottom corner. Nothing happened, but he kept at it, and eventually his claws caught a piece of rubber trim. Merlin pulled hard, there was a decisive metal click, the door opened, and he ran outside, not bothering to close the door behind him, the little shit.

They would find him napping on the driveway, on the front steps, in the backyard, as self-satisfied as any human could be. Blaze eventually found out that the rubber trim running along the bottom of the door was incorrectly installed. It created a miniscule gap between the doorframe and the floor, a space to exploit. Even more mysterious: sometimes the tongue of the door did not fully lock into its catch—it would slip out of place with a light pull. Blaze was dumbfounded, even resentful. Merlin had exploited a flaw he couldn't possibly know about. The family puzzled over this fact, never reaching for the image in the dream, not the action in reality, which came to Merlin first.

Always the inner image comes first.

FA

HE WAS BORN IN a barn under a corrugated roof, next to a snow-capped bale of hay, in a litter of eight, and over the next few months a big red fox killed every cat in the barn, even his mother, except for Merlin and his brother. The farmer, a dairy farmer with rolling pastures twenty miles west of Monticello, found the two brothers fighting in his cow pens and scaring the calves, decided he didn't have time for kittens, gave Merlin to his nephew attending Edgewood in Madison, and the brother, Ram, to his friend who worked as a cellar master at New Glarus. Ram died within six weeks. He had a genetically bad heart, infected with worms and aberrant rhythm, a heart that would require thousands of dollars to fix. Small-brewery cellar masters are not rich—they do it for the art.

Merlin, who still had a bit of country in him, didn't like the nephew's small city apartment or his cigarette smoke and open paint tubes. He'd mew all day and night, clawing up blank canvases. The nephew didn't understand that curiosity was just another name for analysis. The relationship turned sour fast. One night, drunk and stoned, the nephew was creeping up the short skirt of another painter, also drunk and stoned, and Merlin wouldn't stop meowing at the top of his lungs. The nephew threw open the window and dropped him down two stories because he wasn't getting laid with a cat like that.

It was natural for him to climb—a tree, a dumpster, a fence, a drainpipe to the roof, piles of rebar. Whenever he arrived in a new environment Merlin always went for the highest position. He perched there, overlooking his kingdom, observing the life of his domain. He identified objects in his own way—cars, people, animals, alleys, foods, dangers, extreme dangers—and by his understanding of them he made himself rules, a constitution for survival, a system of reasoning with which to negotiate the world. *I will never approach small children. I will investigate every garbage can I see. I will fight when I can, and then I will run.* And the family wonders why Merlin still likes heights, why they find him on top of the kitchen cupboards, bedrooms dressers, bookcases, sitting right at the edge, where nothing can escape his sight.

His eyes are too big for his head and set far apart. Alien. His eyes are rich copper with streaks of lemon and brass, the colors swirling together like some dazzling hurricane on a distant brown planet. There is no sense of "day" ending for him, seeing as well in starry darkness as he does in regular light. The sense of color traded in for sharpness. Certain things are so clear.

After being allowed into the Lyons' house there was a testy and delicate discussion about what to do: keep the cat or take it to a shelter. It went on for a good two hours, Blaze and Donna leaning towards shelter as much as Bremen pushed to keep. Merlin watched the argument from the mantle above the fireplace, watched it grow towards a horizon nobody wanted to see the other side of, so he hopped off the mantle and rubbed on Blaze's leg and skipped over and rubbed on Bremen's leg and then flopped down and rolled on his stomach and chewed on his tail. Even Donna laughed. He was given one week. Merlin slept on Bremen's chest that night, purring softly and rubbing his face into Bremen's face. He did this night after night after night, and when it was obvious the family wouldn't throw him back out into the world, he stopped sleeping on Bremen's chest, and never did it again.

So

MERLIN DOES NOT KNOW Bremen Lyons is dead.

He didn't see a body (nobody did) and couldn't push his nose into a cold unresponsive nose, couldn't cry while sitting on Bremen's chest and hear him not cry back.

What he does know: the house has undergone a rapid and lasting change. Donna used to ignore Merlin as much as possible, shooing him from the kitchen table and spraying him with a water bottle as he pawed at the TV screen, and he used to go to great lengths to avoid her hisses and swats, remaining in a room only if another family member was there, else he'd trot off. Now he's Donna's closest companion. She treats him with a rediscovered innocence—she the kitten and Merlin the mother. He sleeps with her, he eats with her, he coaxes her around the house and rubs against her calf and purrs constantly. Merlin never wanders up to the attic anymore, not even for the view. He'll get his shoulder rides, no doubt, even if Vera forces the issue. Blaze, once so protective of his personal space, now lets Merlin in his work shed, and it's like new shoots have sprouted from the grass. Merlin investigates every nail and chisel, every oily rag and stain, undaunted by the heat of the saws and sting of the copper. He jumps on a planer, content with the novelty of the spot to tolerate the sawdust, blinking and yawning.

What led him to the family was a song. There he was, a five-month old monster of a stray, patrolling the streets, fighting for food, huddled at night in the fading warmth of a car engine, and he heard the song miles away, nearly a whisper, a melody that sounded like a low shaded tree in the cool sun. He was not unhappy. He could be happier. He tuned his ears to the music. The instinct, felis catus, was to set out and search for the song. The intuition, Felis Catus, was the way that led him there.

And now there's another song, a whole new arrangement rising over the noise in the house, heard best when gazing out the window or stretching against the door. His time with the Lyons' is coming to an end. Merlin is searching for apertures of departure—when the snow starts, when the family splits, when the world is green, when the song is irresistible, and when that day comes, he will not go to another house (though he won't discount the option if a favorable one arises), but will live in self-sufficient independence, not looking back at the wreckage he's left behind, no sense of pity for the piteous ones. He inflicts trauma, he doesn't endure it. Emotionally feral one last time.

The family wonders. How could he simply leave like that? After all the affection and shoulder rides and treats and petting sessions and cuddling and sleeping together like lovers? When they held him in their arms during violent thunderstorms? Knowing the security of his house, the people who deeply cared for him and soothed his fears— was there no gratitude, no love? They wonder when he'll die.

Merlin slinks through the kindly falling snow, into the woods, past a thawed stream. He climbs a tree full of fat squirrels. They scatter. He does not know or worry about when his next meal or drink or breath will come. Only that it will come. He knows because Felis Catus knows. That is the only way he knows.

Doubt never led him anywhere.

LA

THE ABILITY TO TELL the difference. The laser pointer doesn't do the trick. He'll play with a rainbow-colored mouse stuffed with catnip, but only for a couple minutes, and then he'll turn his back and lick his paws and ignore the lifeless thing. Give him a shoebox or a wadded paper ball, something he can animate. He'll fetch.

A stranger reaches out to pet him, the hand dropping from above or approaching from below, and right before contact Merlin smells the odor on the skin, in the skin, the scent behind the action, its rot or purity, and he'll recoil and swat at them or move to embrace their reach.

Smell reveals the true nature of the object in front of him. Is this a nice human? Is this a safe street? When Bremen Lyons wore a thick pair of corduroys, Merlin would sniff before jumping on his thigh and holding onto the pants with his claws, and if Vera wore shorts, he'd paw at her leg with his talons sheathed, the downy furs and hard pads always tickling her calves. Many a time Donna and Blaze have happened upon Merlin in the hallways of the house, staring at an empty space on the wall, and they shoo him along, which is a dangerous thing, engaging his contempt. Watch his face smelling blood. Watch it smelling wine.

The ability to tell the difference. Merlin has developed into a world-class murderer of birds who can trade harmless jabs with six month-old babies in gentleness and trust, and while his rage is an unholy fire in a lake, burning up fast and soon forgotten, his love cleaves the particles of darkness to let in playful waves of light. He can intimidate dogs (this is a Cat House) and at the same time maintain his relationships with other cats roaming around the neighborhood: a long-haired Javanese with a penchant for dandelions; a sociable Ocicat who can't climb a fence; a tortoiseshell Bombay, sadly declawed; a brown-and-white Russian tabby with a fear of raccoons. Merlin is helping her get over that.

He can, with one mew, or even a soundless nudge, correctly convey to any member of the family, at any time, that he wants to go outside, wants a treat, wants his food dish in the other room refilled, wants the tap turned on for a drink, wants the curtain pulled back on the window, wants a scratch under the chin. He plops down in front of your path and knows you'll get out of the way. He makes himself vulnerable to your faith.

This means he will lay the *real* dead mouse at your feet because you never would have been able to catch this delicious thing on your own.

Ti

GENOCIDAL FURY HAS NEVER consumed him. Neither has humor. When Donna Lyons steps in a dried-up hairball sitting in a puddle of stomach acid that's eating the finish on the pinewood floor—Merlin feels no shame. When Vera is reading in the attic and is startled by a plant that falls off the bookcase because he tried to chew its leaves— Merlin feels no guilt. When he spills Bremen's cup of coffee on his symphony-in-progress and stains the notation there is no regret. Merlin has a rallying cry that radiates from him when he is warm and full of food—love me as I am or not at all. He does have the desire to be with you.

A fly dances at the edge of a table and he goes for it, misses, falls off, everybody laughs, and he examines his paws. They cackle some more, and he sashays out of the room with his tail straight up, dignity in tact, preferring isolation, for he never had the need to bounce his mind and emotions off another animal, cat or no cat.

Bounce now, at the funeral. Merlin sits atop a bookcase, groggy-eyed, having just woken from a nap by the sound of glasses clinking together for a toast. He yawns and licks his forepaw, brushing it across his whiskers. He stretches deep and long, then walks to the edge of the bookcase, lording over the bodies that mingle in the dining room, and jumps down to the piano top, sniffing the rim of each glass of water or wine. He yawns again, then, mid-yawn, snaps his head back and chews on his thigh. He sneezes, and re-sets his thigh hair in place, before jumping to the floor, where a forest of legs and feet spread out in front of him. He mews, high and insistent. A space is cleared. He trots ahead, a crook at the very tip of his tail, and doesn't stop for the hands that reach out to pet him. The garage door opens. He scans the room and sees Vera.

She smiles and rubs two fingers together and mews softly and he jumps in her lap. She rubs her finger under his chin, a little pressure, so he has to push against it. She scratches his head, his ears, runs a thumb along his whiskers, and begins to pet him in long smooth strokes, building up potential, and at one point Merlin's back becomes a sheet of light, Vera's hand producing a shower of sparks with her stroke. He sneezes, then resettles and finds a nook where his body can rest on the meat of her thighs. He purrs. She just keeps petting.

FELIS CATUS FREQUENCY OFF the air . . . .

SIXTH MOVEMENT

𝄞   "At an afterparty for some atrocious 'modern' staging of a Molière play," Nikki Terling laughed and covered her mouth and then decided, no, I want to remember this the way I want to remember it, and resettled her thin black glasses on the bridge of her nose like a calculating socialite in a 50s French film.

"My friend had a crush on him. She wanted me to work him into our band or something. We got split up at the party and I found myself talking about the play with this random guy who said he actually *liked* it. He had this evil shit-eating grin on his face like he didn't believe a word he was saying. I wanted to break his nose. I wanted to smash his face through the wall. He was so goddamn smug. But then my friend came over and was like, oh, yeah, this was the guy I wanted you to meet. You should let him hear you sing."

What did Bremen expect? Was it a test? Blaze Lyons put the finishing touches on Nikki Terling's screwdriver, slipping a half-moon of orange on the rim, and brought it to her with a hurried smile and then tended to the next guest, asking his or her name and how it was he or she had first met Bremen, and as everybody told their spontaneous mini-epics over the Music, he thought the funeral was most definitely a test, some trial Bremen devised to measure his control and courage and strength, like throwing him in a river full of crocodiles and asking him to swim to safety.

A wave of anxiety hit Blaze, and he clutched his necklace through his shirt. It was there, of course, the memento from Kom Ombo, a flat oval piece of limestone no bigger than a newborn's palm, secured in a black leather knot and hanging down to the middle of his sternum. It was very smooth, with colored bands of orange, red, brown, tan, and white, a mini-Jupiter around his neck. He didn't used to wear it, but the morning after Bremen's death, he found the necklace knotted up and nesting in a pair of grey flannel socks in his top dresser drawer. It took him five minutes to untangle it. His fingers were so stupid, his vision unable to see its way through the blurry twists and turns and into a straight line. He won't even take it off in the shower now.

His trip to Kom Ombo was twenty-nine years ago, six months before he married Donna and seven months before Bremen was born. His travels in Egypt, and his special guide, René Ennogo, had currently set up permanent residence in his mind like a nosy neighbor who keeps inviting himself over for dinner, though he does always bring a killer dish.

"You know why?" René said, appearing behind the bar as Blaze was making a Manhattan.

"You want to show your appreciation?" said Blaze, muddling the drink.

"I want you to feel at ease," said René, writing in the dust on the garage wall.

"What does that say?"

René sang as he wrote: "My friend, you've been weighed in the balance and found wanting. Your kingdom is divided and your kingdom cannot stand. Your house is built upon the drifting, sinking sand."

"That's my favorite song."

"The cherry doesn't get muddled," pointing to the drinks Blaze was building. "It's the orange. You need to get high."

"I am high."

THEY MET IN ASWAN, late summer 1984, in the midst of a tourist boom. It was before the Italian hijacking, police riots in Cairo, and the air raid on Libya made the collective fear greater then the draw of experiencing the engineering feats of the most advanced civilization the planet has ever known. Blaze Lyons, twenty-seven, tasting the fruits of a child's dream (seeded when his father showed him a giant pop-up book of *The World's Greatest Architectural Wonders*), planned to sail the Nile and visit ancient temples along the way. He arrived into Aswan as a child comes into an arboretum, drunk with oxygen and dizzy with wonder. On that first night he bailed from his small hostel and strolled south along Corniche an-Nil. The wide languorous river flowed between black-granite boulders and super green islands. He was seeing actual things, not pictures out of a book. A giddy reck-lessness took hold of him. Blaze searched for a seedy place. He found Ba-Deshret, an underground bar (you walk down thirteen steps) with dingy orange light and exotic music blaring from the speakers. Here, to celebrate, he sought hashish. He asked an old bartender with a skinny moustache and brittle hair, and that tender pointed to a man enjoying a sheesha in a corner booth. Blaze approached. The man looked him up and down. Blaze did the same. The man smiled and said, in soft and flawless English, puffs of smoke accenting each sylla-ble, "I love brave white people."

René Ennogo was thirty-nine and Lebanese. He was sent out of the country by his father, a university professor of Islamic Art, in the late months of '57, just before the insurrection. His father was a man who read the world like a sad fairy tale—his mom died when he was two, from dysentery. René went to Aswan to live with an uncle who ran a successful tourist business, which he learned and mastered and inherited and re-created as a rugged one-man operation catering to fine-feathered Europeans, intrepid Russians, and oddly quiet Americans, whom he liked the best. He had studied Egyptian history from a local Thoth-influenced priest. He picked up sailing and shooting from an ex-guerilla never going back to Algeria. Tall, muscular, with a bald head that shone like a piece of black chrome in moonlight, René spoke perfect English, French, Spanish, Arabic, and the basic syntax of a variety of nomadic tribal languages.

"Do you take travelers' checks?"

"In fact, I do."

Seated on the floor in the back room of René's office, halfway through their second hash session, maps spread out like eagle wings, it was decided the following would take place: Blaze would tag along on the tour René had lined up for three Corsican businessmen; they would drive tomorrow morning to Kom Ombo and see the sights; René would make some excuse/apology to the men and return to Aswan; the next day they would gather supplies and set sail on René's felucca, embarking on an ambitious three-week trip, mooring at as many sites as they could along the way, docking in Al-Balyana and sleeping at the house of René's cousin, who would give them a tour of the Temple of Seti I before they caught an overnight train to Cairo, where accommodations did not yet exist. René would work on it.

Blaze received competitive rates, on both travel and hashish.

In the morning everyone was on time, except for René, who was two hours late and looking seventy-five in daylight. The Corsicans were ruffled. Blaze was jumpy. They piled into the jeep and drove off.

Blaze, sitting behind René, whispered over his shoulder, "The hashish?"

"Seat belt." He was gruff with a side of stale coffee.

Back at the funeral, many things interrupted Blaze at once. A woman was relating an origin story about his son. The Music would not relent. Two people inquired at the same time about the bathroom. He caught a glimpse of his wife gliding through the crowd and was struck with a lust so strong he wanted to mumble an excuse, hop over the bar, rustle her upstairs, throw her on the bed, and devour every last inch of her orange blossom skin. His brother, Terry, slinked up for another drink. Yes, this was most definitely a test.

Kom Ombo was built on a promontory at a bend on the banks of the Nile. They arrived mid-afternoon. It was overcast, unusual for the low summer season, informed René in French, so Blaze didn't understand why he was motioning to the sky. René led them through the eroded courtyard, past the imposing faces of Sobek and Horus, vultures painted over a door, through parallel passageways with detailed hieroglyphs and past two typical antechambers, and finally to the twin inner sanctuaries of the Gods for whom this temple was named. The buildings had been reduced by time to a rocky stone outline of two large rectangles.

"You can barely imagine what the place really looked like," René said in English.

"Un capiscu micca?" said a Corsican, his face all screwed up.

René Ennogo suggested they explore on their own. When they were gone he took out a hash pipe, loaded it, smoked it, and passed it to Blaze, "Anything you are curious about?"

Blaze took a lungful of sweet tarry smoke, held it until his ears popped, exhaled and coughed hard. There was a shimmer in his peripherals, a shimmer of silver light that stayed there for a long time.

"What did they do here?"

"Trained the fear out of you."

"What?"

"Trained the fear out of you."

"What?"

"Give that to me," reaching for the pipe with the grubby hands of a four-year old. "They created situations and put people through tests which they knew would bring out total uncontrolled fear."

René took a hit deeper and longer than Blaze was physically capable of. He did not cough. "I will demonstrate," motioning with his head for Blaze to follow him to the corner of one of the flattened temple sanctuaries. René indicated a small square hole in the ground.

"Hit this. Go in."

Blaze did, and then climbed down into the hole, about eight feet deep. It opened to his left, and he had to squeeze under a large granite slab. Then he climbed up a similar hole, and emerged on the other side of the stone outline, a bit lightheaded and tingly, blinking at René, so?

René led Blaze up a crumbling wall at the backside of the temple, and at the top he could see the symmetry of the whole structure along the axis of the main passageway, with the Nile rushing behind the columns and courtyard. It looked like some sort of optical illusion, as if the river flowed up and into the temple itself. Turns out that's no illusion.

"Back when this place was still in use there was a pool or reservoir that spanned the length of the temple. The wall that marked the end of Sobek's sanctuary and the wall that marked the beginning of Horus' sanctuary created the borders for an open channel, and this channel was filled with water—and crocodiles. They cared for and raised crocodiles here. You will see the mummies after."

"Crocodiles?"

René used a broken twig and drew a makeshift diagram in the sand and rubble. Blaze could see the Corsicans taking pictures of each other by the water, posing as strongmen.

Apparently it was quite the test. Imagine you are a neophyte who, after much preparation, is led by your teachers into Sobek's enclosed sanctuary and brought to a hole in the ground where a flight of steps descends into a dark square of water no bigger than a household door. You are told to go into the water and find a different exit. You get one breath. So you dive in and squirm around a couple protruding slabs towards the bottom, about twenty feet deep, and then squeeze past a low wall and emerge into the light of the open channel. And then you'll see the crocodiles swimming freely. Imagine the fear. Imagine the irrepressible reactions. There's not much you can do at this point other than swim upward, past those killing machines, and hope they don't rip you to pieces before you get to safety. When you find a little ledge and climb out of the water, gasping for breath, the teachers, patiently waiting, tell you that you've failed. You are then put through more preparation. When again deemed ready, that dark hole of water is waiting, and as you swim down to the bottom, squeeze under the wall and into the channel, the crocodiles you have dreamt of will be there. You'll see them in the leathery flesh, see them see you, and at the height of your most intense fear you will have to search for another way out.

"That's the way." René pointed to the hole Blaze had just passed through in Horus' sanctuary. "You had to swim across the channel, down another pitch black corridor, squeeze under another slab, and then swim up the column, and you didn't even know if that was the right way."

René offered him the pipe.

"I'm good." He nodded at the men in the distance patting each other on the back and cackling. "The Corsicans are coming."

Blaze Lyons served cocktails to an older couple, topped off his brother with whiskey, and the very next guest was Jack Galatasinich, shy as the day he was born. His parents, close friends and next-door neighbors, asked Blaze to look after their old Pug, Ruggles, for the duration of their hospital maternity stay. Blaze took Bremen over to play with the dog, and it was so affectionate, so clowning, such a greedy eater, that for weeks afterword Bremen wanted one all his own.

"Do you remember Ruggles?" shouted Blaze over the crowd.

"Not really," Jack said sheepishly. "I'll have another Mud Puppy."

The tap was pouring slow and fine. Blaze returned to Kom Ombo without anyone the wiser. He sat cross-legged on the Temple's rubble, watching the Corsicans bear down upon them, and he realized this might be his only chance to grab a relic, a talisman, some proof of experience. He blindly reached for the nearest stone and slipped it in his pocket.

"How long can you hold your breath?" asked Blaze.

René Ennogo laughed from the belly, infectious and deadly, no human immune. He pounded his chest. "Not long. I have a weak heart."

"But didn't the crocodiles eat anybody?"

"They were pampered. They were tame and too well fed to attack. Like I said, it was a test."

At the funeral, Blaze used a wooden foam scraper to swipe the suds level with the rim of the glass and then brought it to Jack Galatasinich. In the moment of offering, Blaze felt the ridges of his life dovetail together like cosmic cabinet joints. He briefly understood the importance of each individual person (each one holding a piece of his son inside them, a real piece), and he smiled at Jack, now a full-on saint incarnate, bestowing the golden fluidic radiance from brother to brother with a happiness he couldn't explain. It was his son's funeral. How could he be so happy? If Blaze tried to answer that question, well, it would be too much. People would have to get their own drinks. His bones would break from the pressure. He'd lose all meaning his life had ever given him. All plot.

YET IT WAS THERE if he wanted it. Less than an hour before the start of the show Blaze was sweeping up the garage for the tenth and last time. He emptied the dustpan in a five-gallon bucket and hauled it outside, lifting the lid of the dark green trash bin and getting a whiff of landfill rot and cat litter before the kindest and most succulent skunk perfume sidled up to his nose and kissed him with warm and spicy lips. Around the corner of the house this kid was hitting a joint, the cherry flaming up a flat brown face inside an icy shadow. Blaze just stood there, shivering a touch, with a runny nose that could've been a salivating tongue. Somebody had to say something.

"Uh—do you want to hit this?" said the kid.

Blaze sniffed and wiped his face with the back of his hand. "Mind?"

"For sure," handing it over.

"Sativa or Indica?"

"Sativa. Sour Diesel."

"Never got into the names very much," Blaze said, pausing for the hit, talking as he held it in. "It was just the strain that I cared about. Indica always made me a zombie. I crashed hard, just wanted to sleep. I could never concentrate when doing my work."

"Generally, that's true," said the kid, "but it really does depend on the individual strain. Some Sativa's give you couch-lock for days. Some Indica's are like five shots of espresso. You could build a house."

Blaze gave the joint back. "Blaze Lyons. I'm Bremen's father."

"Louie. I brought the fruit and cheese trays?"

They listened to the night and the monastic quiet that overtakes a yard covered in new and falling snow. It's like the open desert—every sound swallowed up as it's made.

"How old are you, Louie?"

"Twenty-two."

"I'll fix you a drink when we're done."

"You got some tequila?"

"Fortaleza."

"Reposado or Añejo?"

"I don't know. Bremen picked the booze. There was a whole list." It was Blaze's turn on the joint again and he felt so much more like himself. What a difference a proper session makes.

"How'd you meet him?"

Louie shrugged. "Wanted to learn guitar. He was volunteering to teach some beginner classes. We just met up."

"I haven't smoked for a month. This is really good stuff."

"Home-grown. My boy in Aurora."

The wind threatened to blow out the cherry so Blaze cupped the joint and gestured with a certain respect to Louie, who pinched it between his thumb and finger and shielded it with both hands like that was the last fire two men could rely on as they huddled in a cave at the top of a mountain, searching for a pass, the countryside so barren and blunted and alien they had lost all sense of direction.

Louie broke into a little bob-and-weave dance to keep his temp up. He asked, from the side of his eyes, "You ever smoke with Bremen?"

One night, after unloading the tools in his shed. He had already taken the first green hit and was zoning-out on the teeth of his band-saw, their oily reflection, Blaze's version of relaxation, where the room was filled with a haze so silky and tenuous that every impression seemed deep as a dream. There was a knock on the door, a knock that didn't ask, it opened, and Bremen stepped inside.

"What's up, Dad?"

Blaze tried to play it cool but when one hand has a blue Bic lighter and the other a smoldering bowl of some stinky weed, dry mouth kicks in hard.

"Can I talk to you about something?"

"Uh—yeah?"

"Relax, Dad."

"I am." Blaze almost took a hit, on instinct, because that's what he did to relax.

"Care if I smoke that with you?" Bremen said.

It was as if all the measurements he had taken at one of his work sites—for a cellar door, floor moldings, wine rack—were off by centi-meters and none of the pieces fit together properly, and Blaze, as the one responsible for the appraisal, was unable to comprehend how the mistake could've happened. This is where he looked like an idiot.

"Does your mother know?"

"About me moving out?"

The hits just keep on coming. He finally took one and didn't care that his son saw him. They were both adults.

"You're moving?" he coughed out.

"She knows. But that's not really what I wanted to talk to you about." Bremen extended his hand, reaching for the chillum.

"When? Where? What for?"

"It's time."

"Time?" Blaze squinted.

"Do you know why I've been living here for so long? Why I didn't move out earlier?"

Bremen tilted his head, mystified, and Blaze had seen that expression before, somewhere, on something not human, on Merlin, when the freaky cat was staring at Blaze on the toilet.

"In no particular order," Bremen counted them off on his fingers, "One, I saved a ton of money. You have no idea how many thousands I've saved by not paying rent. Two, I can have a lot of privacy. You and Mom are never home Monday thru Saturday, usually. Three, since we have the house to ourselves most of the time I can work with Vera without a bunch of distractions. Four, I love the location. It's great for—"

"Wait, wait." Blaze wasn't totally defenseless. In his Father Voice: "How long have you been smoking?"

"I don't. I mean, I have here and there, just to blend into the scene, make things easier. Some people don't like to hang out with people who don't smoke. But normally, no, not a smoker. Not my thing. How long have you?"

Blaze was completely unprepared and couldn't fall back on a believable lie.

"What about Vera? You tell her you're moving?"

"She's the first one I told. She'd be pissed if she was the last." A strategic pause. "That's really what I wanted to talk to you about, Dad. Since I'm not going to be here anymore—well, not as much, I'll still come over, the place I'm moving into is in the north part of the isthmus, like a twenty minute drive. But here's the thing: Vera's going to need someone to help out for a little bit."

A loud meow came from outside, like a probe, seeing what's around. They both perked their ears and heard another soft mew, closer, aimed directly at them.

Blaze had some disjointed thoughts—shaking his head—that slid flush into an idea. "Like what a tutor or something?"

Bremen cracked the door and chittered at Merlin and the cat raced in and pounced up on the workbench, sniffing a lathe.

"Like you, Dad."

"Like me?"

"Yes, like you." Bremen laid out some sketchy plans about Vera's current research projects and her upcoming field trips. A detailed lesson plan for the next six months was alluded to. At least the Mystery Machine was fully explained. In Bremen's blueprint, Blaze was nothing but a radiator to be shifted around the room, its only job keeping the space warm. He saw a circle of hands heating themselves by the fire of his face. It crossed his mind that his daughter was, in some ways, smarter than him. How could he teach her anything?

"What does your Dad do, Louie?" wondered Blaze aloud.

"He's retired. He was an Economics Professor at the University."

"And your Mom?"

"A lawyer. But she quit her firm a while back and started up her own business. Consulting for non-profit groups."

Blaze sensed Louie and him could be great friends, survivors of traumatic experiences. He patted Louie hard on the shoulder, like old warriors do before they storm out to the final battle for all that is noble and holy against armies far bigger and badder, against calvaries of steel commanded by a false light and charging with wave after wave of soldiers propelled by a righteous hate that devours whole races for breakfast.

"Let's have some tequila."

Mrs. Joan Olive Lyons, a lifelong librarian at Milwaukee Central, a woman by no means consumed with the search for Divine Fire, named her son Blaze because she had, on a visit to the family physician, at the beginning of her second trimester, happened to read a contentious article published in a journal of inclusive theology. It was just laying there on the table in the waiting room, an aberration among *Better Homes & Gardens*, *Life*, and *Time*. She lit a cigarette and looked out the window and finally gave in because something had to take her mind off the baby kicking inside, the tightness in her chest when she walked up the stairs, her increasingly short fuse with her husband. She flipped through the pages, genuinely curious, and there it was, *The Destiny of All Nations*, written by a young rabbi who, said the bio in the back, was a farmer running an informal kibbutz for troubled youth in Miami, FL. The general idea, one that Joan absorbed whole-heartedly, in some spasm of grace or insanity, is that God compromises a physical and measurable part of everything in existence, is in fact the most central element of everything in existence, and so there is a seeking from human beings, a desire to unite with this central element. The seeking will always come to fruition, asserted the rabbi, for it has, no matter how long or difficult the path, a one hundred percent success rate. Each single flame is destined to merge with the Blaze of God. The Blaze. The ash tumbled off her cigarette and settled on the black sweater covering her belly. She felt a queasy of sense of panic. The waiting room dissolved into an all-encompassing blur, and then re-focused itself as a clear vision—her son, as yet unborn, on his deathbed. Joan never had a vision before. She would never have one again. The sharpness of the image, the innate sense that she was not imagining this, that she was simply at the mercy of a superior sight descending down—she was being shown. Her son had lived a long life. He was surrounded by his wife, his son and daughter, and their sons and daughters and wives and husbands. The bed was simple. The room was simple. The death was simple. It was shocking how easy the transition had been, on his face and the reposed faces surrounding him, and that was the vision. They lifted her son off the bed, linen sheets slipping away, and then let go. He floated for a moment or two, before flaking apart into millions of dry white pieces, now catching a draft and swirling away into beams of smoky light, hot on arrival from an open window. Joan brushed her sweater clean of ash and took long, long drag. Her boy was meant for great things. He would inspire courage and love in many men and women. He would raise a family of families. He would find the Blaze, be the Blaze. You could say she had high hopes.

—·—

AFTER A SHOT OF Fortaleza Reposado, smoother and spicier than the thighs of a Mexican drug lord's fourth wife, he told Louie about the first time he got stoned, in the spring of '75 when he was only seventeen, in the depths of a city park with four high school friends, Ernie, Derrick, Craig, and Tom, Tom Orlando, who would be dead in less than a year from a head-on collision between his '71 Oldsmobile Cutlass and a small yellow school bus, and who said, after the two blunts were blown and they were leaning against skinny evergreen trees, "Dude, I am in Montego Bay right now." Their laughs brought them to their knees. It became their anthem, something they'd get tattoos about, *Montego Bay Forever*. A code in the hallways and on the phone, "Flights for Montego Bay leaving at 4:20." A shared impossible dream, "We need to get a beach house on Montego Bay when we graduate." And when Tom died, a paradise beyond all human reckoning, "He's burning down where he should be, on the shores of Montego Bay." In the flesh and blood, nobody had ever set foot on that sand, and in fact, Blaze was the last of his teenage friends still living. It struck him that Montego Bay would be the best launching pad if (no, *when*) he decided to travel with Vera.

"You know 'Montego Bay'?" Blaze ventured.

"The Bobby Bloom version or Freddie Notes and the Rudies?"

"Freddie Notes, for sure."

There was no song playing, but Blaze heard the lyrics in his head, and Louie began to indiscernibly dance with the laid-back beat, knocking his knuckles on the bar in rhythm to the inaudible music.

"I like the bar. Where'd you get it?" Louie asked.

"I built it."

The needle slipped—Louie looked at Blaze in that slow stoned way. The bar was ten, fifteen feet long, running the length of the garage, with glossy dark wood, elaborate moldings, stainless steel foot rails, and stocked with a healthy array of beer, wine, and spirits. "Awesome."

"It's amazing what a good sanding job and a quality stain can do for perceived value," Blaze said.

"What do you do?

"Independent contractor. I do general home-improvement work, some specialty jobs." Blaze took a deep breath and wanted to ask this kid if he had anymore smoke. "I'm winding down though. Retiring soon."

Louie puffed out his cheeks and rolled his eyes, "How long have you been doing that?"

"Twenty-five years or so." The blame rested squarely on his father for giving him *Shelters, Shacks, and Shanties* for his tenth birthday, the book becoming his bible, and when he wasn't outside foraging for materials to construct a Chippewa shack or Navajo teepee, he was in school day-dreaming of log rolling and stone fireplaces.

"Must feel good to be your own boss."

"Taxes are a bitch. You'll need a genius accountant."

The garage door attached to the house swung open. Donna appeared. Louie jumped off his seat. Blaze, who had been slouching, straightened up.

"Hello, Louie."

He nodded at her comfortably as if they had had many previous conversations about a number of fascinating things.

She glanced at Blaze. "It's filling up."

Louie bowed. "Thanks for the drink, Mr. Lyons. I'll see you guys later." He tipped an imaginary hat at Blaze and winked at Donna and scooted into the house.

Donna and Blaze, at least it seemed like an honest accident, looked at each other. Their mutual gaze was held for an eternity, relatively speaking. Pupils dilated, pulses quickened, temperatures rose, and what saved them was a shout from the hallway. Donna turned in that direction, just her head, and Blaze, not about to take his eyes off anything, felt a tremendous desire to finger the stitches of her green dress and lick the sheen of sweat off her chest and arms, glistening like expensive glass.

"I'll be right there!" she shouted into the house.

She looked back at him, vulnerable, shoulders dipping in, and his eyes betrayed the memory of their early guilt-free days of fall when she rebelled against the pretense of underwear and pulled up her autumn dress and he could just slide right in, and even after they were done, her legs still wrapped around him, trembling, breathless, she asked, only half-joking, full of sparkle and pep, "Again?"

"I have to go start the Music," Donna said. "Please don't miss the first song."

For a moment, the garage was all his.

"Life just keeps on giving," René Ennogo said, holding a ceramic pipe loaded with hashish in his left hand, and a gynormous bowl of homemade goat curry in his right.

"Am I supposed to take that from you?"

"It'd be the respectful thing to do."

Blaze ignored him, shifting the bottles of beer and testing the spouts on the kegs. René wasn't going away that easy.

"When?"

"Later."

"When's later?"

"After."

"Have you practiced?"

"Bremen didn't invite you."

"Imagine I'm Donna. Tell me how you're going to sell the house, divorce me, and use the money to take Vera on a trip around the world like you're the father of the century or something."

"Did you even have any children?"

"Hey, tough guy, if I don't press you, who will?"

René was just a figment of his mind, René Ennogo was dead, only the stone around his neck was real, but this is what it had come down to: the suave ingenuity of his mind playing elaborate tricks, coaxing him out of stasis, because he was never as good at life as he was at smoothing the surface voids in a foundational wall or a boring a hole by hand. His son was dead. He wife had changed into two completely different women over the course of one month. His daughter wasn't talking to anybody anymore. Blaze developed an instant headache from the thought of jabbering with strangers the whole night.

"Try this," René said, blowing a thick cloud of smoke at Blaze so he had to cough and wave it away. "Ask them how they met Bremen. Ask them for a story. That way, you'll just have to listen."

"First day in the teacher's lounge he shut off talk radio and put on a mix tape of Shostakovich and Nine Inch Nails and old gospel blues, and I remember all the teachers couldn't believe the balls on this kid," said Johan Diletski, once a professional footballer for five seasons in the Bundesliga, holding-mid for Wolfsburg, before breaking his left leg in a horrendous two-footed challenge from a vindictive Polish forward he'd been harassing up and down the pitch.

"He didn't care what anybody thought. I loved it!"

Old Johan, tenured professor of Biochemistry, slammed his hand on the bar and bugged his eyes out more than usual, like he just scored a wonder goal with a half-volley from thirty yards, and Blaze actually took a step back.

"It was great to see things shaken up. But not then, I mean, not at the time. I was under pressure from my department head to raise the average grade of my students. And I was used to talk radio. And I hated Shostakovich. Still do."

The funeral mix was an agoraphobic's personal collection, a string of songs selected by drunks at a jukebox, someone pressing the shuffle button on a four thousand song iTunes catalog, eclectic to the extreme almost on purpose (no, on purpose), swinging from ragas to film scores, Dylan to the Gift of Gab, original dubstep, indie folk, experimental 'scapes, a sample for everyone in this six-hour thirty-seven minute mix, about the only thing missing was death metal. Blaze wondered how Bremen even found the time to put this playlist together—hand-picking the order of every song and loading it on an external hard drive, locking it in a safety deposit box at Sun Hills Bank and giving Donna the key in the Will. Some danced, and danced hard. The last time Blaze danced was at the High Noon Saloon in July, at Bremen's final gig with a ten-piece band called Salsa Verde. The three lead singers were from Colombia, but they were graduating, going back to Bogota, and they'd played the Saloon a few dozen times over years, gathering a good deal of loyal fans, so the farewell turnout was muy épico.

Blaze cruised to the venue in his truck, windows down, smoking a terrifically rolled joint, if he could say so himself.

The Saloon was a dolled-up warehouse with sparkling chandeliers, glossy floors, a huge stage, huge bathrooms, and fifty-plus beers on tap. Mo was there, and Blaze was relieved to see someone he knew, someone that could anchor him in the madness of absolutely rocking salsa, girls in heels and skirts, men in boots and denim, damn, Blaze couldn't help it himself, shuffling like a geriatric Cubano to the beat. He gave up searching for the stairs to the balcony or drinking beer out of a glass. His ears rang like it was 1975. After midnight, between the second and third sets when High Noon let it all hang out, a small black table was free and Blaze sat down in a huff, blown-out. The table hosted empty bottles of Spotted Cow and plastic glasses of water with pretzels and nuts floating on top. Bremen dragged over a chair.

"Need anything?" Blaze asked.

"I'm good. Last set is always the longest," Bremen said.

"How do you do it?"

"Not drink during the show?"

"Play music in places like this."

"I got the stamina part of it from Mom, and the artist part of it from you."

"Artist?"

"Yep."

Blaze bit the inside of his cheek and knew he should've rolled another joint and had it in the breast pocket of his shirt.

Bremen leaned in. "So there's this famous poet. Long dead. He used to talk about architecture being similar to music. He called it frozen music. I've always thought about those arrangements and harmonies in an office door or an opera house or a restaurant kitchen that are similar to arrangements and harmonies in Etudes and Nocturnes and jazz standards. Musicians and architects are really working with the same materials."

"I'm not an architect."

"You're not building a cathedral, but shit, I can't make a window sash look as fantastic as you can."

"Who's this poet guy?"

"Some German dude. He also ended up proposing to an eighteen-year old girl. Keep that in mind."

"What's wrong with that?" Blaze laughed at his wish to be eighteen again.

"He was seventy-three at the time," Bremen said. "He got all pissy when she declined his offer, and then wrote some awful gushy poems about it." Bremen stood up and stretched. "Poets. You take the good with the bad."

Blaze aimed his thumb and forefinger at Bremen and pulled the trigger. "Kids, too."

"Musicians, especially." He slapped Blaze on the back. "Gotta go. Stay for the rest of the show?"

There was no other option. For some reason, young girls were asking him to dance, and in a diverse array of hard drives there exist pictures of that Wednesday night at the Saloon in July (14? 19? 24?), and those scrolling through the images might wonder who, exactly, was that fifty-five-year-old man with a full head of silver and brown hair, a strong jaw, hooded eyes, and a surprisingly fluid frame dancing with all the pretty girls? He counted two million flashbulbs in his eyes so maybe the girls weren't that pretty? He grinned and pointed to the stage, to the guy tearing it up on the double bass and said, "That's my son."

Salsa Verde played encores 'til bar close. In the general milling around after an incredible show, Blaze Lyons told strangers he just met all his fears and desires—like how he could never make a durable rocking chair and that he wanted to live out his golden years in New Zealand. Mo invited him to go somewhere with the Colombians, who wobbled against the bar, tossing back shots. Onstage, Bremen packed up his double bass in the case Blaze had built him. Mo was convincing, but he declined, slipping out the exit without saying goodbye to his son.

Donna's car was in the driveway and the house was pitch dark. Blaze retired to his tool shed and smoked in silence, thinking, wondering if he really was an artist, a frozen musician. His ears were wah-wahing like the band was still jamming in his head. The smoke removed a pound of body weight with every exhalation. Merlin cried from inside the house. Vera was scheduled for a field trip tomorrow to a CFO's lake cabin to watch Blaze wire the lighting for an ivy-lined veranda in the backyard. He hadn't spoken to his wife all day or all night, but all he could think about was building a teepee. Blaze knew people who worked jobs they hated for their entire lives, who hated their families, hated their parents, and hated the places where they grew up. He's met people who've never had a good word to say about anything—a meal, a movie, a sunset—and that sadomaschistically relished the routine of every repetitive day, the crippling boredom of the same thing over and over and over, resigned to digging their rut deeper in the valley of the shadow of death. Blaze told himself he wasn't like that, but even so, here he was, stoned at three in the morning and looking up at the trees because he didn't want to sleep next to his wife tonight or wake up to the day with his daughter.

Jesus, Blaze, you could paint with those tears. Paint he did, back inside the shed where the latch clinked hard on the lock and the light winked out, but Merlin could tell he was home by the clink, by the silence that remained well after the sound. There was no hiding. Christ. Help me in this, my darkest hour.

MR. ROGER HARRIS LYONS, a volunteer, was assigned to the 3rd Defense Battalion in the Pacific Theatre. He shuffled from odd job to odd job on the USS *Saratoga* before an intuitive Lieutenant Captain, seeing the single-mindedness with which Roger scrubbed the walls of the brig (how he let the cigarette in his lips smolder to the nub without ashing—the smoke didn't bother his eyes), re-assigned him to the 432nd Anti-Aircraft division, and soon, not soon enough for Roger, who thought it was about goddamn time, he was loading 24-pound shells into an anti-aircraft gun at the beaches of Guadalcanal, Tulagi, and Bougainville, part of an eight-men crew who grew tight like the jungle vines suffocating palm trees, calling themselves the Kamikaze Killers, notching thirty-two confirmed aerial takedowns from 1942–44 and surviving multiple suicide runs. Except the last, however, while they manned a .38 caliber dual-purpose gun mounted on the desk of the USS *White Plains*. It took out his crew captain, trainer, sight setter, and a pound of flesh off Roger's back. He woke up on his stomach in the med-ward, head bouncing around the ceiling like a balloon off its string, somehow in so much less pain then those screaming and writhing in the beds surrounding him. Roger wished he could take on some of theirs. Not the sight of cratered bodies or rank charred flesh but this was the source of his worst memories of the war: being powerless to help those in real pain. Twenty-two, purple-hearted, marching back to Milwaukee ripped and tanned, sucking down a pack of Pall Malls a day, struggling to keep his cursing under control, mostly deaf in his right ear, lacking the patience to argue with the ignorant or weak of spirit, and so just plain mean to everybody except troublemaking boys and smart sassy girls in floral-print linen dresses.

"Hi. I'm Roger."

"Joan."

"That dress fits you like a second skin."

"Aren't you just the charmer?"

"Cigarette?"

"Light it for me first."

They met at a college football game, Iowa vs. Wisconsin, for the Heartland Trophy. She got it, they married, and Roger, who wanted to be active, independent, and useful, who would rather have died in the waters off Samar then be under the tread of any ordinary civilian's boot, was extended a line of generous credit by a local bank (the owners had invested heavily in Curtiss, Grumman, and Bell) and leased a warehouse near the lakefront and two big trucks. He started his own moving and storage company, The Lyons Den. He grew burly and imposing like a farmhouse cabinet carved from a fallen oak tree. At the end of his third fiscal year Roger had twenty-eight employees and another four trucks and two warehouses in Madison and Waukesha.

He possessed a mysterious organizational talent and could find the perfect fit. Moving crews would call him up, convinced they needed another vehicle, so Roger would drive to the site in his sputtering four-cylinder flatbed truck, study the contents to be moved, and then direct the rearrangement, the last piece slotting into the moving truck with a precision that appeared inhuman.

"Goddamn, Roger. How did you do that?"

"Consistent hard work over a long period of time." That usually shut people up. And then, "Stop wasting mine. Let's get on the road."

He was actually a little ashamed at how simple it was, reluctant to claim too much credit for something that wasn't so hard, after all. Towards the end (he never retired), no longer able to move a Bosch let alone a Bosendorf, Roger limited his involvement to appraisals, visually measuring the materials in a room and knowing to within a few inches how much square feet of storage space was needed. He died fast, from pleural mesothelioma, hiding for decades in his lungs after the exposure in his navy training days when he removed asbestos lagging from the pipes aboard his trooper ship. He wanted to die in Samar, but that didn't seem feasible, so he opted for home, and transformed into one of those soldiers swaying on the beds in the belly of the USS *Enterprise*, delirious and in pain. Roger believed he had passed on to his sons, his two very different sons, the same life lesson, not by brute instruction, but by practical embodiment: seamlessness is real and you can find it. Here is a pile of stuff. Here is a truck. It's moving time. Draw up a plan of action. Play with the materials given to you and have confidence in discovering the right alignment of the pieces. It wasn't a question of intelligence, but desire. It wasn't just the secret of moving, but the end of sadness, poverty, starvation, and war.

Instead, the boys took from their father a deep and meaningful love for the essence of travel. Every summer Roger and Joan took the longest scenic route they could find through the Northwoods to Bayfield and boarded the ferry to the Apostles Islands. They rented a cabin and tramped through the woods, following deer trails off the beaten path, climbing pine trees and swaying with the wind at the tip-top, swimming in the cold mirror of a forest lake, going out for a Fish Fry and smoking and drinking too much. Alone in those woods, no sound but the night predators, Roger built a proper bonfire. It singed the eyes and skin and burned forever. Joan always went to bed early. The boys would stay up with their father, shepherding the fire, and though Roger had no tattoos or photographs of the Kamikaze Killers, nothing he could show by rolling up his sleeve or cracking apart his billfold, he had the proof of stories, which validated a lifetime.

"I had these mosquitoes the size of my fist buzzing around my head..." is how he would begin. Or, "I'd been scrubbing the deck for a week straight, bored as shit, when all of a sudden I saw this ribbon in the water off the port bow, and then, BOOM!!! Knocked me clean off my ass and I almost fell overboard..." Or, "My arms were jelly. I was covered in hot oil. I was moving so fast, loading those shells into the battery as fast as I could. Boys were counting on us..."

To his boys, he spared nothing. Carnage and triumph, kinship and hate. He remembered bloated animals and red-tide beaches and was honest in how they defied his understanding, even now, telling his sons not to worry about it anyway because all the stuff that happens out there (making a dismissive gesture to the stars), isn't as important as all the stuff that happens in here (pounding his fist on his chest).

"The last time though," Roger said, the boys fighting sleep, the fire fighting dark, Axis fighting Allies, "the last time I actually saw the pilot. That was the first and only time. We always blew 'em out of the sky before then. Or else we shot 'em up so bad they couldn't make a straight run. But this one I saw. Them 38s have a different sequence then the 90mm. We weren't as familiar. We couldn't re-load fast enough. So we ran dry, and out across the water comes this plane racing down at maybe sixty degrees to the horizontal, wings burning, propeller sputtering, and I knew we wouldn't get him in time. The crosswinds were pretty strong but the plane held steady. Goddamn hell of a pilot. All of us knew. We watched him fly right in, all ten seconds of it stretched to an hour, and he was terrified. I thought he'd be calm and determined but the sucker was pure fright, probably screaming at the top of his lungs. I saw how scared he was, and knew I'd been that scared before, too, had seen other boys that scared. It's a normal thing I suppose. Being afraid to die. Right before I snapped out of it, before I jumped away and I don't know how the hell I survived, but right before, I remember feeling sorry for him, sorry he had to be in that plane, sorry it got shot up and he had to run it into the side of our ship, sorry he had to die, sorry for the soldiers he was going to kill, sorry for myself. It was the strangest thing, but I thought, as I saw his face, the plane barreling in, I thought, *Fuckin A, Roger. What have you done?*"

"I WAS PROMISED A Mint Julep. With spearmint if you got it."

Foster Clark Baldez was from Taylorsville, Kentucky. He wore a three-piece powder blue seersucker suit with a wing-puffed pocket square, orange and creamy like a dreamsicle. There was a lull in the funeral. Everybody was taking a collective breath. A tuxedoed jazz band played a slow version of "St. James Infirmary Blues." Blaze took his time gathering the ingredients, surprised, but then again not at all, of course Donna carried out Bremen's instructions to a perfect cursive *t* and stocked both spear and peppermint. Foster Baldez leaned against the bar like he owned it, one elbow propped up and supporting his weight, standing at an angle with his heels comfortably crossed. He spoke, in an assortment of stabbing hand gestures, of long-distance horse racing, hot weather, and his sick wife who couldn't be here, never once breaking a sweat, unlike the Collins glass Blaze now set before him, with a red straw and sprig of mint.

Foster took a testing sip. He shined. "Very tasty. Proper and cold."

Blaze hadn't paid any attention to Foster's monologue and asked again, "So how'd you meet Bremen?"

"My wife knew him."

"Nice," a polite pause. "Is she here?"

Foster set his drink on the bar with slow deliberate grace and coughed into his hand, viscerally aware of the present occasion, and so overlooked this bit of disrespect. He had just mentioned Josephine Dalia Baldez and her terminal illness. He was nervous, too.

"She couldn't be here tonight. She's very sick. She asked me to come in her place and pay her respects to your son, Bremen." Foster took another sip of his Julep and smiled from the far corners of his mouth, not at Blaze, but at the drink he made.

"How'd your wife know him?"

Foster took a long sustained breath, but before he could exhale an explanation, Vera appeared at his side, stealing the air like a thief pickpockets another thief.

"Mom says you have all the OJ."

Blaze retrieved a half-gallon of OJ from the mini-fridge under the bar. When he returned, Foster and Vera were deep in conversation. Blaze had no context and couldn't glean any. Foster rambled to no seeming end and Vera followed along and even nodded once or twice, mesmerized by his impeccable suit, and blindly took the OJ from her father and unscrewed the cap and drank from the container.

Blaze Orin Lyons had his physical senses and his interpretive brain, but they weren't ready for this test. On what was becoming instinct, he gripped the stone necklace through his shirt. He remembered the circumstances around Vera's conception, but understood virtually none of it. What remained was a strong emotion he couldn't name and didn't know what to do with. It seriously threatened his ability to mix quality Mint Juleps.

Twelve years ago, in February, Blaze came home from work. He lingered at the front door for twenty minutes, deciding whether or not to go inside and eat the dinner he could smell cooking, or sneak into his shed and smoke himself to amnesia. It was, by far, the toughest decision of the day. Donna had everything waiting. A beet and arugula salad with avocado and walnuts, whipped sweet potatoes with brown sugar and caramel, grilled asparagus, roasted corn on the cob pinned with yellow holders, a sirloin juicy and charred in the criss-cross way he loved. The food steamed with fresh heat, his plate waiting to be filled. Rather then feast, Blaze grabbed Donna with both hands and pulled her against him, kissing her hard. If it wasn't for her skillful maneuvering up to the bedroom—who knows what would've happened to that table of food. The sex was fast and rough and Donna came back from the bathroom and said something sarcastic like, "Where'd you learn to do that?" But her face went slack when she saw Blaze sitting on the edge of the bed, still undressed, staring down at the carpet.

"What's wrong?" she whispered.

"Nothing."

Blaze never told her about the favor he did for a friend that day, a friend he once toiled with back in his office days as a project coordinator for Dane County Public Works. He had stepped in to oversee a thirty-three-man crew razing out-of-code apartments complexes for the Wisconsin Department of Health and Human Services. It was mid-afternoon, clear and hot, and a scoop loader was climbing a mound of rubble and rebar in the center of the work site. But it was too steep. The loader tipped over and careened down the slope, right into the path of a young man hauling loose debris with his wheelbarrow. The cabman was fine, but the loader had slammed into the young man and pinned him to the ground. He bled to death, quick, in front of the whole crew, whispering, *Ari, Ari* again and again until his voice tapered off into wet spastic chokes and finally nothing. He was twenty years old, his name was Ruben, and his friends on the crew explained that Ari was short for Arianna, his fiancée. They were catatonic with grief, crossing themselves repeatedly. After the police, ambulances, fire trucks, and insurance calls, Blaze felt a colossal drag on his body, like he was a piece of shit swirling faster and faster down a toilet bowl that never ends.

Donna touched his face. "Are you hungry?"

He kissed her on the neck. "Starving."

They ate cold food.

Blaze Lyons returned to duty. For a brief second, his daughter took her attention off Foster Baldez and eyed him, covertly, like she knew what he was thinking and could tell that he was scared. Blaze wanted to spark a cigar-sized joint and have no one judge him. His son was dead. His family was in ruins. Give the guy a break. Somebody else want to play bartender?

"I do," René Ennogo held up his hand like a troublemaking eight-year old.

Blaze Lyons hadn't crossed the borders of Wisconsin since 1984. *There was no need*, is what he told himself every year he did not fly, drive, or thumb his way out of all that was familiar and safe. Blaze could stare at a leaf on a tree for way longer than five minutes and think about the shape, the veins, the color, and the taste. He never minded the bugs. Let them suck his awesome blood and become awesome.

June '77: Minnesota, South Dakota, Wyoming.

July '78: California, Arizona, New Mexico, Texas.

August '79: Montana, Idaho, Oregon, Washington, Canada.

July '80: Vermont, New Hampshire, Maine.

July '81: Mexico.

June '83: New York, New Jersey, Rome.

August '84: Egypt.

In the cinema-screen of his mind his travels played out as a montage without any real thematic destination, just a fluid chain of associated images, set to the searing notes of Jimmy McGriff's "I've Got a Woman," the Hammond B-3 superimposing the pictures on top of one another—so the biggest breakfast of his life in the tiny mountain town of Stanley, Idaho, blended with the McDonald's hamburger in the Parthenon Square. The cryptic stuccos of Rome stretched like putty into the tall steel of the Lower East Side where he ate ten-alarm curry in a basement on Lexington Avenue with an Irish girl he met at Battery Park. He took her picture, and the picture of four Jewish boys with pink and purple flowers outside Munich's Park, their yarmulkes dusted with a layer of falling snow, white as the white-tip killer waves off the coast of Maine during a Nor-Easter, a storm which, for all its bravado, couldn't match the wacko in a cave who called himself a shaman and harbored Blaze on the night he was trapped by a deluge in the Etla arm of Oaxaca Valley. The montage ended and into the scene of memory he went.

He had been hiking all day, grew disoriented, and lost the trail in the narrow vertiginous canyon north of Apoala. The sky turned inky black and opened like a waterspout, with lightning brighter than city lights. He scrambled along the scree and just about tripped over the wacko, who was crouched on top of a boulder, barefoot in the piercing rain, with nothing but cowboy jeans and a wooden staff—it could've been a pleasant day at the beach. The man led Blaze into his cave in the nearby hillside and told him, in proficient English, that he would reveal the path back to Apoala in the morning. The fire inside was low and sulfurous. Blaze knew the man was out of his mind—debating the merits of destruction with the storm as if it was in the room with them and also seeking shelter. Blaze didn't dream of going to bed. He stayed up smoking the rest of his stash, ditch-weed procured by a couple of kids whose parents ran the hostel he crashed at in Oaxaca City. The wacko didn't care, even taunted Blaze, telling him to quit smoking, not because of any health incentive or moral code, but simply to exercise the muscles of his mind, to be able to control and limit his appetites, to take an ingrained habit and remove it from his being for the sheer sake of proving mastery over the desires of his body and mind, a practice which would eventually purify his vehicle and allowed a much greater force to pass through unscathed, and rule. The wacko said, *We leave out this force in our estimate of what we are, and so look upon ourselves as crawling pygmies when we might think of ourselves as archangels.* Between the smoke and the storm and the fire he had entered a separate reality and was never happier to see the sun in his life.

These were actual memories of actual things, latent sources of unfathomable power ready and waiting to be accessed.

"Good practice," René said. "Keep it up."

"Some hashish would help."

"You have to practice sober. It's like finger exercises on the piano. If you don't play the scales in private, the music won't sound good in public."

"It's—hard."

"If controlling your consciousness was easy, everybody would be doing it." But people kept talking, over and over the Music pushing to the next measure, as it forever had to do, cycling on to Bremen's next song. Blaze didn't know what to do with all these lyrics. "Don't run," René said. "Mix the drinks."

Someone was rattling cubes in a glass for thousands of centuries. It wasn't Bremen who was dead. It was all the sons and daughters of Earth. The guests addressed each other with honest respect, with a rare attentive tolerance. Not a single person in his scan of the garage was unengaged, and Blaze watched them descend into their own prismatic universe of memory and return to the funeral with the frosted light of some image ("Bremen did this…"), some colorful phrase of the story ("And then he said this…"), a visually tangible souvenir that would symbolize Bremen's presence in their lives and make the whole trip worth it. By pains, because he was the bartender, that was his service, he would interrupt a guest with an empty glass and ask if they needed a re-fresh, something different, and if it was a new guest, to ask his question, "How did you first meet Bremen?" and watch the story unfold in their eyes before it was spoken, trying to keep it steadfast in his head that the trip is the point of the journey, the trip is the point of the journey, the trip

---

RENÉ ENNOGO WOKE BLAZE up with a cloud of peppery Lebanese hashish to the dome, three hours before dawn, as promised. It was a little annoying.

They smoked outside on the balcony and drank strong coffee in the kitchen and prepared their packs in silence: water, flashlights, clean shirts, and candles for the tunnels. René kept looking at his watch, brushing the sand off its face.

"You have everything?" he whispered.

Blaze Lyons wiped his hands on his sandy khakis, checked his sandy billfold, and sure enough—four hundred American dollars in tens and twenties, sticky with sand. It was the equivalent of working eight straight days, ten-hours a day, on top of a roof.

"I'm cool as hell."

René had set-up accommodations with one of his father's old friends, a professor of social psychology at Cairo University, who owned a relatively clean (sand was everywhere here, sand the great equalizer) apartment less than a kilometer from Midan Tahrir and butting up to Café Chire—a volatile place where all the patrons argued with murder in their eyes. René said everybody was more or less, stressing the less, friends, fighting a battle with the desert while living in a city buried by the corrupted weight of its people and history and yet lifted by the generousness and hope of the same. The professor shaved every morning and supported two neat and cosseted sons and a loyal, suspicious wife. René and Blaze managed to leave without waking the house. Outside, the air was heavy as a two-and-a-half ton block of limestone. It was going to be fatally hot. A taxi arrived. They were often one of the coolest and most immaculate environments in Cairo. Blaze loved being in them. There was little traffic, but even at this hour you could feel the pulse of the city, feel it throb through the streets, a living force that goes unnamed but never unnoticed so not even millenniums could erode the outline of the buildings or the tiles on the mosques. Cairo was Cairo because it was Cairo.

They were on Tahrir Bridge, crossing over the Nile, when Blaze thought about the last three weeks and his complicated time on the river: being a tourist (gawking at the grandeur of Thebes) and not a tourist (sailing north of Luxor); an American (skin burnt lobster red) and not an American (sharing a family dinner in a village north of Al-Kab); full of doubt (it's tough to shit overboard everyday) and full of certainty (his life was a river).

The taxi kicked up dust tornados as they passed the City Zoo and Blaze thought he heard a goat bay in terror, as if thrown into a python's cage. They slowed down, taking a hard right onto Pyramids Road, and there was a black-and-white cat in the shadow of a shuttered street vendor, cleaning itself from the dust of eternal recurrence, and it looked up, tongue sticking out, and watched them motor past with that unique feline astonishment on par with a human who's seen a real live ghost.

"We have two hours before the next guard change and three hours before they open up the gate and start selling the first tickets of the day," René explained. "Plenty of time. Just remember what I told you."

He reconciled with the fact that he was going back to the States as broke as those men he saw around town begging for food and wrapped in American flags, whose houses were wheelchairs. And it was a million times worse over here. Blaze had certain advantages, which was a brutal truth for him to contemplate. The whole reason he spent all this money loomed right now in his taxi window and creeping upon him was the shame of being here in the first place. His mother would've given him a tight frown. His father would've punched him in the arm. They rounded an absurdly green golf course, south of the Main Gate, and then the taxi dropped them off on a well-lit street, next to a wild cluster of tin and ceramic shanties, on the doorstep of the Giza Pyramids.

René hopped out. Blaze didn't move. A devil was telling him he should be comfortable viewing the scenery from the backseat. An angel spoke. It told him he had flown many thousands of miles, and sailed, drove, camel-caravanned, and walked many thousands more just to put himself in this very position so buck up and let's do this thing. René, already a few steps away, stared back at him through the window.

"What wrong with you?"

Blaze paid the driver, adding a three-dollar tip.

He ran to catch up with big lumbering steps, sand swirling up and gritting his teeth. He coughed and spit out a wad of sediment that was taken by a thoughtful gust of wind and looped far away.

"I will do the talking. You will give the money. That is all you do. You cannot talk."

"What about—"

"Shut up."

A small boy holding the reins of two sleepy camels met them beyond the line of shanties. He exchanged a few decisive words in Arabic with René, who quickly looked to Blaze, who handed the kid a ten. The kid looked at René and René stared impatiently at Blaze like *he* was the child. Blaze handed the kid another ten and the kid folded the two bills into a perfect square and tucked it in the hem of his sandy pants. René hopped on the saddle. Blaze wasn't so athletic. The boy ended up leading him across the desert for an extra ten.

It was easier then expected to gain access to the Great Pyramid. Feeling and seeing it this close against the night, Blaze wasn't just starstruck, he was overcome by a palpable sense of power emanating from the thing, it's total and unquestioned superiority over everything ever created on Earth. All the movies and books in the world had prepared him, spoiled him, and yet nothing dampened the lived experience.

At the north end of the base, past the usual tourist entrance, they arrived at a steel gate leading to The Well. There were two near-identical guards Blaze had to pay off, seventy-five each, and as one unlocked the gate and motioned them through it the other leaned in and said, "You have one hour and a half, exactly. Set your watch. If you are not here on the dot we will come and get you and we will not be happy. Do not be late."

So there they were, René Ennogo and Blaze Lyons, standing at the top of a nondescript tunnel sloping down twenty-three degrees and descending four hundred feet, finally opening into an underground room called The Well, which was closed to the public by order of the Egyptian government. They flicked on flashlights. The tunnel was about a yard high and a yard wide. They had to waddle like ducks with their packs in front of them. The air was rank with donkey dung. Blaze began to feel a deep and consistent vibration throughout his body, as if very low bass waves were rattling his bones with every beat of his heart. His hands started shaking. The hair on his chest and arms crackled with blue sparks of static. He should have been elated, high as the most diamond-studded twenty-four carat gold kite. Nope.

He waddled further down, the vibration entraining his body to its own intrusive rhythms. A mysterious mounting fear made it hard to move—he had to consciously command one foot to walk in front of the other, mouthing *one, two, one, two*. And that's when he noticed a series of tiny red squares embedded in the walls of the tunnel, one on each side, at intervals of about two feet. As he passed these squares, the vibrations actually dropped an octave deeper and a more profound and complete fear went through him, into the marrow of his bones and the cells of his marrow. Impending death, introducing itself in fertile darkness.

Two weeks ago, after a stopover at Dendara, after hearing about the mythic sailors in little boats who navigated by the stars, Blaze expressed a secret wish to René: to see something, some *thing*, any *thing*, no normal tourist visiting the Great Pyramids would see. René suggested The Well. Many people had died in its tunnels of unexplainable things, things like poisonous spider bites from species that don't exist on the African continent. Blaze wanted to go.

"It's—complicated," René said.

"So?" Blaze shot back.

"It's expensive."

"And?"

"Can you control your fear?" René asked.

"Sure." Blaze was full of pride, sitting on the edge of the felucca like a cat on the ledge of a skyscraper.

"Do you know what happens when you feel fear?"

"I don't shit myself."

"But what does your body do?"

"My body doesn't do anything."

"Time to learn." René Ennogo kicked Blaze off the boat. He sputtered for breath and grabbed the bow. René pushed him back into the water with a wooden paddle.

"Be calm. You're not swimming with crocodiles. You can take a breath."

He forced Blaze, not a good swimmer, to swim alongside the felucca for a few endless miles. He would sputter and sink and thrash and scream while René reminded him to be aware of how his body was reacting, what thoughts were going through his head, what images popped in there. After that, the lessons were toned down and simplified: how to breathe properly; how to keep a sustained focus; what fear feels like; what fear thinks like.

Right now—all forgotten.

Blaze was stuck on scorpions. That made no sense. He'd never been afraid of them, was never stung by one, never touched one except to crush it with his boot. But there are scorpions in this tunnel. There are no scorpions in this tunnel. There may be scorpions in this tunnel. There may be scorpions in this tunnel, but there's not. Can you prove that's not true? It's not true. Prove it—prove there are no scorpions in this tunnel.

Blaze waddled out of the chute and almost fell directly into The Well. It was an opening about thirty feet deep in the middle of the room. He stood and slung on his pack, shining his flashlight around to get a better sense of its dimensions.

The Well didn't seem to have any particular shape, no straight lines, more like a cave than a room. René explained how the Egyptians didn't even build it themselves, who knows who really did, but one of the functions of the Great Pyramid was to protect this very space. René showed him another tunnel, opposite the one they had descended, which the government filled in a third of the way with concrete so nobody could reach the end. Unprintable, otherworldly events had happened in there: teleportations, materializations, annihilations.

"This is it?" Blaze asked, the scorpions still clicking away on the floor of his mind.

"Let me go first," René said.

They crawled on their bellies. The floor of the tunnel was silica sand and soft. The walls and ceiling were covered with small quartz crystals and when they shone their flashlights at an angle the light spiraled down the tunnel in reflective arcs and was lost in the blackness like comets in space.

René stopped. "This is the end."

"What do we do?"

"We lie here."

René Ennogo flipped over on his back and clicked off his flashlight. He cleared his throat with the utmost respect. There was still the problem of scorpions. Blaze thumbed the plastic button and took the longest five seconds of his life to click off the light.

Two things immediately happened.

One: Blaze Lyons realized this was the darkest place he had ever been. There were no spatial distinctions of any kind, no sense of his hand waving in front of his face, not one photon of light was in the tunnel for him to register and use for sight.

Two: there was an impression of immense mass and gravity pressing down upon him. The compound weight of each block, the size of them, stacked so high, and suddenly one dislodges and Blaze becomes a pancake. And then he saw—how he could see was not something he was concerned with, because there it was, he was "seeing" it—a little hole on the side of the tunnel. Out of this hole poured a swarm of scorpions. They covered his body, jabbing their stingers through his clothes and into his flesh. His blood coursed with their poison, his throat seized up, and violent spasms ran through his body, his. head smashing against the tunnel rock over and over until his skull was mush and he was dead.

A soft blue light faded in, illuminating the tunnel with pulsing grid-like patterns. A fishhook, saturated with the same character of light, dangled from above and Blaze reached up with his own etherealized hand, at the moment of contact leaving the confines of planetary orbit, free from the sun's influence and the drag of galactic clusters. In the center of a whirling star-factory, he read the blueprints of his individual-self, was blessed with an omniscient view of not just his life, but Life itself, the infinite marching into the infinite from out of the infinite, and it blew him away, literally, a proper Supernova, scattering all parts of his personality, those habituated traits imprinted by race, nation, family, friends, the world and its weather, until nothing was left but the core of who and what he really was. Winds of gravity swirled the cosmic dust into the shape of a woman and a child held to her breast. Blaze knew that the woman was his wife and the child was his. They turned their eyes upon him and he saw something to worship. He touched them and abruptly returned to the pure darkness of the tunnel. At the very least, he was no longer afraid of scorpions, and deliriously pleased he could breathe and that his body did this without him telling it to. Did what just happen really happen? It doesn't matter, René piped up. You had a moment of transcendence you were not prepared for because you have not developed the organic regions of the brain that would enable you to suitably process the intense energy and information you were just exposed to. It's like a power station. You don't have the correct transformers. You don't have the proper tools to handle the exchange. However, they can be acquired with substantial effort. Am I dead? Blaze wondered. Don't be melodramatic, René said. You have had a tremendous experience of great value. This is what has happened. How it happened, your perception of it happening to you, is secondary. You will, in time, lose the details, the livingness of the experience. You already are. The images are fading. Your story is shifting to fill the holes of a memory you can't comprehend. All that will be left is your emotion, the end product of your forgotten experience. What really happened? Not a practically useful suggestion right now. Instead, I'd ask what you're feeling like. I want to go home, Blaze thought. I want to build my life into something I'm proud to leave behind. Do you have a vision? René asked. Kind of? Blaze thought. You'd better get the details down.

There was a beep.

A flashlight flicked on.

"We've got to go," whispered René. "It takes longer to go up."

Blaze scrambled up the tunnel in a stupor. René had to give him a couple shoves to keep the pace. Upon exiting the shaft, each of the guards shook his hand. It was bizarre. When they reached the camels Blaze was able to mount and direct his own animal, to the quiet disbelief of the boy, and on the ride back to the shanties the boy kept looking over his shoulder as if Blaze would fall off at any time, and Blaze, in mirror movement, looked over his shoulder at the Great Pyramid as if it vanished each time he turned his head and only reappeared at each twist of his neck.

"Thanks for that back there," Blaze said.

"Yeah. What?" René said.

"Talking me down in the tunnel. I needed that. I was freaking out."

"Huh." René looked off into the horizon. It was dawn, a light hue of purple seeping into the sky, air mild, serene, steady, like the breathing of deep sleep. "We'll get a good breakfast. There is a fine hotel nearby that serves fresh juice and cheese."

"I'm a little low on cash. I fly out in two days."

"You do not have to worry."

"He asked me what my favorite piece was. What a stupid question." Back at the funeral, Joy Recioto circled the rim of a beer glass with her finger. "Everybody asks that. People who can't make up their minds ask that, and when you tell them, it's not what they really wanted anyway. But it mattered to him, which one was my favorite, like it would somehow tell him something important about me."

Donna appeared at the far end of the bar and raised her arm for attention. Blaze excused himself from Joy and rushed over.

"Are you very busy?" she said.

"I am," he said.

"The heat's not kicking on. Can you fix it?"

"Who's going to bartend?"

"Can't it wait a few minutes?"

It's not like a riot would break out. People wouldn't just help themselves to a bottle. Bremen wouldn't allow that. His spirit was the authority at the door for what is and is not allowed, the bodybuilding bouncer in everybody's mind. "Lead the way."

She did. Boy, she did. Blaze made the mistake of trailing too close, and in her wake he could smell her skin as it exhaled some evocative perfume of jasmine and musk that stirred up the lust and invincibility of his youth.

Donna stopped in the front foyer and showed him the gauge. "See?" She spun the dial back and forth. "Heat's not turning on."

Blaze pretended to examine the thermostat. Her smells distracted him. Guests in the vicinity were dancing and laughing and singing and drinking and a ditzy blonde girl bumped into Donna who bumped into Blaze. The girl couldn't stop apologizing with dramatic intonations. Donna gave the blonde a quick hug and whispered something in her ear and the blonde hugged Donna harder. Blaze watched the girl melt back into the mercurial flow of the funeral, her body losing its distinctions in the mass of limbs. Down the hallway, Mo was standing alone at the door, chin high, hands held politely in front of her, much as he was tending bar, and Blaze lifted his head in acknowledgement, a subtle lift, executed with the precision of a professional spy. Mo decoded his gesture and lifted back: *yeah, this is outta hand*. Blaze grabbed that which he intuitively knew so long ago as the love of his life and threaded with her through the crowd and into the basement.

The pilot light was out. Mystery solved. "Matches?" Blaze asked.

"Kitchen drawer," Donna replied. "I'll get them."

Blaze floated around the basement he hadn't worked on since Bremen died. He discovered the remains of a broken bottle with a familiar wax red top. Where are my father's habits? Where is my mother's mentality? His eyes glowed with the issles of smoldering anger that a thousand pounds of sand couldn't put out. Donna trotted down the steps and Blaze took the matchbook without meeting her gaze. They crouched beside the furnace. He turned the gas knob to the *off* position, waited a beat, then turned it to *pilot*. He struck a match.

"Press the reset button," showing her where, "and hold it down until I say."

She did. Boy, she did. Blaze shared the flame with the pilot opening and an orange light flashed into being, skimming along gradations to a bright white blue. He shook out the match.

"Let go." The furnace kicked on amid the rising smoke, and they stood together, sulfur mixing with silence. Then Donna retreated a few steps. Her eyes flitted around Blaze, but never straight at him. She adjusted the chopsticks in her hair.

"You're right," she said.

"About what?"

"You don't have any more time for me. And I don't have any more time for you."

"You're right," Blaze agreed with a subdued and desperate sincerity.

"I thought it would happen differently, under different circumstances, at a different time. But I knew it would happen."

Do we vow revenge on torrential rain? Do we vow revenge on a falling tree? Change is swift and change is slow, so-hum, so-hum, and on we go. Blaze pulled his wife in and kissed her. Donna bit down, a hard bite, but he pulled closer, for there is no substitute for the taste of iron. He raised her green dress, lifted her against the concrete wall, and she softly twined herself around him, a movement as natural as smiling when you hear a song you love, falling into its rhythm, shouting the lyrics, and at the end, you just want to hear it again. A thunderous applause resounded from above, voices cheering, feet stomping, one anthem ending, another ballad beginning. Blaze and Donna were a little embarrassed, each panting hard, still connected.

"What now?" he said.

"We go upstairs," she said. "You know somebody needs a drink."

SEVENTH MOVEMENT

DOOR

🎼 Mo Tipper just wanted to paint something that would make people look at it like their eyelids had been sliced off. Friedrick was her favorite, the most solitary of the Expressionists, and a re-pro of his *Monk at Sea* was the only thing hanging on her studio walls, something other painters in the Grad House got weird about and made pointed, sarcastic, uniformed comments about (even getting the period and his name wrong: it's Caspar, like the fucking ghost, ok?) and which made them question her entire artistic sensibilities, probably. The lack of decoration meant she had to concentrate on her canvas, which she never told them, or, at times of brush-block, project herself within the cloth folds of the monk, that Rükenfigur, get swallowed up by the size of the landscape, make little valleys from the draw of her fingertips across the sand, taste the salt riding on the wind with the gulls who dissolved all her anxieties, and poof! not too long until she could paint again. Never questioned why or how, but knew it was something of a cure-all, because what would happen, as she went about working, was the appearance of an image, for no apparent reason, without any allusory force behind it. She had the impression she was a conduit and the image, abstract or concrete, a Dadaist landscape or a pair of pearl earrings on a table, would paint and express itself in its own form and style if only she could stop thinking, stop being *her*, just react and let flow. She scribbled them down first thing, and wished she could develop those initial fleeting images into fresh masterpieces, but the fullness of them always eluded her. She felt the sting of failure and threw them away. Mo wondered if she was a good enough painter, if she had the talent to go tampering with these beamed-in, mysterious forms and try to make of them something (dare she think it?) beautiful, something with substance, something with spirit, like the texture and color on the outside of the Lyons' front door which she had been staring at for two straight songs.

Guests had been arriving thick with snow. She bundled up and went outside and shoveled a path from the front walk to the street. She paused before going back inside, a little hot and sweaty, kicking the snow clumps from her knee-high boots and brushing off the hem of her dress, scarlet like the shade on her fingernails. Snowflakes drifted onto her golden tights, melted and tickled her thighs. She leaned the shovel against the house and unwound her scarf and was at the right angle to appreciate the door.

It became so much more than a door at that moment. Mo turned and looked at the night and imagined the scope of Friedrick. She re-faced the door and imagined everything Bremen had waiting inside.

Maureen Eileen Tipper (*Mo T*, as she signed her work) wanted to paint that door more than anything right now, fuck the funeral, she wanted to grab her keys and drive to her studio and abandon her other panels and get down the door's tenuous bruised blue color, the snowflakes falling in coal grey shadow upon it's face, the angles of the frame, thin and absolutely black, the muted brass curves of its knob and lock, the densely grained surface of its wood. She had never painted wood. More: she wanted to impress each layer and brushstroke with a deep mental energy, so that every person who stood before her Door would get that feeling you get when you're facing a portal into the unknown, one you either go through now or never see again, and there's a twinge in your whole body when you finally decide, a fear and excitement, a panic and calm, a horror and peace: you're inhabiting both poles at the same time. She loved that feeling. It was intoxicating in the headiest sense of the word. It was eyelids sliced off.

Tomorrow she'd go to the studio and burn it down with everyone inside. Alone, with all the other painters dead, she'd reset her panels on the black and white ashes, en plein air, and paint this door and paint it over and over until it was like this, as it is now, over and over until it was like this, as it is now, over and over. It might be the start of a radical New Period. She didn't move from the porch. She didn't want to do this anymore, take care of shoes. She hated that he loved Free Jazz. Just a bunch of junkies swinging their dicks in the wind. She shivered.

Go back inside, Momo. It's your best bet.

RUG

SHE WIPED HER BOOTS on the rug. It was a green wool rug with a border of intricate grape vines framing a ground of elegant plum blossoms. It was soaking wet from the slushy snow. She shook it out on the porch, took one last glance at the night, and shut the door as respectfully as she could.

When she re-set the rug, careful to line it up with the doorframe, more out of an aesthetic predilection than for any courtesy on Bremen's part, she had a sense of the rug being, like the door before, a symbol or glyph or effervescent concept of Rugs itself, which only existed because some person had an idea to clean the bottom of their shoes. The Lyons' rug was the Lyons' rug, fine, but it was also anything anybody has ever wiped their feet on, ever. She took that as confirmation. She took that as challenge.

She slipped off her boots and into a pair of stylish white slippers, the only one allowed to wear shoes. Bremen made all this shit up, not her.

WILL

So many warm delicate shades of orange, yellow, and red in the house you'd think it was mid-fall. Mo felt cupped by the soft clean hands of Hell.

Donna Lyons appeared out of the crowd like a shy girl from a high school hallway. "I saw you go out for a while. You're freezing."

"I'm fine. The walk needed to be shoveled."

Donna cowed as if insulted. "Next time it gets like that, I'll shovel. Do you need anything to drink?"

"Some water?"

"Anything else? I can bring you some food."

"I'm fine."

Mo wasn't thirsty at all, except for some blueberry vodka with that water, some limes. That's what she was drinking when she got a call from a 414-number she didn't recognize and ignored because she was downtown with friends, but then listened to the message and stepped outside to call Blaze back. She left her friends without explanation and bounced to a different bar, The Pampered Thug, where Bremen used to play jazz with this lame quartet. She tried to blackout with Tequila, succeeded like she did at all the things she singularly set her mind to, woke up on her bathroom floor totally naked, hair knotty and wet like mountain moss, not wanting to get up because the tile was so cool and therapeutic and the day—the moments she could see strung out one by one at infinite rest, moments that required a living breathing person with a will and desire to do them—was asking way too fucking much of her.

Mo Tipper told no one of Bremen's death. She entered a period of prolific artistic creation. Nothing salvageable, most panels destroyed before completion, but she was basically living at the grad studio for three weeks straight, eating nothing but Thai food, pissing off the other painters in the house by not setting up proper cross-ventilation when heating her resins and solvents. When working, Mo wore black gloves, a black gas mask, and a black bandana, looking like an anarchist adequately prepared for the apocalyptic riots of the 21st century and despite threats of defacement, of setting fire to her camelhair brushes, nobody ventured even a sneeze in her direction.

The Will reading was the first time she had been in the presence of Bremen's entire family. Over the course of three years she had met Blaze, Donna, Vera, and Terry in many variations, but never altogether. Mo once had the idea of doing some sort of hybrid family portrait of the Lyons' with encaustics and organic materials like dirt and blood and cotton and animal skins, the kind of painting that would decompose over time. She didn't ask because she thought he would say yes.

Donna called her up a week after the reading. "We're having a funeral."

"I thought so."

"Are you free tomorrow afternoon?"

"You're having the funeral *tomorrow* afternoon?"

"The funeral is December 9th. Will you meet me tomorrow?"

"I don't understand."

"It's best if we talk in person."

"I'm pretty busy. I've been painting a lot."

"Bremen always said you were very dedicated."

"I don't think he was talking about me."

"I could drive to you? You wouldn't have to go anywhere?"

Mo drew in and forced out a gigantic breath, over the phone, on purpose. "Sure."

SHOES

Section X – Greetings

1) Every guest must take off his or her shoes upon entering the house.

> *a. If the guest has some sort of disability that requires corrective footwear, then he/she is allowed to keep their shoes on.*
> *b. Said guest must be reminded to be careful not to step on any toes.*

2) Maureen will be stationed at the front door and will be in charge of making sure everyone takes off his or her shoes upon entering the house. She should be the first person a guest sees when they come through the door and hand her their shoes, and the last one they see when she hands them back.

> *a. To streamline the process, a shoe rack should be built or acquired (possibly two depending on the number of guests) and small rugs should be laid down to aid in the transition from shoe to socking foot.*
> *b. Mo will also be responsible for giving the Funeral Program to each guest upon entry. If the guest refuses said Program, then she has a few options.*

Mo read the instructions at her kitchen table, rubbing one bare foot against the other and absently scraping dry flecks of wood stain from her forearm. Or were those freckles? Bremen could never tell. Donna Lyons stood to one side and leaned against the sink counter and stared out the window.

"I don't want to do this," Mo said, still reading, not looking up from the page.

"Any particular reason?"

Mo didn't answer, only read, and Donna let her. After a few more pages: "What did he ask you to do?"

Donna Lyons smiled, pointing at the instructions, all seventy-two pages of them. "I'm responsible for putting it all together. Coordinating the different aspects. Making sure it all goes according to plan."

"And you're just going to follow along," wagging the instructions back and forth in the air, "with whatever he says?"

"Yes."

Mo thumbed through the rest of it. Reading it would be a chore she hated doing, like eating breakfast. She just wanted to go back to her studio, its bare walls, Friedrick, the beeswax, her panels, the heat of the colors and the people who wished she would die in a car crash. It was the only place she could concentrate.

"Read the rest later. Call me tonight, if you can?"

Mo did not touch it for a week. She ignored Donna's calls. Every night in bed she couldn't stop her hamster wheel from revolving around the vortex of Bremen's nonexistent life. It was 3:57 am. She phoned Donna and left a long rambling message agreeing that she'd do it without necessarily saying outright that she'd do it. At 4:22 am, Mo read the rest of the instructions. What hit her most, besides the obvious insanity and blind assumption you'll go along, so typical of Bremen, was that despite the seeming precision, he hadn't really thought everything through. For example, at one point he said he wanted cigarette smokers to go out the attached garage door and smoke on the porch but declined to say how they would get their shoes. Would they have to get them from Mo at the front door, walk through the house to the garage, put them on, smoke, take them off, and then walk them back to her? Why would he ask her to be that person? How could you ask that level of attention from everyone else?

So Mo improvised like Bremen on a Saturday night at The Pampered Thug. It's what the occasion called for. By now, her slippers had become a bit soggy. Two shoe racks, Blaze-made, were stationed on either side of the door, salt and snow dripping off the leather and laces, soaking into the highly reflective wood floor. Cocky son of a bitch. He didn't think he'd die in winter and the funeral would fall on the night of a snowstorm that was smothering three states like thick white paint over a wall of brilliant graffiti.

There was a muffled knock on the door.

Mo snapped to and opened it in less then a second.

COUPLET

AN OLDER MAN STOOD at the threshold, alone, without a coat. He had bronze skin and acne scars along his cheeks. His grey striped suit was refined and polished without ornamentation, and his grey shoes, hand-stitched, aerodynamically pure, had no snow sitcking to the soles.

Mo nodded hello and said, "Welcome." She offered him a Program.

The man had long lashes that cast thin shadows over the whites of his eyes. He took Mo's free hand in his, a clammy hand smelling of olives and roses. She had the sensation he was going to say something she didn't want to hear, although not in the accent he spoke it in, some susurrus Latin American accent reminding her of a visiting painter from Uruguay who lectured about the virtues of being born in an atelier.

"Light will someday split you open, even if your life is now a cage. Behold the beautiful drunk singing one from the lunar vantage point of love. He is conducting the affairs of the whole universe while throwing wild parties in a tree house on a limb in your heart." His arcadian tone matched his outfit. "For Bremen. I'm sorry for your loss."

"Yeah," leaning back and looking at his snow-caked shoes. Perhaps she hadn't shoveled as well as she thought? "I'm sure the family would love to hear your condolences."

"You are not family?"

"No."

The old man dropped her hand, looking puzzled, as if he had stumbled into the wrong story. "Who are you?"

"I'm...Maureen."

He was shaking his head back and forth. "You have welcomed me to his funeral. You must be family. A cousin?"

"I've known Bremen for a very long time. May I take your shoes?"

SHALL WE NOT TAKE WHAT WE ARE GIVEN

THREE YEARS AGO, Mo Tipper stood outside Starling Depot on the corner of Bedford and Main and listened to a man tell her she was crazy. They both smoked Pall Mall Menthols. Passing strangers craned their necks to watch the train wreck.

"You're bat-shit crazy," the man said calmly. Todd Young was thirty-five years old and hailed from Salt Lake City, had pierced nipples, ear plugs you could fit a buffalo nickel through, and when drunk he joked, too often, about machine-gunning down psychotic Mormons (which sooner or later in his schemata meant all of them) and the advantageous reasons, seen from a long-term evolutionary POV, for doing so. He made explicit anti-religious themed paintings in Mo's MFA graduate program, mixed media hybrids modeled after his hero, Andres Serrano, and especially his *Piss-Christ*.

"I told you I was never going to be exclusive. Is there some word in that sentence you don't understand?"

Within the first month Mo and Todd had hooked up multiple times when all of a sudden he decided to stop answering Mo's texts, right around the time she called him out in their Modern Techniques Seminar and told him Serrano was a practicing Christian. He didn't believe her, nobody did, until she whipped out her cell phone and found the quote from his *NYT* interview and interrupted the class to read it out loud with excessive pride and contempt. When she saw Todd Young at the Depot (a painter hotspot she soon stopped going to, obviously) with Sara, an attractice Vietnamese girl who was also in the program, third year, Mo flipped. Todd had to take her outside.

"You're a douchebag," Mo said, finding elegance in the phrase, somehow.

Todd bowed like he was in a tux and in the presence of a president.

"I'm such an idiot," Mo said.

"Yep. I'm going back inside now." He flicked his half-smoked cigarette into the street. He scratched the side of his face. "So I'll see you in there?"

Mo took a swing. Todd ducked it easily and laughed and opened the door, holding it for a moment in mock gallantry, before disappearing inside.

It would've taken Caspar himself to get her back into the Depot. She walked along Main Street to the Capital Square. She popped into Bruiser's, a hedonic bar for bestial undergrads, and unbuttoned one button on her top so the cup of her black VS bra would peek out, and turned on this kind of sociopathic charm and accepted every single top-shelf shot of Vodka and Tequila that men wanted to buy her. Conversations were performed on autopilot (smile here, laugh there, push away now) while the bigger part of her mind was consumed with a new idea, a new project: encaustic paintings with testicle blood. She'd leave Bruiser's at bar close and go to Todd Young's house on East Mifflin and sneak inside. She'd hide in the closet, and when he got home and passed out she'd tie him down and stuff a gag in his mouth and then cut off his balls with a serrated blade and collect his blood in a five-gallon bucket, using it as pigment to mix with her filtered beeswax. She'd make a series of fayum-like portraits, after Jean Denis. She'd stalk men from Bruiser's and take them home and tie them down and gag them and cut off their balls, and depending on their death mask and the subtle properties of their blood she'd give the individual portraits long titles (which was her M.O. and greatly informed the artistic statement she submitted, along with her encaustic-on-panel portfolio, to twelve different grad schools, from SCAD to UCLA), titles that described, in essence, who these men were: *The Knight that Could Never Be a Knight Because it was Born a Bitch; The Orbit of Your Pathetic Electron is Not Even Platonically Attractive; You Got Me Where You Want Me, Baby, What You Want Me To Do.*

She remembered white lights that flicked on like a splash of cold water, but T.I. still bumped through the speakers and she was talking to a beefed-up Media Studies major who wore a lacrosse shirt and quoted Kierkegaard. She almost threw up on him. Next thing she knew, she was on her ass on the lawn in front of her apartment. She must've fallen, hard. Both her wrists were stinging bad and her head hurt. The door was wide open and some guy was standing there. She reached out for help. She couldn't stand on her own.

They were in his bed, a few months later, when Mo asked him where he had found her that night. She knew pretty much all the rest. It had been their first topic of conversation (since gone unmentioned) after she awoke the next morning and saw a small gash just above her hairline (somehow cleaned up) and an email address written on the dry-erase board on her fridge with a message: *I can tell you what happened last night and where your phone is. My name is Bremen.*

"I was at the crosswalk on the Square," Bremen said. "There was nobody else around. I didn't hear you walk up, just saw you zip past, whoosh. And when you got to the other side of the street you stopped cold on the corner, like you were lost and didn't know the way."

"So you followed me?" Mo said, pulling the sheet closer.

"No, the light changed. I walked across the street. You were still on the corner."

"Did I say anything?"

"You asked where Mifflin Street was." He laughed and inched farther up the headboard. "You were trying to get to some house and we started walking in that direction. Didn't I—"

"Yeah, you told me all that."

"You seemed so lucid. You were walking fast. You weren't stumbling or slurring at all."

"So what did you first think of me? Seeing me there in the street?"

Mo had small feet and ankles (bright red as if she always scratched them), somehow made smaller by the tattered white Toms she was wearing. Though standing relatively still, there on the corner, her long skirt (also white, bone white) was drifting about like a stage curtain being played with by a fan. Her black cami fit her frame as smooth as a basecoat of paint and he'd be lying if he said he didn't want to peel it off. She had no visible tattoos. Bonus. Her brown hair was up and attractively dishabilled. The line of her neck and shoulders reminded him of the neck and shoulders of his double bass. She wore little pearl earrings, and the dust mote of a sapphire on the left side of her nose. Very little makeup, just a few smoky green flourishes around the eyes, for effect, not affect, like Satie, he told her, not Cage.

"And I thought, well," shrugging against the headboard, "here's an interesting looking girl. Let's see if she likes me."

WATER

"Nasazzi—I can't believe you made it." Donna grabbed his arm with her free hand, squeezing hard. "When did you fly in? I would've picked you up at the airport. Don't tell me you rented a car."

Nasazzi deftly took Donna's hand off his arm, cupped it like he had done with Mo's earlier, and recited his couplet again. Donna tried hard not to cry, and Mo, seeing this, seeing the surface of the water tremble in the glass she held, understood for the first time how much more heartbreaking it is when someone tries hard not to cry, versus weeping at top volume, full of snot and tears.

Both women succeeded in not crying. It was admirable and sad. Nasazzi kicked his heels clean of snow and removed his shoes, grey loafers with black scuffs on top. He handed them to Mo without looking. Donna passed her the water like a baton in a relay race, and then escorted Nasazzi into the funeral fray.

Mo examined the shoes in her left hand, the glass in her right, and wanted to continue her New Period, and paint the stubborn luffa texture of the scuffs and the ineffable limpidity of water in motion. She was in love with the past masters. She hated Modern Art.

DOOR, AGAIN

THE REASON MO HATED Modern Art was complex, like the plot of a classic detective story or the contrapunto style of Bach's violins. She considered history and motive and desire. Warhol was clearly a vampire. Breton was tolerable—for a few seconds. Duchamp was a child playing pranks his whole life and at least he admitted it. Marinetti was a speed freak. Futurism, Abstract Expressionism, every bastard boy and girl of the Moderns could go the way of the passenger pigeons for all she cared. Their masterpieces wrought from house-paint were falling apart now. What does that tell you? Shoot the fuckers out of the sky and strip them for canvas meat. Give Mo the useful enchantment of a pencil-drawn wolf, dressed as grandma, and sleeping in the bed of a little girl in red. Give her the morgues and prairie fires by Deas and Calcedonia. She got it, ok? Transgressive techniques jolted the artist out of their programmed routine. Absurd performances shocked the audience out of their perceptual complacency. Radical manifestos, audacious revisionism, and self-conscious experimentation encouraged the flight into the high skies of creativity so as to re-chart the evolution of the individual personality and the socio-cultural body of the earth. Whatever. The depths of subconsciousness were not a place she wanted to live her life. She admired the movements from a certain political perspective, but emotionally, she might as well have been starving of thirst in the desert. It was a barren place with murderers running free, attempting to lay waste to the very air she breathed, redefining the meanings of love and hate, flipping the polarities of matter and spirit—the world was horrible, people were horrible, we all make our playground, this is ours, play with us if you like, if not, fuck off. All the art and all the theory only served to exacerbate what was mindblowingly cynical about life. Let's gather round and laugh at the meaninglessness. Laugh at the bile of humanity reflected back at us in the frame. Maybe this is why it's so entrenched, so lionized, such a pervasive influence. Maybe this is what we actually want. Bile.

And then there was her door. Still figuring out what to do with that. She thought she heard a knock and perked her ears, but there was nothing.

She drank the entire glass of water in three gulps. Nasazzi's loafers found a place on the rack, seventh shelf, next to a pair of kid's sneakers with Spider-Man decals, and she stuffed the empty glass into the heel of the shoe.

BEAT

WHEN MO WOULD MAKE eye contact with a guest, if she knew them, she would smile and nod. If she didn't, she would stand straighter and wave. Everybody had their memories of Bremen, biomusicologically speaking, and though Mo would never be familiar with that catalog of songs, it didn't stop her from wanting to hear them. Who was Nasazzi? Who was this funeral really for?

Here comes Odetta. "Waterboy."

Some of the guests stopped dancing. One by one, and then as a group, they began to stomp a 4/4 beat on the hardwood floor, as an accompaniment to Odetta, who sang a cappella. It was infectious like the wave at a Mexican fútbol game. It felt like the whole house was stomping in unison. It shook the shoe racks back and forth, the shoes dancing by themselves, possessed pairs jumping off the edge and onto the floor, itself shaking so hard and ready to give way beneath Mo's feet. Somebody, amid stomps and whoops and cheers and claps, actually turned the music up. Odetta towered over the communal beat of the house. Her voice could split the sun in half.

Mo almost screamed at them, at every single stomper, and would've broken their ankles with a sledgehammer if she had one in her hands. Her whole body was a lethal coiled spring, but she didn't move a muscle. The tension made her lightheaded.

Hey, Momo, you should sit down.

BLUES

INSTEAD THERE WAS A knock on the door. Two policemen. They stepped a few feet back from threshold, the interior lights not quite reaching their knees, but silhouetted by the waxy streetlights and waning moon—they could've been demons. Mo did not invite them in. She stepped outside as is, nothing snaps you alert like subhuman cold, and closed the door behind her.

"Can I help you?"

The two policemen, one with a beard, and one clean-shaven, glanced at each other the way parents do when they aren't entirely confident which one of them should speak to the children. The clean-shaven one finally spoke with a clinically authoritative voice. He was stiff and bulging at the chest and arms. He looked in pain. Did he wear tight clothes on purpose?

"We received a noise complaint about twenty minutes ago."

He put his right hand on his hip, on the butt of his gun, and looked to his bearded partner, who kicked one of his shoes against the step. He had a potbelly and the fine hairs in his beard were sparkling from the cold.

"From the neighbors," said the bearded one.

The clean-shaven policeman pointed to a house three doors down and across the street. The yellow streetlight shined on his silver nametag. Officer Eyce. His nose was runny and he wiped it with a black glove, sniffing. He looked at his partner again, who brushed a layer of white fuzz from his shoulder.

Odetta and the stomping played for a few moments over the otherwise silent night. Even with the door shut it was very loud and Mo imagined walking up the block as a stranger and thinking *what the hell is going on in there?*

"I realize it's only," Eyce glanced at his watch, "seven-fifty four in the evening. But it is a Thursday?"

"Yeah." No trace of compliance.

"What is your name?" said the bearded one. Mo heard wheezing when he spoke, like a werewolf with asthma.

"What is your name?" Mo repeated back, as fearless as she had never known herself to be.

"Officer Barn."

"Barns?" thinking of Wyeth and Grandma Moses. The desolation so appropriate.

"Barn," sharpening his eyes.

"We're having a funeral."

"Who died?" Barn said.

"My cousin."

"What was his name?"

"Bremen Lyons."

"Sounds like one hell of a party to me," Barn said, flashing his teeth, in pouncing position.

"It is."

Officer Barn shifted his inquisition to the exterior of the house, trying to see through heavily curtained windows, leaning to the side without lifting his feet.

Odetta hit her last note. There was an eruption of greater volume than anything that had previously occurred.

A crackling voice, possibly human, sounded on Officer Eyce's shoulder radio. He responded with indecipherable code speak. Then it was quiet again. A bird chirped. A staccato of car horns echoed in the night. The crackling voice returned with directives.

"10-4," mumbled Officer Eyce. He gave Mo a deferential nod.

"We can't keep getting calls like this," Barn said.

"We did alert the neighbors." Mo hadn't moved this whole time.

Officer Barn put both hands on the front of his belt. "Keep it down."

"I'm not in control of the Music."

He stepped closer to Mo, but Officer Eyce coughed and opened his body in well-rehearsed angles. It was convincing enough. After one last sneer from Barn, the policemen walked back to their idling cruiser double parked on the street, which had two kids behind the grate, one white, one brown, in t-shirts without coats. Handcuffed, they stared at Mo through the window. She waved, mouthed sorry, and as the cruiser sped off she thought they nodded, in solidarity, in understanding, in her direction.

THERE'S ALWAYS GONNA BE
A DARKER HOUR, A BRIGHTER DAWN

"As an artist, you're not one *in* a billion, like your lost in some hypothetical haystack, never to be found, never to be discovered, never to be appreciated for the precious self-important needle you think you are. You are one *of* a billion, like you're a weave running through a quilt that illustrates four generations, or a note in a folk song that's survived centuries. It's basically an eternal unbroken line of creativity we're talking about here. But everyone's trying to be so Singular and Important."

"I don't even want to hear you right now."

"But this is my apartment."

"I'm not leaving."

"I'm not making you leave."

Mo, who had been skinned alive and hung upside down in Critique that day like the Comanches did to spiritually trespassing enemies, quit her pacing and sat down at the kitchen table. She wanted to accuse Bremen of many things she would, tomorrow, five years from now, maybe, regret. Mo wanted more people in her life she could be brutally honest with, people who loved her like she loved the molded tips of beeswax that were layered, with unbelievable pain and time, on her panels.

"Nobody stepped in. Nobody defended me. Not even Erikson."

"Then he's useless," bringing out a plastic bag of carrots from the fridge. "I wouldn't listen to a word he says."

"They were all piranhas and I was this huge elephant that fell into a river. I think some of them died from feeding on me." Her face was a mask of disgust, remembering her own disembowelment in slow-motion detail. "I don't even want to think about it anymore."

Bremen shut the fridge with his foot. He cradled a small Valencia orange, two Chilean pears, a hunk of ginger, and a big red beet. He arranged everything on the counter and washed the carrots in the sink.

"Tell me what else you want to do."

Mo, with effort, broke free from the afternoon's strong psychological grip. She suddenly laughed and jumped onto him, clinging to his body while he continued to wash the carrots, unfazed.

"I want to take your pants off."

"I'm making juice."

"That can wait."

"I know you like it after Critique," Bremen said over his shoulder, "and I love how it calms you down, but Vitamin A won't get into my body all by itself." He began washed the beet.

Mo let him go and crossed her arms defiantly, stomped once, bit her bottom lip, gave him hungry eyes, which he didn't even turn around to see.

"Give me ten minutes. Beet juice is a vasodilator. I'll last longer."

Mo turned into a deliberately alluring snake, wrapping her hands around his chest and smelling the back of his neck, her nose pressed to his skin, standing up on her tiptoes with her whole body a sunfresh pink linen sheet draped all over him.

Bremen turned and faced her, orange in one hand, pears in the other. She kissed him and he let her. "You have to make me juice after."

"Deal," Mo said, suppressing a smile that would tell any speck of paint on the wall who received the better end of the transaction.

SMILE

THERE WAS THE SENSE of having missed out. On the funny Super Bowl commercial with talking pandas and luxury cars. On the series finale of a popular TV show. On the cute guys that just walked by. On a rapper's concert, on a famous artist's exhibition. On the confession of a family secret that's been buried for generations. On the adventure, on the sunrise, on the coolest thing to happened that night. Mo didn't care. When told breathlessly of all she missed, she was happy she missed it. The more people who saw it, read it, felt it, spoke about it, the more grateful she grew at having no part in it.

That summed up her and Odetta.

Mo Tipper, free of the cops, returned to her post with no focus, like a stoned teenager staring at a lava lamp. She peered into the distance of the middle hallway, and her eyes drifted to a young girl in blue. Mo waved automatically. The girl in blue waved. There was some sort of pull. Mo couldn't stop looking at the girl in blue, who couldn't stop looking at Mo, and was in fact walking straight towards her right now.

A gray blur, scents of floral and brine, and Nasazzi appeared in front of her, a condensation of a dream Bremen must've once had. He held out his hand. It was weightless and content to wait, so Mo shook it for the second time tonight, surprised at how much warmer it was. The girl in blue stopped behind Nasazzi and retreated a few steps back. He didn't notice.

"I've known Bremen for almost twenty years. We first met in Chicago, during the World Cup in the USA. I went with my family to see Bolivia play Spain at Solider Field. Do you remember?"

"Um—"

"Before your time, maybe." Nasazzi waved it away. "In front of the stadium they had a little fútbol field set up. You know, for the kids to play. My son, Horatio, was playing there." Nasazzi laughed and Mo assumed she was supposed to laugh along. So she did. So did the girl in blue. Very quietly.

"There was this boy running around the field like a lightning bolt. Not much intelligence on the ball, but his speed—he dribbled around the other kids like practice cones."

Mo was split between Nasazzi and the girl in blue, who hung back, dangled her wrists, pretended to study the ceiling, the thermostat, the crowd, her gaze flitting to Mo's with ease, with patience.

"Bremen and my son became friends very fast. For many years after, whenever we visited family in Chicago, my son made sure to meet Bremen somewhere in the city. Bremen always wanted to visit Horatio in La Paz, but he did not get the chance." Nasazzi half-smiled, a smile of pain, a smile that knows intimate and prolonged pain and sees, somehow, the other side of it. Mo gave him her full attention.

"My son died five years ago. Bremen came to the funeral in La Paz. He stayed with me for a week. I appreciated that. And so, here I am now."

Mo, out of knee-jerk politeness, nodded *yes* mechanically.

Nasazzi understood this as confirmation he could continue with his story, or tangents of it, soon reminiscing about his roots, his country, his city, and his upbringing with the kind of reckless abandon that overtakes certain strangers when they find themselves in the presence of an attentive Listener. Mo didn't like being a Listener. She hated imprisonment. Her greatest fear was being buried alive.

Mo caught the eyes of the girl in blue's eyes. She begged for an intervention. The girl in blue smiled. It was a conspiratorial smile. It said, *I know.* It said, *You don't have to tell me.*

There was a knock at the door, solid and true and not in her imagination. Though she didn't believe in anything resembling the concept of God, Mo silently thanked a higher authority at that moment. Who else could've dropped its grace on her like a laser-sighted bomb?

DOOR, AGAIN AND AGAIN

WHEN HER HAND TOUCHED the knob, Mo had an intuition and pressed pause. In obedience to hidden laws, her universe paused.

The door, her idea of the door, her paining of the door arose in her mind clearer and with more propulsive force. She was, as usual, the Monk by the Sea and comprehended the image in pristine form. She thought of running to the kitchen and grabbing a notepad and pen to sketch it down, but there was a feeling of confidence, a certainty that she knew what the door looked like and would never forget. This was unusual. She'd paint each side of the door, both front and back, on two separate panels, and then join them seamlessly together. One door, two planes, infinite portals to the unknown, because even if you thought you knew where you were going, no, you never really did.

A^3

THE WOMAN WAS VERY old, quivering in open-toed shoes. She wore a long black dress and wrapped herself in a thick shawl. She must not have read the invitation. Mo debated letting her inside. The middle-aged man who held the old woman's arm, not so much for balance as for the attentive perception it produced, wore a heavy tan overcoat and dark brown suit. He shook like a bird in a curbside puddle and the snow flew off him and drifted to the floor. He glanced from Mo to Nasazzi, nodding hello, while the old woman scrunched her eyes and pursed her lips.

"Questo è il posto giusto? Questo è il funerale? Cosa sta succedendo?"

The man sighed, his patience had, at some point, run thin and translucent. "You ask them, Mother."

The old woman tightened her shoulders and stared hard at Mo, as if this was a schoolyard and intimidation was the name of the game. Mo was unfazed. Most people are ashamed of what will be seen if another human being looks closely. Most people don't want their personal dynamics to be known by others. Mo Tipper, however, had been torn apart, multiple times, by a pack of ravenous narcissistic beasts, so this woman was just a drop of wax on a giant panel.

Mo forced kindness into her voice, "Welcome to Bremen Lyons' funeral. Please come in. Let me take your shoes."

In response, the old woman unpredictably shed whatever animosity she carried like dead petals from a flower, and hobbled past Mo, mumbling pleasant incoherencies of thanks. Nasazzi was already introducing himself.

HAWK IS ON THE WING, WOLF IS AT THE DOOR

A YEAR AGO Mo woke up completely unsatisfied with every aspect of her life. She had Critique that day. She had lunch with Bremen. She skipped town and did what always made her feel better. She went to a museum. She drove to Milwaukee and parked near the Lakefront and went to the Art Museum. She dropped four bills on a Donor Membership for no reason at all. The cashier strongly recommended the Italian Masters exhibit. There was Botticelli's *Annunciation.* There was Mancini's *Sulky Boy.* It was a Tuesday and the galleries were deserted. Mo, violating the sacred laws of the institution, took the opportunity to brush the canvases with her fingertips. She ignored the texts and calls and emails of the stupidest people on Earth. She wandered through five hundred years of naturalism and rationality and religiosity and cityscape secularism. It was only half-past noon. On the Main Level, sharing a wall with New Realism and Pop, was a gallery of American Masters before 1900. She sat down at Eastman's *Indian Scalp Dance.* She remembered when she was a little girl and her parents would take her to museums and let her sit for as long as she wanted. That was the way she fell in love with art, by looking and looking and looking, sinking all her senses deep inside the frame, but when Mo tried to enter the dance now, to feel the wonder, joy, and thrill of scalping, there was only the dread of an onlooker. Could she even call herself a painter anymore? She no longer thought so. The Indians would forever dance for the dead. It wasn't their problem she was losing her life in no direction.

Mo moved on.

An empty frame hung on the wall. Posted inside was a hand-written sign: Artwork Under Restoration. It was Homer's *Hark! The Lark.* Mo knew that brooding pink sky, the plump faces of the girls, and the power of what was not painted. Mo had no idea what Restoration actually entailed. She raced to the front desk and explained her MFA status as if it was the highest government security clearance, pretty much demanding to see a Restoration in progress at that very moment. The receptionist was serene, telling Mo no such thing was currently possible, but that perhaps, maybe, here's an email, see what you can do? It was Gabrielle Socorozini, Head of Art Restoration at the Milwaukee Art Museum. Mo drove home composing the introductory email along the way. She called Bremen.

"I might quit the MFA program and transfer over."

"Who is this?"

"I'm going to apply for the Fine Art Restoration track." Mo heard the whirr of his juicer. "Hello?"

"I'm here."

"Well?"

"Why would you do that? You paint. You're a painter."

"I'll be there in five minutes. I'll explain everything."

It was fifteen and she explained the intoxicating possibilities of bringing art back to life, a metaphorical fountain of youth, restoring paintings so they never looked aged or worn or neglected. It was a chance to honor the originality of the artwork and the intentions of the artist.

"That'd be like me categorizing old compositions instead of playing them."

"It's what I want to do."

"You're just going to give up painting?"

"I'm sick of people talking shit all the time. People just talk shit. I'm done with it." This was a reason but not the reason. Mo was just happy she came up something.

Bremen wasn't buying it. "Shit is the basic unit of verbal currency. Why do you think I play an instrument?"

"Because you're a coward?"

Gabrielle Socorozini responded in a timely manner. There was an extensive explanation, based on Mo's inquiry, of what it took to become a Fine Art Restorer. There was lots of chemistry and anthropology involved. There was a PhD. But it was a statement from Gabrielle on the practical philosophy of Restoration that clinched it. The Restorer, she wrote, must not have any attachment to their work, for it is always in flux and should at any moment be capable of extermination or change. The Restorer does his or her work on a thin layer of varnish, so that it is possible to wipe off and erase thousands of hours of effort in as little as ten minutes if a better technique is invented in the future, or if some previously unknown detail of the painting is unearthed from antiquity. Mo, as if in flight from a bank robbery, escaped to her studio and had no problem with its modest Friedrick and her paintings done, half-done, and not even started. She missed them and hugged the frames and felt, she could definitely feel, all the paintings hugging her back.

ANNIE

THE GIRL APPROACHED ON cue. She had fluffy blue socks, tight blue pants, a plaid blue shirt with the cuffs undone and rolled up to her dry red elbows. Her earrings were topaz, her eye shadow baby-blue. She wore a blue iris headband with dark green lilac leaves. Hair blonde as straw. Eyes tiny as peas.

"I really wanted to meet you."

Mo tilted her head. "Why?"

"I feel like you should know who I am."

"Uh—okay."

"I'm Anastasia. But you can call me Annie."

"Maureen. Call me Mo."

"Oh, I know."

Mo leaned back on the balls of her feet. "How do you know who I am?"

"Bremen—he was my teacher. He would talk about you sometimes."

"In class?" Totally horrified.

"No." Annie dug a fluffy blue toe into the floor.

There wasn't a forthcoming explanation. The distance between them widened—a thousand feet, five. They couldn't see each other over the curve of the earth.

"Look," said Annie, her voice suddenly broken and tired beyond all human reckoning. "There is something I have to tell you."

I WILL KILL SOMEBODY
JUST TO HEAR MY JUKEBOX SONG

JUST SAY THE WORDS and ghost him with a complete communications blackout. She never did, never believed it was possible to do, or believed it was possible but not that she could do it. Maybe she loved him more then she consciously realized. Would he see how much better he could do before she succumbed to her naturally submissive desires and threw away her own goals to fuse in one with his? Fuck. That. Better to be bitter and on the lukewarm side of lonely for the sake of her own freedom. Bremen could invade her mind like a virus and disintegrate the neural pathways that made Mo, Mo. One day she'd wake up and be his clone. All that was a dream. All that was a nightmare. She woke up for real, and he was snoring like a baby dragon. She poked his arm and then he was awake. She put her head on his chest and listened to the flames in his lungs and that was how she fell asleep. Dreamless. She woke alone, curled up in the crumpled sheets. Mo was twenty-four and was going to meet millions of men. Bremen brought in two cups of coffee and offered her a mug. She wanted to be alone and didn't want him to leave. "Get in bed." They passed two hours that way because it was Sunday. The window above her bed was open and they listened to the upstairs neighbor's haltering interpretations of Liszt on a twangy piano that hadn't yet grown past puberty. Mo really didn't want to leave this room, this bed, this man's arms, and didn't know what she would do when she had to, and maybe for the first time she admitted, to herself, that she didn't know what love was or if she knew how to love or if she even loved herself. He kissed her temple and got out of bed. Let's go, Momo. You can't paint in your underwear.

ANNIE, AGAIN

"It's about Bremen."

"Of course."

"You don't understand."

"Well…here I am."

Annie scanned the room to make sure nobody was near and nobody could hear. "He wrote me a really good recommendation for my college application. I got in to USC. I'm pretty sure I got in because of him."

"USC, great."

"Yeah."

"What do you study there?" Mo didn't allow a pause to slip in.

Annie, with the coast clear, came clean. "Six months ago, in the summer."

"Uh…you study in the summer?"

"I slept with Bremen."

Mo was a rock, a slab of perfect natural strength. "This was in the summer?"

"I'm sorry."

"When?"

"I'm so sorry."

"It's ok. I'm ok. When?"

"This year."

"That's all?"

"I'm so sorry. I had to tell you. This is probably the only time I would've been able to tell you. Ever."

"Probably."

Mo hid her reaction. She didn't see how Annie could understand. It wasn't jealousy. It wasn't rage. It wasn't relief or despair. It did not rejoice. It's most coherent expression was an action—Mo wanted to hug Annie at that moment. If not Annie, anybody, anybody at all would do.

WITH YOU IT WILL SINK,
WITH YOU IT WILL RISE

A MONTH AFTER BREMEN went down with the ship and five days before the funeral, Mo was up for Critique. She presented an encaustic painting with an abstract rationalism unlike anything she had previously attempted. All bets, it could be said, had been decapitated. She wasn't in love with the painting herself but took a hard pride in the disciplined process by which it was created. The painting, on a 12x16 panel, was a painstakingly symmetrical arrangement of *5 Order-Three Venn Diagrams*, evenly spaced apart so no two diagrams were touching. The circles, alternating dark yellow, light yellow, deep purple, seemed to bore into the panel and rise up off the surface, concave and convex at the same time, depending on the perspective. Mo, out of character, ever so briefly explained, during the swish-swish sound of the class sharpening their knives, that *5 Order-Three Venn Diagrams* took her twenty straight hours to do, sometimes, by her timing, painting a single circle over and over for ninety minutes to produce the best impression she could. Erikson scribbled on the note cards in his lap and turned to the frothing eight-person class and shoved his glasses up his nose. "So what do we think?" Mo didn't explain how she had twelve other paintings similar to this (different only in shape—triangle, hexagon, parallelogram) and hadn't slept more than ten hours a week for the past month and was just trying to find something to distract her mind from pulling apart her flesh, something to seize and harness it like a country boy does to an ox when he straps it to a mill on the unforgiving Wyoming ground and the animal grinds the grain in peace with its existence stripped to pure rhythm.

The customary silence at the beginning of Critique was ignored. Kent jumped right in. "I think it's boring. We did this before, didn't we? Decades ago? Lifetimes have passed. The Mayan calendar ended a couple years ago. There's not much new here."

"The initial impression of aping previously revolutionary but now dogmatic techniques is interesting." Johanne took off her high-heeled red shoes and twisted a finger in her fishnet stockings. "But I don't think this has a purpose. It strikes me as purposeless. Which can be interesting." She sniffed and consulted the state of her stockings. "But I don't think this is interesting."

"I hate circles. A circle is a lie. A circle tells you there's no end or beginning. That's a lie."

"Explains your over-reliance on splatter, Olenya."

"Splatter is the essential method by which the universe sustains itself, Gene, thank you very much."

There followed a two-and-a-half hour discussion on the practical, commercial, philosophical, cultural, and political value or not-value of Splatter, and out of this discussion a Platonic understanding was distilled and brought into the sphere of Art, and the class, unsure but unanimous, decided upon the nature of Splatter and its attendant aesthetic truths as they bear upon human aspirations and conditions. *5 Order-Three Venn Diagrams* passed by without further comment. Erikson never said a word until the end. He now wrote, for the second time, upon the note cards in his lap. He thanked the class.

"Anything you'd like to add, Mo? You've been quiet this whole time." He smiled, big and broad. "Quite a different tactic from you."

"I feel great," Mo said.

Erikson glanced at the class—they were stone-faced. "You feel great? Care to elaborate?"

Mo knew exactly what she was going to say and why she was going to say it. She knew as soon as Kent uttered his first syllable. It was the first time she truly believed the inner meaning of the words and that she was capable of saying them without sarcasm or irony. All during Critique, as the Spatter discussion reigned, Maureen Eileen Tipper remembered running through a field after a rainstorm when she was a little girl—the bristling air, the wet tall grass—a screaming fit of freedom so powerful she could've torn off her clothes and run naked and bloody for miles. That's what she was feeling, there in Critique, the desire to strip nude and howl and race the sun to the horizon. She was on the brink of incredible laughter. She bit down on her tongue. Erikson asked her again to elaborate, on this feeling great thing?

"Because," Mo snapped, "I don't give a fuck what any of you think."

DOOR, *AGAIN AND AGAIN AND AGAIN*

"Also," Annie said, holding her breath, her face frozen for a moment in fear, "I'm responsible for Bremen's death. It was my fault."

Mo's laugh was accidental, a reaction to Annie's ludicrous claim, but it seemed to cut the girl in half. She faltered, and could not meet Mo's eyes.

A couple of guests muscled in on them, chattering about the upcoming meteor shower.

"It's supposed to be clear."

"How clear?"

"The storm is supposed to pass by ten pm."

"And it lasts twenty minutes? Hi, Mo. Boots. Black. Size seven."

Mo, on autopilot, retrieved their shoes without comment, and when they scuttled away, Annie was gone.

There was a sudden run for shoes, and everybody was talking about Bremen. Bremen this, Bremen that, Bremen Bremen Bremen. It occurred to her that they presumed him infallible. Mo was the sober girl in the land of blind drunks. She didn't fix him on a golden pedestal and kiss his feet. Was delusion that strong with death? How could people not understand that this whole funeral was an event to make up for all the surreptitious shit he did, things nobody knew about, things he didn't have to take responsibility for because he was dead? His secrets large and small. Mo knew one of them now. It made her feel stronger than death, for a little bit. It made her think of death as a false show, a futile weapon in fighting the truth of a person's life. She imagined some people repaired electrical lines or sorted mail or opened expensive restaurants or wrote travel brochures. She wanted to completely master the Art of Painting, and eventually she'd figure out that she could never reach that goal, never fully master and know the Art of Painting, and then she would die. And that would be fine. It would be enough. The Lyons' door was the beginning. She'd give up her signature encaustic style. She'd toss her panels, and work with gouache on paper, or oils on canvas. She'd build a frame with Basswood and buy Belgian linen with the tightest weave she could find, and paint simple objects with repetitive meditative strokes to invest them with a sense of anguish, delight, spite, bliss—all the paradoxes of our nature. If this wasn't a funeral, if she did not have certain responsibilities, Mo would've slipped on her jacket and boots and stomped outside and stood in the cold as a test of her will against the world. *Let's see what you got*—a zombie apocalypse, the second coming, pole shifts, tsunamis, or the blue beams of an alien invasion. Wind goes around the stone. Fire doesn't cross the lake. No matter the strength of the elements coming at her she was stronger, stronger, stronger.

BY LAW YOU WILL GO THERE, BY LAW IT WILL COME

SPEAKING OF RESPONSIBILITIES. IT'S been twenty minutes and nobody's knocked on the door or asked for their shoes. There's a classical dance playing, something folksy from the Highlands, and it reminded her of Steen's painting where a man was blowing smoke in the face of a drunk woman. Mo had the urge to explore. She deserved a break. She drifted through the dining room and kitchen and hallway. She toured the bar-garage and waved to Blaze, who waved back. Donna didn't track her down. The guests parted before her. They smiled when she drew near and nodded when she drifted past. Everyone seemed to know her and act like she was a friend, and they did know her, she was a friend. In the living room, Mo lingered at the edge of the crowd. It swayed before her, securely knit. She didn't force her way into the dancing—it came to her. The crowd recognized Mo and opened itself and drew her in with its tentacles, and when the Music felt so good her eyes shut by themselves and she was cat-pawing the air, it closed behind her.

EIGHTH MOVEMENT

I see you, Vera, in a man's grey overcoat, and you are saying that I am your sister. This I will remember for the rest of my life. I will remember it was tweed and double-breasted. I will remember the charcoal-colored buttons and the chalky stain on the left arm I thought was snow. I will remember how you wrapped it around yourself and how it covered you completely and dropped to your ankles, hovering like a magic carpet. You, Vera, snug in wool. I will remember the steadiness of your hands that clung to the coat in the cold. I will never forget how cold it was. You had barn-red hands and fingernails you must've chewed on. I will remember the cloud of my breath wafting in your face, but you didn't blink. It was intimidating. Only Bremen has looked at me like that. I was very happy to be your sister at that moment. This is what I will remember. This is what will carry the entirety of the Bremen's funeral in my mind. I have chosen this picture and I am fixing it in me so it will be a source of constant power.

I see you, Vera, because I must, because this is how I've trained myself to think long before Bremen talked about a Musical Imagination. He was my teacher. In Bremen's Musical Imagination, you, the musician, must develop the ability to imagine yourself as part of the audience that's watching you play. Teach yourself to see in a third-person perspective as you practice singing or playing your instrument because this lets you see more clearly how your body takes part in the creation of the music, and if you can make the body memorize how it sings or plays you will never forget. The clearer you know your body the clearer you know your music and the clearer you know your music the clearer you know your body. I am creating my confession. I am going to confess. I must have an audience, and that's you, which I decided at the funeral when you said that I am your sister.

My full name is Anastasia Elena Jones and I hate it so that's why you call me Annie. I'm twenty. I grew up in a bubble of no history. I was born in Wisconsin but didn't come from any place or time. My father was born in Texas and that's all I know. He's never told me anything about his life or what any of the ugly faded tattoos that cover his arms mean. He's a Crisis Counselor. My mother is forty and has a limp. She says she was born without some supporting bone in her foot but I don't buy it. The rest of her body is beautiful and she doesn't carry herself like she was a cripple from birth. I've seen old pairs of high-heeled shoes buried in her closet and overheard her talk about dancing, about swimming in the lake, how she misses it. My parents were deliberate ghosts somehow able to make meals and work at jobs. But they didn't try to haunt my thoughts on the slightest matter. I was, if I wanted to be, left alone. They allowed me to be who I am. They did not try to shape me as they wanted me to be.

The Little Duck is a children's book. It was a present for my fifth birthday. I'm looking at it now. There's no cover—it's long since disintegrated. The edges are brown and mushy, with food stains and faded marker doodles ruining some pages. Still, the stapled binding remains strong despite the millions of times I've read it. Each page contains one or a series of photographs along with captions and narration about the life of a duck named Ronny. This book was the beginning of my life. I don't remember much before it. After: I wanted ducks. Baby ducks, preferably, yellow fluffballs with rubber orange feet, hordes and hordes of them. There is a photo on the first page of the book, a close-up of an egg nestled in the grass by a pond. That was the dominant image of my childhood. If I think of that, I can recall years and great spaces of my life. My mother still keeps a picture I drew at that time: a white piece of construction paper filled with ducks of all colors and shapes. There is barely any white left. At the top of the drawing I scrawled in black marker *Yes Ducks More Ducks*.

We had no pets. My father did not trust animals. I read every single duck book from the library, twice. *Yes Ducks More Ducks*. I would always be saying that around the house, at breakfast, lunch, and dinner. It drove my father insane. He'd escape to the back porch or sit in the garden even if it was raining or too many mosquitoes were biting. I was seven.

Every night before going to bed and every morning when I woke up and every spare moment in between—I thought about finding an egg and raising a baby duck. I memorized the photograph of the egg nestled in the grass. I re-read *The Little Duck*. I imagined going to a pond and searching through the tall itchy grass, bugs zipping by my face, sweaty, hopeful, and there it would be, a pearl in the shade of a thicket not ten feet from the water's murky edge, my egg. I'd bring it home in secret and incubate it at the perfect temperature and when the hatchling broke out of the shell, poking a little hole with its beak and pushing to get through, it would look up and peep at me, blink like a tired old man, struggle with its matted wings, almost there, and at the moment of freedom I'd say, *You can do it*, and he'd bust out and stand up and fall over and stand up again and shake his wet fur and clean off the blood and fall asleep. I named him Ducky and imagined taking him for his first swim in a kid's plastic wading pool, feeding him homemade duck mash, stroking the stiff white feathers that grew over his yellow down. I lived in a state of quiet expectation, as if at any moment these images might materialize around me. *Yes Ducks More Ducks.* I remember spending a lot of time at city parks and lakes, searching.

It happened when I was nine—not the way I imagined, but still the way I imagined.

A baby duck wandered into our front yard.

Now, we live in the suburbs. There are no ponds or rivers or small-forested areas nearby. We don't see ducks unless we go to a park or a lake. But when I opened the front door to go to my friend's house down the street, and saw the baby duck rummaging in the nearby grass, well—love, Vera, can happen in one sixty-fourth of a second. I took him inside and washed him in the sink and dried him on low with a hair dryer and fed him mashed up corn from a metal can, by hand. I called him Ducky. My mother said we should wait to tell my father. I said it was useless to hide. She pleaded with the ceiling cracks like they were stained glass windows in a church. I helped her cook a fat steak with potatoes and roasted vegetables. My father's death row meal.

When he opened the front door, Ducky began piping his head off.

I lifted him up and calmed him down and he carved out a place in my chest. I approached my father, who was still standing in the doorway, and surrendered.

There was a very specific look on his face. I don't remember seeing it again. Though I hadn't said a word, and neither had my mother, my father looked absolutely beaten. Defeated. His face was slack and helpless, holding no anger or surprise, as if he knew this was going to happen, as if he had, just last night, dreamt some horrible prophetic dream of this very situation and here it was in waking life. My father confronted the demons of addiction, self-hate, and self-destruction on a regular basis. He saw the black convoluted heart of humanity in close-up, examining the sludge in arteries and veins. I'm certain he tried to talk people out of suicide, and failed.

He spoke to me, but was glaring at Ducky. "Not at the table or in the bathroom." He climbed upstairs, showered, poured a tall glass of iced tea, and sat outside on his lawn chair and didn't even come in for dinner.

That night, in bed, with Ducky burrowing and burrowing in the nook behind my ear, vibrating his happy little body in sleep, I thought about all the circumstances that brought him to me, and became convinced I had a great and fantastic power. Over and over, for years, every day and every night, I would think about finding an egg and raising a baby duck. And then a baby duck came to me. All the strangeness and complexity of his arrival could be reduced to a simple motive: I wanted to feel his body against mine and now I could feel his body against mine. My devotion caused Ducky to appear. I made a promise to myself. Whenever I wanted something, something of major importance, wanted it more than anything else in the world, I would create a very detailed image of what I wanted, make it crystal clear, fix it in my mind, and fuel it day and night and night and day with a vast and eager desire for it to appear.

Funny thing—it worked. Sort of.

When I was eleven I wanted singing lessons, so I created a situation where every day in my mind I had singing lessons.

I enter a large studio room with bare walls and a hardwood floor. There's a highly polished microphone stand in the middle of the room. An upright piano, wheels locked down, top up, is off to the left. There's optimal warmth to the room, a sonic richness palpable to the touch, allowing me to easily resonate with the space. I stretch my neck and shoulders and bend deep at the waist, warming-up with lip bubbles and tongue trills, nay and nee, gee gwee go no no go no. I have a free and flexible larynx and perfect sound pressure in my head. As I sing, my teacher, a man with a beard and slick black hair, imparts instructions with a wave of his disfigured hands. I have smooth golden tone.

Three months passed. At the 70th birthday party of a distant uncle, there was a young man with long snaky fingers and he started to strum folk and blues on a guitar. My mother nudged me. I sang along with him. We meshed well. He applauded me with a thump-thump-thump on the wooden body of the guitar and asked if I took singing lessons. My father, who had an arm around my shoulder, explained how there really wasn't any time for me to do that.

"I know someone good, really good, for cheap."

My father shrugged and said, "The days are just packed."

The man turned to me. "Find the time." He wore a grey T-shirt with the phrase *Stop Vowel Abuse* written in rainbow-colored letters across his chest.

Nobody relayed the specifics to me, and I didn't ask, I think I was in shock, but a week later my mother drove me to an Art Studio Collective west of the University on Monroe Street. It was an old brick building and I walked up five flights of cold iron stairs, my arches burning, my armpits damp. There was only one room. Jo-Ellen Savoire, Vocal Coach. She was a middle-aged woman who looked and smelled like a brand-new ulta-chic designer handbag.

"My friend told me you had a talent for singing."

"Oh."

"Sing your favorite song."

Ten bars into it she held up her hand, and it was a beautiful hand, as faultless as her face was crinkled. "How much do you like singing?"

"Um. A lot?"

"We must find out if this is something you, and more importantly, I, am sufficiently committed to go through with."

After an hour-long interrogation, I became her student for seven years. She built the confident foundation of my voice and etched her initials into the concrete before it dried.

Here's something you have to know about me, Vera: I grew up in very regular circumstances. My mother has always been the most positive influence on my life, and my father, in his own distant way, is proud that his daughter sings. It's amazing just to be able to say that. I did not crawl through thirty-nine kinds of green and purple shit for mysterious reasons. I was never abused, assaulted, violated, or harassed. I've heard many stories and have many friends who swam, and are still swimming, through that river of shit. The scale of suffering on this planet every day is not something I'm capable of imagining. The trauma and depravity is visceral and unforgettable and evident in the faces I pass on the sidewalk, in audiences I sing for. I haven't gone through such things. I'm not a victim of anything. I wasn't born one or raised to be one. I do not self-identified as one. Everyone has their cute go-to phrase about how all people can be lumped into this pile or that pile, category A or category B, and this is mine: people either think themselves to be at the mercy and whim of the universe, or they don't. I don't. Do I believe this because I didn't have to crawl through thirty-nine kinds of green and purple shit? I think so. If I were verbally abused by my father or violently raped by a friend would I believe myself to be a victim? I believe I would think that, yes. But at the same time I believe every good thing and every bad thing that happens is not as important as how you think about those things, how you make sense of them, interpret them, value them, the story you tell yourself to understand them, because good and bad might be different for different people in different contexts, no matter the lightness or severity of the event, and nobody can see each piece of thread in the massive weave or the beginning and end of a single line of cause and effect.

I don't want to forget why I'm here. Bremen pulls me into wild tangents, grabbing my hand when he jumps off the path and breaks into the undergrowth at the edge of a hot jungle. But I want to take you through my cold forest and its open spaces of clean permafrost. I grew up a normal teenage girl. I sang in the choir, even solos. I had a minor talent for Ceramics and English and Social Studies. I wasn't popular but I wasn't anonymous. There's not much to say about this side of my life. The other side? I developed what I called my Major Talent.

I learned that the picture in my head would only appear in the outside world if I pictured it accurately and in the correct situation. Yet however clear and detailed I made my pictures they never appeared that exact way in real life. What I pictured in my mind—singing lessons, Ducky swooping through the clouds—were blueprints or patterns and whatever force creates the universe presses these patterns into happening like a silkscreen print, but in the pressing there must be some sort of variation and leeway so that the event in the world is similar to but not identical with the picture in my head. This is how I tell it to myself.

The true power of my Major Talent was obvious after I had sex. The first two boys were about three weeks apart, played soccer and hockey, and were dumb as rocks. I started getting attention from a lot of people I didn't care about. This went on for a while. After one of our homecoming football games, I walked to a neighborhood pizza joint and sat on a bench, waiting for my slice to heat up. There was that wet flour smell and yeast baking in a brick oven at seven hundred and eighty-six degrees. Suddenly I felt really, really lonely. There was no one I could talk to and connect with, no one who could understand and appreciate all of who I was, all the things I was proud of and ashamed for. Nobody knew me or desired to know me. The pizza arrived on a white picnic plate already translucent from grease. I ate half and threw the rest away. The garbage can didn't have a top and I could see my half-eaten piece was the only thing in there. It also seemed very lonely and sad. I remember the moment clear: I was looking at my pizza in the garbage, teeth marks on the crust, melted cheese sliding off the sauce, and I thought, I can bring a better person into my life, another real live human being, someone I actually want be around.

Mind is future. Matter is past. You have an idea, Vera. And it's a miracle it ever happens.

I imagined myself with a man. Not a boy. A man. I listed every attribute I wanted, mental and physical, wrote the details down on paper and read that paper every day, slipped it in the back pocket of my jeans, the waistband of my underwear, the cup of my bra, and if I lost it or it somehow became unreadable I'd copy it out again and carry it closer then before.

Two years later, at the beginning of my senior year of high school, I was allowed to take classes at the local community college—a Modern Literature class for college credit, and Music Form/Theory. You know who taught this one.

He wasn't exactly the man I imagined.

Bremen was a bad teacher, bad in the sense that he couldn't connect with anybody who didn't share his enthusiasm for the subject. If the motivation didn't come from you he wasn't going to provide it. Certainly you would fail the class. The first day he warmed us up with singing scales. It was stupid. This wasn't Vocal Performance. Half the class wasn't singing (me included) and the rest sang awful. He waved his hands and cut everyone off. He cupped his ear and said, "Listen." We did for a very long time, maybe five minutes, which in a room like that is Infinity. People were fidgety and nervous in their seats. Bremen was composed at the center of the class and in what seemed like a random moment he drew in a deep breath and sang a low b-flat and held it for about twenty seconds. Impressive. He had everybody now, even me. He talked about tone, about body, about posture, about breath, about voice as energy and the emotional effects of a *directed voice*, about everything it takes for a human to generate sound and what the sound says about the human who generated it and that this is what we are going to learn.

When the room emptied out after class I snuck up to his desk and asked straight to his face if he believed what he was saying or if it was just bullshit.

"Oh no," he said with a smile, "It's total bullshit."

But you must know all about this. What he's like. What he was like. *Yes Ducks More Ducks*. Musical Imagination. I am confessing. I see you, Vera, and it's cold.

I was irritated by every little thing he did: the way he pointed like a poisoned arrow at a student texting on their cell phone; the sappy inflection of his lecturing voice; the disgusting smirk on his face when somebody asked a question he thought was beneath him, a cockiness beyond all doubt. In every class there would be at least one moment, usually more, during lecture where he'd speak and look directly at me, through me, into me. I found myself slipping. Sometimes, Vera, you'll find this out, sometimes a girl just can't help moving her body a certain way, intentionally, how she lets an arm dangle off her desk and changes the rhythm of her walk down the hallway and how her head turns when her name is called and how she raises her eyebrows during a high-C and lingers after class and thinks of smart questions to ask and when she gets a response she angles her head in a pre-scripted gesture, so that the tantalizing line running from her chin to her neck to her shoulder is bare and open and wanting to be open. You can't hide this because it's what your body does when it craves another body.

It's not worth recounting details, the hows and whens and wheres. There's only one conclusion. I went absolutely crazy for him. It wasn't fleeting and it wasn't floozy but it was very fast. Sometimes, when I'd stay over at his apartment, he'd be softly snoring and I'd be wide-awake, staring at the ceiling, totally paralyzed, reminding myself, among other things, to not ruin his life by going to my friends or my parents with a psychotic meltdown or his unborn child. My mind flew in circles like a bird on fire attached to a pole. This was what I wanted, a man who I could spend some high-quality time with, so why was I so scared? I was eighteen. He was twenty-six. I was his student. He had a girlfriend. Nobody knew about us. We met after dark and I left before morning. None of that bothered me. What bothered me were the pictures forming in my head—without any prompts from me. I was ready to follow him, without being asked, into gypsy poverty, unexplored Arctic tundra, small Pacific islands, or an old folks home. Every second he was not with me was a second I was waiting for his return and even though I felt a great possessiveness the waiting didn't have any tinge of worry or jealously, more like an exciting expectation. My blueprints of the future were filled with his face and I was tethered to his presence, loose at first, then the slack was taken away, and it was very difficult to separate Bremen from myself in my own head.

At this point, I was applying for college. I wanted to major in Vocal Performance. I wanted to be an opera singer. I researched the best public and private universities, but I judged and ranked the schools by one key criteria: their distance from Bremen.

I applied to eight in total, and even though it was, in the beginning, very hard to imagine, I pictured myself alone, unlinked to Bremen's presence, as an undergraduate student majoring in Voice at the San Francisco Conservatory of Music. I took virtual tours of the Oscher Salon and the grand Atrium staircase, read bios of the entire faculty, talked to alumni about their experiences via email, applied for a dozen scholarships, viewed documentaries of old San Francisco, studied turn-of-the-century photographs of The Mission District, The Castro, Chinatown, studied BART routes and bus schedules, pictured myself, every day, walking down Oak Street in the chilly morning sun and pushing through the doors of SFCM's main campus building and skipping up the staircase to the one of the vibration controlled floating rooms where I'm sonically isolated from the dissonance outside. My instructor plunks a few notes on a brand-new Steinway grand. A sepia portrait print of Debussy watches me from the wall. I warm up my vocal chords. Out the window, the city is on fire at nine am and this is exactly where I want to be burning.

I live in Nob Hill with three roommates and one bathroom. I attend the required classes listed in the freshman curriculum. I practice the songs for my first college recital. I wake up into my senior year of Madison High School but live in my mind as a freshman Voice major at the San Francisco Conservatory of Music.

I did this for four months, until March, when I got a letter from SFCM—application denied. Three days later, three depressingly long days later, an acceptance letter from the USC Thornton School of Music arrived. Five days later, the Jacob School of Music in Indiana accepted me for the Fall Semester and, after that, Bucknell.

Bremen most definitely did not want me to go to USC. He hated California. It was a self-righteous hate. He's never been there. Neither of us talked about my departure and nobody said goodbye. We both acted like I wasn't leaving even as I flew to L.A. for my vocal audition and registered for classes and got my money set-up from student loans and scholarships and found a house off Figueroa Street with two girls and three guys. I definitely didn't want to live in the dorms and made a good case for it with the lie that my singing would suffer. On September 1st, I drove out to California with my mother and father and began the semester a week later, transported from one planet to another, just what I wanted.

Funny thing—it didn't quite work.

Distance doesn't always mean escape. Bremen and I emailed back and forth. An occasional text or phone call. He wasn't physically in my life but he was always present. Every lecture, every voice lesson, every party on the beach, every concert at the Bowl, every gaudy storefront on Wilshire Boulevard, every time I felt satisfied or frustrated or wondering what I was doing, in the middle of class, in my bed—he was the voice inside, commenting, judging, baiting, questioning. I came to think of his words as a recording of rain on the river playing in the background while you study. It wasn't necessarily a distraction, until it was. The desire to be with him, to follow him, was alive and kicking.

After the first semester, on home for Christmas break, I broke it down and figured out my mistakes. I pictured myself away from Bremen, but I didn't picture myself free from his influence. Distance is not escape. We kept in contact. This was a mistake. We slipped into familiar patterns across half a continent. This was a mistake. I didn't explore great portions of Los Angeles because I was fixated on a man playing bass in Wisconsin, a man who possessed me, a man who didn't have a good influence on me, kept me bottled, in his clutches, in his dissonant lair, a man who didn't want me to express the full range of my life. I made up my mind not to have any more contact with him, in any way, shape, or form.

But I saw him in January, after New Year's, before I had to go back to California for the start of Spring Semester. We parted again without saying goodbye. I thought of myself as a weak and terrible person, which I had never done before. I couldn't stop what I wanted to stop. On the flight back, over the Rockies, with the last dark pink of day capping the mountains, I knew I needed to picture my life completely void of Bremen.

I resorted to blacking him out of my thoughts. I didn't answer his emails, calls, or texts. I resisted the urge to write or call or text him. I resisted the urge to even think about him. I pictured myself as a hulking samurai warrior in heavy armor, a sheathed sword on my right hip and a spear in my left hand, standing at the top of hill in front of a large wooden torii that marked the start of a path winding up into misty peaks, white sun was at my back, and before me the big bad world, so when a thought came rolling up I let the white sun expose all shadowed parts, and if it found a dark and stormy aspect connected to Bremen, I sliced the thought to pieces.

I had never been so tired in my life. My voice broke in the middle of a scales exam. I had trouble maintaining even tone. I couldn't relax my throat and normally hit the notes I used to hit and move through the registers with the smoothness I once did. The choice was: give up guarding my mind or give up trying to sing.

I wanted to sing.

Bremen returned to my thoughts and, soon enough, to my life. Nobody's fault but mine. I called but didn't speak. He called. I didn't answer. He called again. I answered. I felt myself falling from a plane and didn't care one way or the other if I would die, the falling felt so scary and so good.

I saw him over the summer and everything was the same. In August I flew back to L.A. and bribed one of my roommates with a smuggled six-pack of Spotted Cow to drive me up to Point Dume. I walked the seaside trails for miles and miles. My feet would get sore and I'd stop and sit and an ocean breeze is the healthiest thing in the world. I thought about my Major Talent and what it actually was and how it really worked—I created a picture, I fed that picture with a spirit of constant expectation, and the picture, or a variation of the picture, would appear in my life.

It was like my desire was a fuel and my mind was a focus, and I sent out into the world this tentacle web that attracted and captured the specific things I needed for my picture to appear. It all depended on how clear-cut the web was and how strong I sent it out into the world and how effective it was at capturing what it was designed to. People are echo chambers attuned to certain wavelengths, bouncing signals off other people on the same frequency, and my net captured the signals at the level it was attuned to. And that's when it made sense. Bremen and I shared the same level. He was in my head because he was alive and thinking thoughts, feeling emotions, acting in space, and no matter how hard I tried to cancel him out, we were too strongly attractive. It wasn't enough for me to stop thinking of him. I needed to stop his thoughts from having an effect on me. It would be best if I pictured him out of existence entirely, and so, right then, I began to picture his death.

I didn't actually want him dead. I wanted him to have a long fulfilling life and die old and warm but he needed to be amputated from my body and this was the way it had to be done. Board the vessel. Sail out of my mind forever.

In the beginning, the pictures were very general. A natural disaster like an earthquake or a tornado would take him away. I had a dream the Earth flooded and Bremen was at the top of a mountain peak with the waters rising, I was the water, and I rushed in on him and sat up in bed in a hot sweat. Sometimes a plane crash or a bomb would do the job.

My singing voice hit a streak of excellent form. My teachers commented that something must've changed over the summer. They pushed me to keep doing what I was doing. It was working.

The pictures of his death became more detailed, more violent. There could be a break-in at his apartment and the psychos might have a nail gun and they end up crucifying Bremen on the bedroom wall with his cat right beside him. Or Bremen became a soldier in war, captured and tortured. He's dowsed in gasoline and I light a match and watch how the skin curls off his bones. I throw him from the top of Sears Tower and listen to the sound of his splat and the sticky peel of his gory pancake from the sidewalk. Ultimately, I whittled it down to one polished image. There was a river I visited with my father when I was young, canoeing downstream twenty-two miles in three days. I took the memory of those waters and put Bremen in them. He floated facedown that river until it emptied into the ocean. It was simple and direct and I seized it, I pictured this with a frequency and a flame I can barely describe because I attached it to the first thing I ever remembered wanting. *Yes Ducks More Ducks*. The center of the sun has nothing on the power of a child's perfect desire.

Most people have no idea what goes on in their own heads. I have the opposite problem.

Everything I have described and shared, everything I have explained up to this point is in order to have you, Vera, think about and take seriously and eventually come to believe what I am about to tell you.

I killed your brother.

I am responsible for his death.

I imagined him floating down a river to the sea and he drowned off the coast of South Carolina. There is no excuse and no other conclusion. I imagined him dead and now he is dead. This would not have happened if I did not pour myself into picturing it happening. Sometime after his death, in my survey class of Modern Lit, I read a poem called "Rounding the Horn", about a merchant ship sailing around Cape Horn in Chile, which was described as a place "that tramples beauty into wreck / And crumples steel and strikes the strong man dumb." Cape Horn, as an idea, as a destination, wormed its way into my mind for a very good reason.

It's a graveyard. It's where the massive bodies of the Atlantic and Pacific confront each other on equal footing. The continental shelf rises fast and the deep ocean trips over itself and wave upon wave builds up into notorious rogue swells. The winds blow clear all the way around the world and when they are funneled into the narrow passage of Tierra Del Fuego and the Prime Head of Antarctica, a six hundred mile stretch of the roughest water on the planet, they can reach monster hurricane status. Here, at this Cape, hundreds and hundreds of ships have been destroyed, and thousands and thousands of men have drowned.

It sang to me.

And this is the reason: the pain I saw in everybody else, the pain they wore like tattoos or flashy clothes, this pain I once hovered above is what I'm now swimming through. It has shaped me into a strong person with a strong mind, has given my voice a depth and texture I was not born with. Pain did all this without me aware of it because I have always tried to avoid and forget the source and effects of pain as long as I had the ability to do so. My trip to Cape Horn will be hard and difficult because I want it to be. I want to experience the pain of the world without a buffer. I am aware of how suicidal this sounds.

But I don't want to be an opera singer anymore, or go back to USC, or stay in Madison. I don't know what to do with my life. No superior and lasting answer will come without the pain involved in the act of answering.

I will travel by foot and by car, by plane and by ship, through North and Central and South America, and I imagine myself seven thousand miles older, stepping off a charter boat at the bottom tip of Chile, scrambling up a stony beach onto the island of Cape Horn. This is a test of my limits, what I'm capable of, what I can bear—I don't know my threshold on any of these things. I have killed a man. I must search through my own life and discover how I am going to take responsibility. I can do this if I travel through the Americas and step off a charter boat and touch the stony beach on a late afternoon and taste the sea-spray whipping up the air. I am tired and wet and it's as cold as the night of Bremen's funeral. I have eight new scars on my body. I'm very hungry. The island is treeless, but lush from frequent rain. I walk to the far southwest side and hike up a granite bluff, the very same one that has meant death to so many men who have seen it abeam from their ships. The walls are steep and contoured by the waves into organ pipes. They are playing a hymn. The winds chant the chorus. The sea keeps rhythm with its whitecap swells. In this song, I feel the weight of the life behind me and the raw power of the waters stretching into a future blue I can only sing about. To the west lies a solid wall of blackness, a storm of ominous legend rolling towards the Cape as if to swallow the island in one gulp. It is so beautiful that I have no more energy to stand. It is here, at the edge of the bluff, on my knees, at the door of everything, where I can finally say I'm sorry, to you, Vera, and to Bremen. To be completely hollowed out and then filled with an understanding beyond anything I can comprehend right now. It is here where I will be able to stand and steady myself in the middle of primal forces and say it was worth it.

Everything that has ever happened to me has been worth it.

One hundred years from now I will see things in a different light, but you called me your sister in a man's grey overcoat and this I will remember for the rest of my life. I will think of you every time I am drained, afraid, and suspicious, at every low point, at every moment of despair and hopelessness, I will remember the lines of your face and the tone of your voice and believe with all of my heart in the sister I have back home in Wisconsin, living the cold and snow.

We'll meet again, Vera. I don't know where. I don't know when. Maybe you're a marine biologist and maybe I teach Spanish to children, but we'll hug like old friends and talk about my letter and our past. You'll show me a picture of your family, and I'll give you a phrase that I memorized ever since the Cape. It was inscribed on a plaque beside a lighthouse on the Island and strikes a personal note for both of us because I don't get the chance to speak much English anymore and you spend a lot of time underwater.

I am the albatross waiting for you
at the end of the world.

Love,
Annie

NINTH MOVEMENT

"Hello! And welcome to—"

"Hello yourself. When is the next flight to Milwaukee, Wisconsin?"

An efficient female attendant behind the Delta Airlines ticket counter tapped the keys on her computer.

"Seven-twenty this evening," in a gravelly voice, as if she'd been a professional bartender for decades. Her tag said *Jeanne, Flight Coordinator.*

"You got to be kidding me."

"I'm sorry, sir?" Jeanne spit out.

"Are. You. Kidding me."

"No, sir. The next flight to Milwaukee is at seven—"

"When's the next flight to Chicago?"

She was less carefree with her hands over the keys.

"Three-forty five but—"

"When does it arrive?"

"Scheduled arrival time is five-thirty pm. However, sir—"

Maxwell Herbert Bachoven raised the sword of his hand and cut Jeanne off.

The general sonic swarm of Atlanta International washed over them both like an ocean riptide. It was peak time at the airport. Jeanne breathed shallow. Maxwell remained in his thoughts, undistracted.

"Book me a ticket for the three-forty five to Chicago."

Jeanne didn't move a fingernail.

Maxwell, for the first time, looked at directly her. "Don't tell me."

"I have been *trying* to tell you that that flight is fully booked, sir. I can get you on the next available flight to Chicago at six this evening."

"No. No. No. No."

Each 'no' was more menacing the softer and more inaudible it became. Nobody, none of the other Flight Coordinators along the polished silver counter, none of the passengers they were successfully assisting, none of the travelers lined up like an endless Amazonian snake behind them, nobody heard him except Jeanne.

"Listen to me carefully." Maxwell leaned in close and pressed his lips tight. "Are you listening?"

Jeanne sneered.

Maxwell became impassive. "I'm not going to tell you my story. You don't want to hear all that bullshit anyway. But I am going to try and impress upon you how important this flight is to me."

The staring match continued.

"I am on my way to a funeral. I cannot miss this funeral. If I am not on the three-forty five flight to Chicago I will miss this funeral." He smiled the defeated smile of a man about to jump off a building. "If I miss this funeral, then I am going to kill you."

Jeanne backed up and widened her eyes. "Sir, you're going to have to—"

Maxwell held his frame. He did not have to raise his voice. He spoke his words in the tone of an adult addressing a child with precocious intelligence but no life experience.

"Please understand. This is a matter of life and death. *Your* life and death. You have two options, Jeanne. One, you generously bump someone off the three-forty five flight to Chicago and get me a ticket, after which you'll never hear from me again."

She crossed her arms and scowled.

"Two, you can refuse to issue me a ticket, and if you do that, then I will kill you. Not here, not now. Your name is Jeanne. You work for Delta. I might wait here until you get off work and follow you home. Or I'll hire a private detective to find you for me. Shouldn't be too hard. I will find out where you live and kill you. I'm not a violent or perverted man. I don't need to chop you up with an ax and eat your organs. I don't need to drag you behind my car for twenty miles on a gravel road. I'm just going to quickly and quietly take your life. And it won't matter who you tell. Call your supervisor over. Call them, Jeanne. Pick up the phone right now. Call the TSA. There they are. Wave your hand and they'll come running. Explain what I've said to you. Explain how scared you're feeling. Explain how I've threatened you. I won't deny it. I'll repeat my threats. Word for word. Sure, I'll miss the flight. I may get arrested. I may have to pay a fine or even serve jail time. I do not care, Jeanne. I don't care. I will find you and I will kill you."

Jeanne glanced to the right and the left in a soft growing panic, opening her mouth to call over one of the Flight Coordinators. Maxwell tapped two fingers on the counter. It sounded like the thud of a broken piano key.

"I'm right here."

She came back to him.

"You have to understand, Jeanne, my life doesn't matter to me. I don't care if I'm caught after I kill you and have to spend the rest of my life in prison. I don't care if I get the death penalty and sit on death row for a decade. The police can't help you. They can't guard you twenty-four hours a day seven days a week for the rest of your life. You'll die by my hand, whether it's next week or on your 80th birthday. I will risk my death and the deaths of other people to be on this flight. These are the consequence of your decision right here, right now. Think of me as a dispassionate judge and executioner. As the legitimate Angel of Death. You're having a brush with a power that will wipe you off the face of the Earth like dust from a bookshelf. Look at me. Look. You will not see any human feeling. I am not human. Your life holds no special meaning for me, and neither does my own. So believe me when I say, Jeanne, believe every word I'm saying to you: if you do not get me on this flight, I will kill you."

Jeanne had collapsed into a blank helplessness, like a small child who has done something very wrong that she didn't know about and was just beaten by her father for doing this very wrong thing she didn't know about and had turned into a puppet that only responds to commands and manipulations.

Maxwell straightened himself and put both hands on the counter. He waited a respectable amount of time. "Jeanne?"

She kept her eyes down on her grey Delta pantsuit and made no sudden moves, speaking in a voice more feeble than the neck of a sparrow. "Yes, sir?"

"Please check me in for the three-forty five flight to Chicago." Maxwell pushed his identification and credit card over to her.

Jeanne did not immediately move. Maxwell didn't ask her to.

Soon, of her own accord, she took his ID and credit card and tapped the keys on her computer, tapped them deliberately, afraid of making a mistake, so that her eyes welled up and a few tears rolled like lightning down her cheeks.

"Window or aisle?"

"Window."

"Baggage to check?"

"None." Maxwell tilted his head at her. "Breathe, Jeanne. Just breathe normally."

She let out a breath and tried to take another but her chin and lips began to tremor like someone in progressive shock. She wiped each side of her face with the palm of her hand. The boarding pass dropped in its slot from the printer.

"Hand me the ticket, Jeanne."

She did.

Maxwell Herbert Bachoven eased without further incident through the TSA Checkpoint and into Terminal B, where at Gate 29 he found an empty row of seats and sat down in patch of sunlight that had made the leather hot, shedding his travel bag and reclining like a lion on a rock after feasting.

WHO WILL SAVE US from Western Civilization?

This was the question he had been asking himself most of his adult life, and now he didn't give a shit. Its presuppositions were philosophically insane. Nothing could save anybody from anything, which meant, for Maxwell, death, pain, decay and whiplash change. *Western*

Civilization will end. *Us* will end. The appeal for salvation (and that was the lie he swallowed hook, line, and delicious sinker—don't we all want to be the Savior?) was an act of ignorance, because saving is not possible if there is nothing to be saved from, and there is nothing to be saved from. Of course, Maxwell knows this now.

In the midst of his second hour at Gate 29, ninety minutes before boarding, a woman wheeling a petite suitcase and shepherding two boys, took over a section of seats opposite Maxwell. He pretended to read a book, but went into stealth assessment mode. He was very good at watching people and not calling attention to himself. You need that ability as a university provost.

The mother, without her children, would never be mistaken for a mother. Besides rocking peep-toe red stilettos, she wore a long burgundy summer dress with a white leather half-coat that made the most of her scaled down but harmonically proportioned body. Her face was plump in the best places and perfectly made up. There was a ring on the correct finger, yet Maxwell sensed an air of indifference and exhaustion. She shushed the kids and brought out her phone and fell into a tapping hypnosis. Maxwell pictured his daughter at the beach feeling entitled to another virgin piña colada whenever she deigned to lift her head during those endless sun-tanning sessions.

The two boys couldn't be older than four and seven. The older boy wore Falcons sweatpants and a Matt Ryan jersey and had what looked like scratches from tree branches all down both arms. He was rooting in a bag. The younger boy was in the seat next to his mother. He had a curly mop of black hair and was constantly sniffling and wiping his face on the sleeve of his sky-blue Oxford button-up. He wore khaki shorts and Timberland boots that kicked the air with happy apathy.

Maxwell very much wanted to be back in the time when he was just a kid too small for his seat.

The older brother unearthed a tablet and shooed his younger brother off the seat, assuming a pose similar to his mother. The boy tugged at his brother's sweatpants and was promptly swatted away. This happened two more times in quick succession before the boy, when hit the hardest, made a noise like a squeak toy. The mother snapped at them both, searching in her bag more frantically then Maxwell thought necessary, and bringing out Welch's Natural Grape Fruit Snacks and Lays Potato Chips and two cans of Tropicana OJ. She shoved the bribes in children's direction and rattled off empty threats. Then weirdly softened and petted them each on the head, lovingly as far as Maxwell could tell, and issued a last gentle warning before slipping back into her hypnosis.

The boys noticed Maxwell watching them. Kids always notice. He burrowed into the book and attempted to read but realized, today, the letters did not make words and the words did not make sentences. The boys were still watching him. Each had the same curious detachment, a kind of fascinated boredom, as if they were trying to figure out what kind of creature he was, but didn't care if they ever finally did.

Maxwell didn't want their attention, and sent out pulses of hostility.

Their glances scattered away. The older brother tapped on his tablet, sipping his OJ and munching his chips, the crumbs falling on his jersey. The younger brother drank his entire can of juice at once, jammed five chips into his mouth and a whole pack of fruit snacks, wiped his hands on his shorts, placed the bag and the bottle on the carpeted floor, ambled like a first-time drunk down the aisle, past Maxwell who had to lift his feet to allow for clear passage, and climbed onto the last chair of the row. He stared out the window at the airplanes on the runway, landing and refueling and taking off. He hopped around in his seat. He climbed down and ran to the window, slapping his hands on the glass, looking back at his mother and brother with a face of tremendous joy. They didn't see it. He pressed himself hard against the glass. His mother noticed and muttered something to the older brother, who nodded at his screen, and then she went back to hers. The boy slapped the window again, looked back again, for someone, anyone, to share his delight. He caught Maxwell's eyes for a brief instant, and then a far more interesting thing interrupted them: a 747 inching along outside the window. It was very close. The boy was utterly transfixed—the shadow of the beast blocked out the sun—and like an insect catching the scent of its favorite flower he followed the plane along the glass as it taxied down the runway. Very quickly the boy was out of sight.

The mother and older brother both smiled at their screens like they had been told the exact same joke. Maxwell discretely followed the boy and caught up with him at Gate 33. One boot was untied, and a few cowlicks swirled on the back of his tiny head. There was a lull between flights and only a handful of travelers were in the terminal. The boy followed the plane along the glass until he hit a concrete wall at Gate 42. The plane wheeled slowly out of sight, but the boy, face pressed to glass, remained that way some time. Maxwell thought he might have fallen asleep, but the boy spun around with wide over-stimulated eyes. Maxwell made a show of looking at something else, the floor, the ceiling, the hanging TVs, like the kid meant nothing and held no interest for him, like the kid was dumb animal that would pay him no attention if he didn't pay it attention.

It worked.

The boy slid away from the window and drifted along the closest row of chairs as if he expected to find his mother and brother along the line. He didn't, and so ventured out into the main walkway of the terminal. Maxwell tailed him.

The boy set out in the wrong direction and stepped right into the thick of it. People swerved around him like he was a traffic cone at a race-driving course. The terminal was much more congested now. Maxwell received a number of stares, and realized he was being mistaken for the father. He played along. He shrugged his shoulders in a confident, fatherly, *fuck you this is my kid,* and nodded at those who gave him a weird look, *yep, I know it's weird, but I'm just taking my son on a little walk through the airport—it's his first time! And he's so excited!*

The boy, for his part, would occasionally stop dead and look back at Maxwell the way a driver might look at street signs for directions. Maxwell was certain the boy recognized him, dimly, had pegged him as a non-threatening presence, some sort of guardian, maybe? Whatever it was, the boy seemed reassured each time he looked back. Twice he lost balance and landed on his ass. Maxwell didn't help him up. Emboldened, somehow, he scurried forth through the Terminal in that hell-bent-can't-stop-them-but-with-a-leash-way boys his age always want to go, if you just gave them a chance.

Maxwell dropped off his tail. Ten feet. Twenty. Far enough so that it should have been obvious to anybody that a little boy was lost. Nobody noticed. It was a perceptual thing. The boy was truly invisible. He could not actually be seen, and not because he was at knee level. Maxwell observed the faces of people walking past, faces bent and contorted by varying degrees of pressure and time, by the different tests and trials of every moment of every day of every specialized life. It was difficult, living. Maxwell acknowledged this. He wondered what his mug looked like to a stranger, what they could decipher in the lines and arrangement of his features. Yet the desire persisted, the desire to grab each passing face by the ears and shake it senseless and shout, *what have you been eating? What have you been listening to? What have you been watching? What have you been thinking and doing, all this time, over the course of the last decade? All this time, where has your attention been?* Maxwell figured he wouldn't get much more than the same dumb look he had been giving the boy. People had been trained since birth (Lord knows Maxwell helped train) to see themselves as separate objects randomly interacting in accordance with no objective laws. Alienation was blissful and pervasive and complete. The good old days were extinct and the bad new ones were here, now, where a lost little boy actually was a traffic cone. This is why nobody can be saved. It is not a situation to be saved from. It is situation to be lived through. Ever since the first funeral, Maxwell had taken into his heart (which he never would've taken before) the idea that life and death were just the tests and trials of a single punishing day, a day that can have no end or salvation.

The terminal opened onto a circular commons area and branched off into three different corridors. Maxwell crouched down and pretended to tie his loafers. When he stood he could no longer see the boy.

The expected satisfaction didn't arrive. Instead it was panic, seething panic. The speed of its arrival was compounded by the mystery of its origin. Perhaps it was a strong paternal animalistic instinct.

Perhaps it was guilt. Perhaps it was the certifiable idea that the boy really was his son. Perhaps it was his memory of Jacob when he fell in the autumnal lobby of the Renaissance Hotel and cried, reaching in the air for somebody, anybody, to lift him off the ground. The panic could only be alleviated by one thing: going after the boy.

Maxwell went after the boy.

He plowed through couples holding hands, groups of student travelers, suits on cell phones. He scaled a sandwich cooler near a kiosk to get a better view. He raced along the branching corridors and found no traces. He was heading back up the central corridor when he saw the boy at a boarding gate, standing on a chair with his face pressed to a large window, watching an airplane taxi across the runway. The next thing anybody knew, Maxwell was carrying the boy like a sack of potatoes with their twiggy sprouts curled around his neck. He broke into a slight jog. The boy began to moan, frightened for the first time.

You could hear desperate high-pitched weeping starting at Gate 32. He set the boy on his feet and they walked the rest of the way. The mother's make-up was destroyed. She was surrounded by TSA and Delta personnel. An outer circle of interested passengers whispered to each other, texting all the while. The older brother, standing to the side, looked genuinely traumatized.

Maxwell was smooth in his approach. The older brother was the first to see them. He tugged at his mother's dress. She screamed like she had just been stabbed in the back. The TSA and airline personnel breathed visible relief.

She ran to them in her heels, a shuffled staccato run. When she was near, Maxwell positioned himself between her and the boy. She pulled up short and stared at him, leery and confused. Maxwell took a step towards the mother, forcing her to look him in the eyes, and then, in one fluid motion, he slapped her hard across the face, gathered the boy in his arms, and held him out to her like a toy to be taken.

She took him.

Maxwell's palm print and the outline of his fingers were already starting to show on her cheek. He brushed past her and acted as if the rest of the airport did not exist. It was a self-fulfilling prophecy. The passengers were in shock. Not a single person said a word. He could've been a spiritual savior or a deadly virus—either way nobody touched him.

He returned to his original seat at Gate 29. A miracle it wasn't taken, and still warm from the sunlight. There was so much pleasure to sitting down and unburdening yourself of your own weight. He even took pleasure in the sting of his palm, the beauty of the fizz of pain spreading on his skin. Maxwell knows how to count his blessings. It took his son's death, but hey, he knows now.

MAXWELL DOZED ON THE flight. He dreamt he was at a funeral, his own, that he was a ghost threading through the mourners, able to take in all things at once from anybody and anything he ghosted into and out of. The seatbelt light dinged on. They were descending. Maxwell had a powerful moment of amnesia. His heart tripped over its beats and went numb in his legs—because he didn't have an exact idea of who he was and where he was going and what he was supposed to do when he got there. The passengers sitting in the rows, the drone of the engines, the clothes on his body, the leather bag under his chair, the sunlight burning the edges of his drawn window shade—he could not use these clues to solve the mystery of himself. Maxwell put his head in his hands, rocked back and forth in his seat, and murmured to himself that his son, Jacob Gregory Bachoven, was dead, (*my son is dead, my son is dead, my son—*), that he could at least count on this as a foundation for his reality, and if he traced the line of this thought everything else would flow into the sense of himself.

Not really.

All that flowed was a recent memory of Maxwell, not a drinker, extremely drunk and wandering around Meridian Hill Park at some nameless hour of a night just after the accident, pulling from a pint of Absolut Vodka and pissing in the stone basins. He stumbled into Dante, wearing a laurel crown and scholar's robe. Maxwell, too drunk to care about embarrassment, poured out his problems at the poet's feet—his son's death, the disintegration of his family, the lost of his job as the Provost's Assistant at Georgetown. Dante, sympathetic, came down from his sea-green granite pedestal and asked for a drink. They ambled through the brown grass of the park and Maxwell confessed everything. It felt good to share. Dante listened with attention, agreed, disagreed, said *perhaps* twice and *maybe* three times, killed the Absolut, shrugged when Maxwell said he had no more, and climbed back up on his pedestal, offering no advice. The memory ended somewhere between him puking in the shadow of Joan of Arc and passing out in the marble lap of Serenity. It was enough. The amnesia evaporated. He knew who he was and where he was going: his name was Maxwell Herbert Bachoven and he was going to a funeral. He sat up in the airplane seat and could feel the waves of revulsion coming from the two passengers in his row. They stared straight ahead and cleared their throats like cocking pistols. It did appear, when Maxwell thought about it from another point of view, that his behavior could be described as aggressively abnormal, but these shallow evaluations were beyond him now.

He flipped up the window shade and leaned into the glare of the late afternoon sun bouncing off the plane's wing. Maxwell could see no future after Madison, no solid existence for himself, his vision just flatlined. Though he was not contemplating the suicide his family and friends believed was imminent, he had a foreboding feeling he could not explain, a small stable voice kept telling him this was the end, this is it, a snap of the fingers, a puff of smoke, and no more, no more Maxwell after this.

Bremen Lyons is the last one.

THE COAST GUARD CONTINUED to search for possible survivors, out of professional duty, but they couldn't even locate any hull wreckage from the charter boat the musicians had rented. Maxwell purposefully stayed away from the details. His son was dead—what else did he need to know? Jacob Bachoven's funeral was three days after the sinking. His wife and daughter, digging through rocky soil, planted an acorn next to Jacob's favorite tree in the backyard. People said their peace, said things so unremarkable that Maxwell, when it was his time to speak, turned his back on his family and friends, kicked off his shoes, peeled off his socks, and marched into the public park behind his house like a medieval martyr seeking punishment. He tramped for hours, cutting his feet on twigs and stones. When he was washing off the blood in a muddy creek, a flock of ducks waddled into his orbit eager for bread. They quacked, disappointed in his empty hands.

That night Maxwell rang old friends: the editor of a Charleston daily newspaper; a Junior Lieutenant in the Maryland Coast Guard; an analyst in the Maritime Division of the Department of Transportation. The men spoke very low and clipped their responses at two or three words. They knew. They knew what he wanted and what they had to do to make it happen. Maxwell had the impression they'd been sitting around the phone waiting for his call. He preempted the conversations, else he might break into a blubbering mess.

At five in the morning his friend from the DOT phoned back. Maxwell should expect an email soon. He refreshed his Gmail page every twenty seconds until it finally arrived. The email, forwarded to him by an anonymous agent in the Intelligence Division of the DOT, contained an extensive theory of the cause of the sinking, the list of all thirteen men who had drowned, their names and addresses, and the names and addresses of the next of kin.

Maxwell noticed an address in Vineland, New Jersey, a few hours away. He fixed a pot of light roast coffee and poured it in a giant mason jar and drank it as he drove to the house of Xavi Alejandro Lucas. By quarter after nine, Maxwell was banging on the Lucas' front door. Nobody was home but that didn't stop him.

A neighbor lifted her window.

"They are at church."

"But it's Friday."

"Their son has died."

"So has mine."

She gave him directions to Centro Evangelistico Los Hijos De

Dios, where they were having Xavi's funeral. The church, on an industrial stretch of road next to a boarded up gun shop and a nail salon, was blindingly white and skinny. A plain red cross of careful artistry was nailed above the double doorway. Maxwell knocked, with no idea what to say.

Nobody spoke English. They were reduced to making hand signs and Maxwell couldn't think of another symbol for death besides drawing your finger across your throat. The mourners surrounded him, impertinent, combative, but then a small girl in a dandelion yellow sundress squeezed through the crowd and volunteered to translate. Pella had learned English from cartoons. She was Xavi's ten-year-old cousin. When she relayed the reasons for Maxwell's appearance—who his son was and how he knew Xavi—the church adjusted it's attitude and Maxwell was rewarded with many hugs and ushered up front with the immediate family.

It was a full Service, with readings, songs, prayers, candles, poems, and flowers. Then the mourners traveled to the burial site at a local cemetery. Maxwell shuffled along with the procession, an improbable guest of honor. They buried an empty coffin with a pair of drumsticks on top.

It was here that Maxwell said to Pella, "I think I should be going."

Xavi's mother, sensitive to Maxwell's every move, fired off a series of bewildered phrases at the girl. Pella responded swiftly and at length. The mother beamed, trembled, reached for Maxwell's hand, and he suddenly found himself escorting her through row after row of tombstones and into her car and back to the house. In the cramped kitchen, he cooked beans and rice and learned from eighty-two year old hands how to pound corn tortillas, and who her son was.

Xavi Alejandro Lucas was twenty-five years old and a drummer that lived in the Bronx, picking up freelance studio sessions or jamming at loft parties when on a break from his main gig playing for a jazz band that performed at black-tie events in Manhattan. He had a bulldog named Marcelo. His favorite food was shrimp pasta. He loved Real Madrid. No one asked why he died, no one fell to their knees and begged for an explanation, no one besieged a higher power for justification, and this was a huge relief to Maxwell—they just told stories around the dining room table. Pella, caught up in the memories, no longer translated, and Maxwell didn't mind, content to watch their gestures and note their inflections, and when he closed his eyes a light shined directly into his brain and illuminated all they were saying.

On the ride back to D.C. he sketched out a plan: inform his wife of his intention to divorce; pack three bags of clothes; secure a room at the Renaissance Washington; contact the eleven remaining families; arrange to attend the funerals of the other dead sons and daughters; tell his story, be embraced, appreciated, again and again and again. So he's journeyed to Boston, Savannah, Tuscaloosa, Lansing, O'Fallon, Modesto, Sarasota, Scottsdale, South Bend, Billings, and now, finally, hurtling through space like an asteroid on its fateful course, to Madison, Wisconsin.

Maxwell, running two hours late, rented an Infiniti M56 at O'Hare and drove with a boiling rage through Rockford at rush hour and pushed the needle to ninety-two just over the border on I-39 North, and if a Wisconsin state trooper happened to clock him along the way Maxwell had already arranged his Driver's License, Rental Information, and Insurance Card on the passenger seat, had arranged the tone he would use, the emotions he would project, the words he would unleash when the cop tapped on his window with a gloved fist or a loaded gun.

—

LOST AT THE INTERSECTION of Walter and Atwood, Maxwell squinted at the map on his phone, the screen dimmed from low battery. Snow floated down in heavy feathers like all the angels and demons in heaven and hell were having a pillow fight. Somebody beeped. The light was green. Maxwell rolled down his window and motioned for the truck to pass, and when it did, an old woman in the driver's seat flipped him off and mouthed *asshole* with her face in permascowl, while her husband gazed out the passenger window, as if it was all happening on another planet. Maxwell imagined chasing down the truck and smashing the old woman's head into the hood ornament and telling the husband, "You're free." The light turned red and Maxwell took the chance to program a route into the Infiniti's navigation system, something he should've done in Illinois, and soon a British woman's voice instructed him, turn by turn, to the Lyons' front door, estimated time of arrival, twenty-nine minutes.

464 Newhall Avenue was lit up like gangbusters. Both sides of the street were filled with parked cars, no open spaces for many blocks, and Maxwell didn't have boots to tramp through the snow. He pulled into the empty driveway and his headlights flared up two girls who stood at the end of it—a small girl wearing a man's grey overcoat and a teenage girl in a bright blue jacket.

He killed the engine and scrambled out of the car.

"Is it okay to park here?" Maxwell shouted to the girls.

The teenager spoke. "Yep."

Maxwell expected something more. The two girls stared at him in the same way as the boys at Atlanta International. "This is Bremen Lyons' funeral, right?" He was hesitant, and the girls glanced at each other, their faces cryptic. "Well?" Maxwell said with a touch of impatience.

"This is his funeral," she said.

"Who are you?" asked the girl in the grey coat.

"My name is Maxwell Bachoven. I don't know Bremen personally. But I wanted to come pay my respects all the same." It was vital to speak exclusively with the immediate family about the exact nature of his attendance. Nobody else needed to know. "Are you family?"

"Yes," the little girl said. "We're his sisters."

They looked at each other again, even more ambiguously than before, and his confidence drained away.

"Do you have anything else to wear?" the teenager said, waving her hand dismissively at his black wool suit and tie.

"I have a change of clothes," Maxwell said, wanting to please, confused but wanting to please.

"We're not supposed to wear black tonight. Bremen's wishes." She presented her blue outfit for his gaze. The little girl opened the overcoat and flashed her purple dress.

"Can you change?"

"Um—in the car?"

"We'll wait."

Maxwell was indecisive. He gazed into a nearby pile of snow whose wind-blown contours could have been, in miniature, a giant swath of Arctic Tundra. His son and Bremen were dead, and if respect was to be paid it should be paid in every way. He smiled self-consciously at the girls. "I'll be right back."

Shivering, contorted in the back seat, wool slacks stuck on his ankles, the freezing car leather goosebumping his ass, Maxwell remembered how hard it was to discover the details of this funeral. Out of all the families he contacted and out of all the fathers and mothers and brothers and sisters and daughters and sons he spoke to it was the Lyons' family that was most uncommunicative. Maxwell called every other night for three weeks and nobody answered or returned his messages. It was only two days ago that Donna Lyons phoned and explained there would be no burial, no service, just the funeral at their home as Bremen wished it to be. There was no further contact. His repeated attempts to check-in went unanswered as before. All the other families made him feel truly welcome, had foreknowledge of his journey and shared an eagerness to engage, but out the front windshield he could see the sisters at the end of the driveway, facing his direction, waiting, as tough and inscrutable as the chimerical statues that guard temples built in antiquity.

Maxwell changed into dark wash jeans and a zip-up windbreaker. He gathered the bits and pieces of courage spread over the detritus of his life, gathered the bouquet of flowers he purchased at a florist on the isthmus (he knew how important flowers were), and scooted out of the Infiniti with more poise then he had any right to possess.

They were amused when he returned, as if he hadn't changed his clothes right, but said nothing, only shared another look at Maxwell's expense, as if he was their private joke.

"All set?" said the girl in the grey coat.

A shoveled path wound around the house and opened onto a wide porch in the backyard with a side entrance to the two-car garage. A man in a silver suit was smoking by the door. The sisters slipped inside, and in the space between the door opening and closing Maxwell felt an urge to retreat. He looked to the silver suited man for, what, inspiration? The man tipped an imaginary hat and grinned and motioned with the stick of his cigarette to the door like indicating to a pet that it's all right, it's all right, it's safe. Go inside. Go on, boy.

———

MAXWELL RECOGNIZED THE SONG. John Prine's original version of "Angel From Montgomery." In his college days at Cornell there were parties at the Phi Delta Phi mansion, the one with a high basement ceiling where they played a lot of disco and did a lot of coke and Maxwell would get irritated and slink to the garage that was the designated weed smoking section, low-key bluegrass like Prine on the record player, with dudes passed out in beanbag chairs, and girls in hazy states of undress who pined for free-rambling cowboys, who let the years flow by like a broken down dam, who went to work in the morning and came home in the evening and had nothing to say. This was the spirit of Bremen's funeral, even down to the homemade bar and thrift store sofas, people laughing and leaning on themselves in their own insular groups and greeting Maxwell as if he was cool, but not cool enough to be in their circle.

He stepped on the tail of a cat. It mewled and hissed and raced away. More than a few people looked him over. There was a light touch on his arm and Maxwell whirled about. It was a woman in a green dress. She wasn't startled.

"Donna Lyons," offering her hand. "Bremen's mother. Did you

just arrive?"

"Maxwell Bachoven." His skin was raw and dry. "We spoke over the phone a few days ago?

"You're the one," Donna said. She squeezed him on the upper arm. There was heat coming from her palm. "Maxwell. You made it."

"I made it," Maxwell said quietly. "I met your daughters. They showed me inside."

"My daughters?" Donna jerked her head to the side, the way a dog listens for a sound beyond human ears.

"They were very nice."

"Were they?"

"You must be proud."

Donna Lyons glanced at her bare stocking feet, and it drew Maxwell's attention to his own saddle brown loafers caked with snow.

"Do you mind taking your shoes off?"

He did, and stood there awkwardly with the flowers in one arm and his shoes in the other, wondering if this was a movie set and these were actors and there were hidden cameras and a director off-stage giving commands through secret earpieces, manipulating the mise-en-scène in order to draw out the desired reactions from him.

"You can give them to Mo at the front door. I'll take those," reaching for the bouquet.

Maxwell flinched.

This was the moment he'd been waiting for, it was the moment he always waited for at each funeral he attended, this incredibly fragile moment when he could communicate with the only people who could possibly understand what he was going through, when he could offer them a display of his own understanding of what they were going through, and by this mutual support they could achieve a closeness, however small and fleeting, a feeling of security that emerges from acceptance, but Donna's look of doubt erased the heartfelt speech from his mind, and he gave her the flowers, shamefully, without a word.

She looked at him like mothers look at sons when they want them to go play outside, no matter if the boys feel like it or not. "I'll put them in water. You go have fun."

"Evening," the bartender said. "What can I get you?"

"What do you mean?" Maxwell said, setting his shoes on the bar.

"Would you like anything to drink?" The bartender stared at the loafers dripping snow on the polished countertop.

"What do you have?"

"What do you feel like?"

"You have a full bar?"

The bartender coughed into his hand and put on a kind obvious face. "How do you know Bremen?"

"I don't."

"Lots of people said that tonight."

"Are you family?" Maxwell asked.

"I'm his father. Blaze Lyons."

"You don't know who I am?"

"No."

"Your wife didn't tell you who I am?"

"I don't think so."

On the tip of Maxwell's tongue was a torrent of verbal abuse, but it was muted by the recollection, getting harder and harder to remember, that both Blaze's son and his son were dead, had died together, so how could Blaze not know the nature of their association? And how could Maxwell explain himself now, with the vital weight of other guests actually waiting for a drink? With the rowdy music he had to talk above? There was no intimacy, no space for connection. It was all slipping away.

Maxwell swiped his shoes off the bar and stormed into the house, through a jam-packed main corridor and towards the front door where a young woman in a red dress was flanked by two large shoes racks filled to capacity. Her attitude, so far removed from the somber sentry you'd expect at the doorway of death, resembled a cheerful hostess at the grand opening of a restaurant.

"Would you like a program?" she said breathlessly.

"What do you mean?" His shoes disappeared from his hands.

The young woman thrust a single sheet of paper at him and gestured to the living room. "Everyone's already here."

There was a free space along the wall and Maxwell slumped against it for a number of songs. He read the program, again and again and again, but the thing remained a piece of total gibberish. A multitude of bodies danced about with a laughter and delight that made every fiber of his being burn with incandescent anger. They were supposed to be having a funeral. They were supposed to be revering and lamenting the loved one who was no longer with them. All the other families acted appropriately shell-shocked, hushed, allowing the event to be what it was designed to be: a safe place to grieve. Maxwell was an atheist, but this was sacrilegious.

Suddenly the music cut off. People stopped dancing. They milled about like aimless cattle. Some sort of announcement seemed to be imminent.

"WE WILL HAVE THE eulogy in five minutes," Donna Lyons shouted from the front of the room, the message soaring over the low chattering crowd. "Exactly five minutes. Let's try to accommodate everyone. It'll be a tight squeeze."

Guests began to spill into the living room from every corner and crevice of the house, and Maxwell had to hold on to the shirtsleeves of the man in front of him to keep from getting swept away. Everyone else knew the drill. Small white fold-up chairs were snapped open and arranged, each steel frame snug against the other, in seven rows of five. Three long wooden beams, 2x6x10, were brought in and set flush against the surrounding walls. People stood on these beams and other people stood in front of them, people kneeled, and yet more people sat cross-legged before the kneelers in a human terrace of efficiency. People carved out spaces between each row of chairs and some guests lucky enough to snag a seat had a person in their lap, including Maxwell, hosting an old woman who weighed no more than a pile of freshly fallen leaves.

He was beset on all sides, fourth seat, fifth row. To his right was a man with an expressionless samurai face. He reeked of booze, as did the man sitting on Maxwell's left, one with serious eyebrows and blonde hair rapidly receding. He cradled a glass of golden liquid to his chest and wasn't bothered by the young boy bouncing on his knees.

"Can we bring it down please?" Donna Lyons raised her hands, then gradually lowered them.

It was quiet.

"My daughter, Vera, will now read the eulogy for Bremen. We thank you so much for being here tonight." She ceded the floor.

The sister from the driveway, the one in the purple dress, tentatively stepped into the center of attention, framed by two tall black speakers and a square table with a sleeping laptop screen. She did not raise her head. The papers in her hands shook ever so slightly. Vera Lyons cleared her throat. The crowd held her and held Maxwell, too, held him tighter and tighter, pressing out every last millimeter of mental space, and there was a distinct possibility he could blow and leave behind a crater with finally enough room to think. Before Vera finished her first sentence Maxwell wished on all that was decent and good in the life of his son that the eulogy was already over.

"Bremen was my brother, and he was my teacher. He taught me about music, about astronomy, about history, about anything I wanted to know, as long as I had good reason for wanting to know it. One day, I wanted to know about the light switches on the walls of our house. I wanted to know how you could control the light going on and off from so far away. So Bremen taught me about electricity. He said it could do so many different things. If an electric current passes through the filament of a bulb it creates light. If it passes through a coil in the stove it creates heat. It powers the computer and fridge and the garage opener.

"I wanted to know what created electricity, and where it came from. Bremen said the universe is basically at rest. It's just a rubber band lying on the table. But if you take that rubber band and stretch it—that's electricity. And if you let the rubber band snap back to its regular resting place—that's electricity. It's just motion, the most basic kind of motion. And really, really smart people have found out how to take this basic electric motion and use it to power my toothbrush.

"I remember going to a science museum and watching the video exhibits of what an atom and electron were supposed to look like and how they were supposed to move. I had trouble trying to imagine how fast they were actually spinning. Bremen told me they spin so fast it probably looks like they're not even moving, and I wondered if down there, in places that small, there was electricity. And he said, 'Why do you think they call it an elec-tron?'

"He always made dumb jokes like that. Maybe you heard them. He thought every time he told the same joke, it was different.

"I remember my brother. And I am made of atoms. You remember my brother. And you are made of atoms. And they are always in some kind of motion. They always have electricity. Bremen is my brother. He is your friend. He is your teacher. He is a musician. He's the electricity that makes all our different memories real. We think of him and we are sitting here and he is alive, moving through us."

Vera Lyons lifted her head to the crowd for the first time, letting out a huge breath, glassy eyes gazing beyond, not in tribute, but in brief relief from her deepest fear, and then turned to the low table, woke the computer, cued up the Music, and the speakers blasted out "Your Silent Face," Bremen's favorite New Order song.

The people obeyed Vera's unspoken cues and began to fold up the steel chairs and take away the wooden beams and exit from the living room in a tidy rhythm. Maxwell Bachoven did not play along. He dumped the old woman off his lap and bulldozed through the chairs and guests, bracing his chest and arms so that any obstacle in his path just careened off his frame.

"Whoa, easy there, son."

"Stop pushing!"

Maxwell shoved through a loose cluster of bodies, adding to the trail of wreckage behind him. He approached Vera, doubling in size, transforming into an archangel of moral vengeance, fearless and at full strength.

"You think he's still alive?" Maxwell screamed.

Vera had the frazzled overstimulation of a child who's seen enough of the adult world today. The Music continued and not a soul rose to stop it. "My son is dead." Maxwell made sure the whole house could hear. "He's dead! You think he's here?" He stomped three times on the floor, hard enough to fracture his foot.

Blaze clamped a hand on Maxwell's shoulder—who slapped it away without a second thought. Vera made a move to retreat, only with her eyes, but Maxwell denied her escape, only with his eyes.

"Tell me," clenching his whole head.

Vera stood there glaring at him, defiant and certain.

Maxwell went blind, white spots blotting out his view. He couldn't breathe. He thought he had passed the pinnacle of what he could endure, he thought this was the end, but then his vision swam into focus, Vera his center point, and he rushed at her, grabbing her by the throat with both hands, lifting her off the ground and pinning her against the wall.

Maxwell immediately felt better. He felt more than better. He felt ecstatic. Her faint pulse, her windpipe squeezing like a hard balloon, the knowledge that he would never hear her voice again—it was an enormous pleasure and relief, it was a long sigh at the end of a long day, it was a bench he could sit on, a fountain he could drink from, and then he could sleep, because he was tired now, floating out of the action, and the further away he floated, the less and less he cared about the outcome. The men, seven of them, Blaze included, who had been trying to wrestle the beast down, finally succeeded in peeling him off Vera and slamming him to the floor. Maxwell roared at the top of his lungs, kicked out, fought for his life. They swung at him. He threw wild elbows, some connected, some didn't. A large circle cleared around him like a force field, and though Maxwell had already tossed off the men, he threw haymaker after haymaker at nothing but air until he flopped on the floor, sweating bullets, winded, his eyes darting everywhere and landing nowhere. Donna Lyons was bent over her daughter, checking her vitals. She put a hand on her Vera's red cheek and wiped away her tears. Then Donna stood, stepping into the space between Maxwell Bachoven and the crowd. In her there was a readiness to receive, in her and no one else.

Maxwell prepared himself, cat-slitting his eyes, feeling his killer instinct. She walked right up to him, walked right through an area holding so much violent potential, and all she had to do was touch his bruised knuckles with her fingertips and, like an alternating current, the dynamic was reversed. A gentle shudder ran through Maxwell and his body went limp. His head dropped onto Donna's shoulder. She caught his weight, tucked her arms around his waist, and embraced him.

Let the countdown begin.

Ten...

They fused together and were immobile, their essential natures gravitating towards a new center of harmony, for Donna had engulfed her polar opposite, was actively dissolving his constituent parts, and Maxwell, his form altered, his authority gone, surrendered to the bliss of a different kind of wisdom.

Nine...

Blaze took one step towards them, and that was all he could take. Vera coughed, her face dark and red, her eyes watery and wide. She pushed herself off the floor. In Bremen's sheet music, the bass became the lead for guitar licks to wrap around, and a melodica flooded into the song with all the beauty of a prime Augustus Pablo track.

Eight...

Donna and Maxwell emitted a soft luminosity which absorbed the crowd's attention, gathering their brightest rays, drawing them back to the center, back to the crowd, back to the center, the whole movement a pulsation of increasing power.

Seven...

Emerging from the crowd was a woman. She wore fitted denim jeans and a pastel pink tank top, long golden hair hanging at her shoulders. She promptly strode towards Maxwell and Donna and flung an arm around each of them. Mo was next, then Annie, marching towards the embrace with the same fierce purpose as the woman already there.

Six...

The pulsation promoted a sympathetic vibration, one that entrained the minds of the living with the intuitions of the dead, and this established an equilibrium in the heartbeat of every guest, schronizing the movement of every breath and every thought.

Five…

They trickled into the embrace, one by one, Joy, Nasazzi, Jack, Louie, Foster, Sado, each guest distinct as rain droplets as they streamed by a stationary Blaze like serein down the face of a statue. Even Vera was washed along, her breath raspy yet undefeated as she swam through the waves of people, arrived at Donna's side, and easily bonded to the bodies in her midst.

Four…

The vibration equalized, the pulsation amplified, the ray of every guest was now magnified, streaming into Donna and Maxwell, an accretion of materials around a vital center—mouth of the volcano, eye of a hurricane, Delta of the Nile.

Three…

There is nothing we haven't done. There is nothing we haven't been. There is nothing we haven't thought. Blaze didn't need to move. Terry took him by the arm. He was in the embrace whether he wanted to be or not, next to men and woman with their heads bowed, hands on each other's shoulders, and the consciousness of this crowd now took control of his current.

Two…

All flowed without friction, the energy growing exponentially, moving toward ignition and radiant release, that burst of the visible from an invisible source, for nothing could ever hold such a luminiferous pressure.

One…

All throughout the house they were in touch, eyes closed, mouths shut, everyone at Bremen's funeral was linked with everyone else in the kitchen and the garage and the living room, and in this state of harmony with the chords of creation there was only the silence that accompanies a pure transmission from the Ineffable.

And we have detonation.

The explosion blew through all the bodies at the funeral, traveling through blood and brain and bone. It traveled with intensity and speed, flash-freezing the mind of every guest with the memory of this moment, with the feeling of profound closeness, the magic of human contact, with the understanding that nothing which comes into this world can or should persist, and that humanity was not made to mourn. The shockwave passed through the Lyons' home with no loss of strength, moving through the neighboring houses down the street, through the cars and trucks on the expressway, through the bars and factories and bright lakefront cafes, gliding over the waters, rippling their darkly mirrored surface. The wave induced in all who felt it the admirable idea that it was wonderful to be alive, before the droning keen of earthly necessities returned from banishment to divert their attention once again. With no end in sight, the wave bloomed out beyond the city and into the frozen white forests and fields, whistling through dairy farms with stiff clapboard barns where livestock roamed for warm pockets of air. It disturbed a mound of snow near a sleepy calf, who jumped to its feet, alert and unafraid, watching the flakes waft up in a cyclone, disperse in a cloud, settle, settle, and be still.

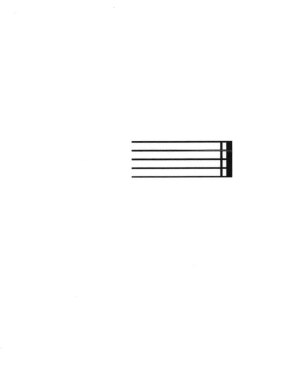

ACKNOWLEDGMENTS

I'm grateful for every single person in my family, my mother, sister, father, step-mother, brother, aunts, uncles, cousins, grandparents, who provided me with nothing but love and encouragement.

For the entire editorial and publishing team at Ad Lumen, who spun gold from a handcrafted loom—Michael Angelone, Christian Kiefer, Michael Spurgeon, Karen Quirarte—it exceeded all my expectations to work with a group of warriors like yourselves. For every student who read the manuscript at American River College, it's stunning to know you enjoyed it this much. For Elissa Goldman, an intuitive editor who first picked the novel apart, and gave me the greatest writing compliment of my life. For Thomas Fox Perry and Matthew Limpede, and their detailed perspective of the book at an earlier stage. For the formative experiences of the Iowa Writers' Workshop, along with Sam Chang, Connie Brothers, Deb West, Jan Zenisek, Ethan Canin, James MacPherson, Paul Harding, Charles D'Ambrosio, Cole Swenson, Marylinne Robinson—thanks for making all your shadows a breeze to stand in.

I'm grateful to Sarah Pogell, who revolutionized my literary perspective, and if not for a dozen or so words she addressed to me, we probably wouldn't be here today. For G. Christopher Williams, who showed me, actually, unequivocally, how to read. No one before or since has made it so clear. For Pablo Peschiera, who released a depth charge in my subconsciousness—the degree to which you open your heart, and craft the outpouring, is the measure of the power of your words. For Ben Percy, who saw the potential in my feral prose. For the poem of BJ Love which got this whole ball rolling. For the classical salons of EJB. For Gerardo Herrera, his hilarious hot takes, his scintillating prose, his infectious love of books and movies. For Anthony Marra and keeping the bar epically high. For Matt Null, an extraordinary critic who can write his Appalachian ass off. For the sublime Charity Stebbins, who took me by the hand, led me to her bookshelf, and introduced me to Julio Cortazar. For Marcus Burke, the most humble, hard-working, inspiring writer I know, because every time I leave his presence, I just want to channel the best within me.

Over the long years, I'm grateful for the literary support system of Alex de la Pena, Brian Dunigan, Mike Herndon, Alex Bauer, Chris Rush, Chuck Lyons, Karl McComas-Riechl, George de la Pena, and all the friends who let me poke around inside their heads. And for John's Grocery and Wally Plahutnik, who offered me a parallel life in the wine realm.

I'm grateful for the One Life, in which I live and move and have my being. I'm grateful for the miraculous shack on Bloomington street, and for Brown and Alien who roamed the greenery around it. I shan't forget Lela Falcon, the cowgirl who literally wrote me into her life. Baby, it's been one long ride into the sunset.